"So what happened?"

He stepped closer—close enough to see the tiny, convulsive shudders that vibrated her body. "Hey..."

He touched her arm, closing his fingers around the bones just above her wrist. His hand felt heavy and strong and warm, and before she knew it, she'd pulled her own hand around to grab him in the same place.

They stayed that way, too close to each other.

"Lately, I've been having panic attacks," she said. "I can't even remember how I got out of the room." Without planning to, she pushed her forehead into Callan's shoulder, somehow needing to be in contact with his rocklike steadiness.

When he made a movement, she thought he was letting go, and the cry of protest escaped her lips instinctively. She wasn't ready yet. He felt too good, too right.

THE RUNAWAY
AND THE
CATTLEMAN

LILIAN DARCY

Silhouette

SPECIAL EDITION

Published by Silhouette Books

America's Publisher of Contemporary Romance

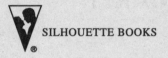 SILHOUETTE BOOKS

ISBN 0-373-24762-1

THE RUNAWAY AND THE CATTLEMAN

Copyright © 2006 by Lilian Darcy

This edition published by arrangement with Harlequin Books S.A.

® and TM are trademarks of Harlequin Books S.A., used under license.
Trademarks indicated with ® are registered in the United States Patent
and Trademark Office, the Canadian Trade Marks Office and in other
countries.

Visit Silhouette Books at www.eHarlequin.com

Printed in U.S.A.

Books by Lilian Darcy

Silhouette Special Edition

Balancing Act #1552
Their Baby Miracle #1672
The Father Factor #1696
The Runaway and the Cattleman #1762

Silhouette Romance

The Baby Bond #1390
Her Sister's Child #1449
Raising Baby Jane #1478
Cinderella After Midnight #1542
Saving Cinderella #1555
Finding Her Prince #1567
Pregnant and Protected #1603
For the Taking #1620
The Boss's Baby Surprise #1729
The Millionaire's Cinderella Wife #1772
Sister Swap #1816

*The Cinderella Conspiracy

LILIAN DARCY

has written over fifty books for Silhouette Romance and Harlequin Mills & Boon Medical Romance (Prescription Romance). Her first book for Silhouette appeared on the Waldenbooks Series Romance Bestsellers list, and she's hoping readers go on responding strongly to her work. Happily married with four active children and a very patient cat, she enjoys keeping busy and could probably fill several more lifetimes with the things she likes to do—including cooking, gardening, quilting, drawing and traveling. She currently lives in Australia but travels to the United States as often as possible to visit family. Lilian loves to hear from readers. You can write to her at P.O. Box 381, Hackensack, NJ 07602 or e-mail her at lildarcy@austarmetro.com.au.

Chapter One

He looked like a cowboy, against the backdrop of rust-red outback dirt and endless blue sky.

Or to be more accurate, like every woman's fantasy of a cowboy.

An ancient, broad-brimmed hat tilted low over his forehead. It shaded his face so that the color of his eyes was impossible to read, but one look at his profile would tell a red-blooded woman all she needed to know. Strong jaw, firm mouth, an intensity in the way he watched the world...even when he looked as if he wasn't really seeing it.

His body was even stronger than his jaw, but he wasn't the type who needed to wear his T-shirts too tight to emphasize washboard abs and bulging biceps. The muscles were just there, hard and motionless beneath faded denim and stretch cotton. He'd learned to conserve his energy for when he really needed it—for a long day of boundary riding, cattle branding or herding his animals to fresh pasture. Right now, since he didn't need it, he leaned his tanned forearms on the wooden rail in front of him, the way he would have leaned them on a stockyard gate.

Yes, any woman who'd picked him as a cowboy would have been close. He was a cattleman, an Australian outback farmer, owner of his own huge spread of acreage. He was no one's wage slave, but answered only to his land, his animals and his family.

Nine out of ten women took a good look at him as they walked past. Eight out of ten were impressed with what they saw, and would have liked to find out more. Just what color were those eyes? Did he have tan lines around those solid upper arms? What did he have to say for himself? Did he like dressy blondes or down-to-earth brunettes? Was he available? Was he as good as he looked?

But if the cattleman noticed any of the female attention he was getting, it didn't show. You would have said that Callan Woods's thoughts were at least two hundred miles away, and you wouldn't have been wrong.

"Look at him, Brant! What are we going to do?"

Branton Smith felt helpless at his friend Dusty Tanner's question. Like Callan himself, they both lived most of their waking hours out of doors. They worked with their hands. When they struck trouble, it was something physical— drought or flood or fire or an injured beast—and the solution to it was physical, also.

They just worked harder. They climbed on a horse and herded cattle or sheep to higher ground. They got out of bed two hours earlier in the morning and fed their animals by hand, dropping feed bales off the back of a truck until their hands were calloused like leather and every muscle burned. They were big, strong, capable men, and they had brains. They looked for active, assertive answers.

But what could they do about Callan?

"Just be there for him, I guess," Brant said in answer to Dusty's question.

He wasn't surprised at Dusty's bark of derisory laughter. "You sound like an advice column in a teenage magazine, mate!"

True.

Had to be cruddy advice, too, because they'd both "been there" for Callan since his wife Liz's death four years ago, and he only seemed to have folded in on himself even more this year.

He stood, as they did, with his forearms propped on the rail that kept spectators back from the racetrack, while around him swirled the color and noise of Australia's best-known outback racing carnival. Judging by Callan's thousand-yard stare, his slumped shoulders, his tight mouth and his silence, however, he barely knew that he was here.

The three men had been best mates for years, since attending Cliffside school in Sydney more than seventeen years ago. Then, they had been three strong, shy outback boys, boarding away from home for the first time, in the company of the sons of stockbrokers and car dealers and property tycoons.

Now they owned racehorses together, five sleek beautiful animals at the present time, of which two were racing at today's carnival. Three of their horses were trained at a place near Brant's extensive sheep-farming property west of the Snowy Mountains, while the two running today were with a trainer in Queensland, near Dusty.

As a hobby, the racing syndicate just about paid its way. As an exercise in mateship, it was solid gold.

Their spirited two-year-old mare Surprise Bouquet had put in a reasonable performance in her maiden event this morning. She'd placed fifth in a field of sixteen after a poor jump from the barrier, and she should do better next time around. Saltbush Bachelor was the horse they had real hopes for today.

Callan, Brant and Dusty couldn't meet face-to-face all that often, given the distance between their properties, but this race carnival was a tradition they kept to whenever they could. Callan had missed a couple of years when Liz had been ill. She'd died at around this time of year. A couple of weeks along in the calendar—end of September. Maybe that was part of Callan's problem. The Birdsville Races and September and Liz's death were all wrapped up together in his heart.

"He's thirty-three," Dusty muttered. "We can't let him go on thinking his life is over, Brant."

Standing beside his two mates, Callan wasn't thinking that.

Not exactly.

But yeah. He knew Brant and Dusty were concerned about him. They weren't all that subtle on the issue. Those frequent anxious looks, the muttered comments he didn't always hear but could guess the gist of, the over-hearty suggestions about going for a beer, the occasional comment about a woman—nothing too crude, just "nice legs" and that kind of thing—after which they'd both nudge him for an agreement, which he would dutifully give.

Yes, she had nice legs, the blonde or the brunette or the farmer's daughter with her hair hidden beneath her hat.

Brant and Dusty both thought it was time he moved on, found a new mother for his boys.

Callan had thought so, too, once.

Three years ago, to be exact, here at this same annual racing carnival.

To him, it felt like yesterday.

He could still remember the panic, the loneliness, the physical hunger, the ache for his own loss and the even harder ache for what his boys would miss without a mother, after that first endless year without Liz.

But, sheesh! What the hell had he been thinking that day? Had he really thought that a party-going, city-bred twenty-something with "nice legs," carrying a glass of champagne in one hand and in the other a race guide she wasn't interested in, could possess the slightest power to help him move on?

There had been a nightmarish wrongness about that woman's body. The freckles across her nose weren't Liz's freckles. Her hair wasn't Liz's shade of blonde. Her curves weren't right, or her voice. He'd been looking for all the wrong things, and he hadn't even found those.

"They're in the barrier," Brant reported, his voice rising to cut across Callan's thoughts. "He looked lively but not too wound up."

"And Garrett is hungry for this win," Dusty added. "He'll ride him just right."

Both men had binoculars pressed to their eyes, now. They didn't want to miss a second of the race, or of their horse's ride. They wanted Callan to care that Saltbush Bachelor was running with a good period of training and some successful starts behind him, and actually had a shot at a win.

The silk shirts of the jockeys shimmered with color in the bright sun, the way the desert air shimmered on the horizon. The nearby airfield had light planes lined up like minivans in a shopping mall's parking garage, and the population of the tiny outback town had temporarily swelled from a few hundred to several thousand. Callan could smell beer and barbecued sausages, sunscreen and horse feed and dust.

He roused himself enough to answer his two friends. "Yeah, Mick Garrett's a good jockey." But he didn't lift his own binoculars and barely noticed the anticipation that knotted their bodies and their voices as the race got underway.

Instead he thought about his boys back on Arakeela Creek

with their grandmother, thought about what he'd need to do with the cattle next week when he was home, thought again about three years ago here in Birdsville and that disaster of a nice-legged woman who could never in a million years have looked—or felt—or sounded—enough like Liz.

He thought about the other woman, too, a few months later—a blond and freckled Scandinavian backpacker whom he'd permitted to camp down by the Arakeela Gorge water hole, and who had been happy to make all the moves in what had soon turned out to be a limp disaster of a one-night stand.

Lord, he hated remembering! He'd been so crazed with grief and loneliness, but how could he have thought that hooking up with some stranger would do anything to heal him, let alone anything to provide him or his boys with a better future?

Watching Callan's mental distance and his thinned mouth, Brant and Dusty looked at each other again. Didn't need to speak about it, but spoke anyway.

"Does he even know it's started?" Dusty muttered.

"Knows," Brant theorized. "Doesn't care."

"If Salty wins—"

"Won't make a blind bit of difference to him. Hell, Dusty, what are we going to do? *Being there* is just bull. You're right. We both know it. He needs action."

"Action? We're doing everything we can. When he wanted to pull out of our racehorse syndicate, we basically told him he couldn't."

"And his mother talked him round on that, too."

The race wheeled around the far curve of the track and the jockeys' colors blurred. From this angle, it was impossible to see how Saltbush Bachelor was running. As long as he wasn't hemmed in at the rail. As long as Garrett didn't leave his run too late.

Beside Brant, two would-be Paris Hiltons were screaming for the horse they wrongly thought they'd bet on. Van Der

Kamp wasn't running until the next race, but neither Brant, Dusty nor Callan troubled to give the two overexcited young women this information.

"Kerry's worried," Brant went on, still talking about Callan's mother. "She phoned me last week and asked us to look out for him this weekend."

"Like we wouldn't anyway."

The momentum of the race picked up as the horses came around into the home straight. The Paris Hilton girls had realized their mistake over Van Der Kamp and were cheering for the correct horse, now—Salty himself.

"He's going to do it!" Brant yelled. "He's up there. It's going to be close. Can you see, Dusty? Callan?"

Callan didn't answer.

The horses thundered past, their legs a blur of pistonlike movements, their jockeys' colors once more tangled together. Just twenty meters to go, then ten.

"He's there, he's...no, he's not going to win, but second. He's—hell, he's losing ground, but he's going to get—" Brant stopped.

Second place? It was too close to call. They'd have to wait for the official result. Brant listened to the distorted sound of the PA system for several seconds and managed to catch winner and place-getters' names. Even allowing for the distortion, none of them sounded remotely like Saltbush Bachelor. Their horse had lost out for third place by a nose.

"So much for omens," said one of the Hilton types to the other.

"Guess we're not scoring ourselves an outback bachelor today," the other one replied.

Beside them, Callan didn't even react—despite their nice legs—and Brant and Dusty could only look at each other helplessly once again.

"Talk to your sister, Brant," Dusty suggested. A small, irritating bush fly buzzed near his lips. Like most outback-bred people, he'd learned not to open his mouth too wide when he spoke, which was an advantage in confidential conversation. "Maybe this needs a woman's touch. Nuala has a good head on her shoulders."

"A good head full of crazy ideas," Brant said.

"Maybe a crazy idea is just what we need."

"Yeah, because the plain, ordinary ones haven't worked, have they? Okay, I'll talk to her about it when I get back. But I'm warning you, it might not be an idea we want to hear."

Dusty got a stubborn look on his face. "If there's a chance of it helping Callan, mate, at this point I'll listen to anything."

Chapter Two

"So we're going to pay Nuala back *how*, for coming up with this dream scheme?" Dusty drawled to Brant, almost six months later.

The Birdsville Races had been held on the first weekend in September. This was a Friday night in late February. Their horses had had a couple of promising wins during the spring season. Brant's property had received higher than average rain, while Dusty's had sweltered in the intense Queensland summer heat. Kerry Woods had talked again to both men about how worried she was about Callan.

"You were the one who said you didn't care if it was crazy, as long as there was a chance it might help Callan, you'd do it," Brant reminded him, a little defensive on his sister's behalf, even though he'd had a few payback fantasies himself over the past couple of weeks, since the appearance of the February issue of *Today's Woman* magazine.

"And I'm here, aren't I?" Dusty retorted. "I did do it. I had my photo in that damned magazine. I had to list my hobbies and my background, and—" he hooked his fingers in the air to show the quote marks coming up "—*what I'm looking for in a woman and why I believe love can last*. And then the magazine didn't use a quarter of what I'd said."

"You did a better job with all those questions than I did," Brant said.

Dusty shrugged and grinned. "I was more honest."

"Yeah, mate, don't you have any self-protective instincts?"

"Plenty of 'em. I'm just not a very good liar. Does your sister really think Callan's going to find what he's looking for this way?"

Both men looked around the room. It was just after six in the evening, and the air-conditioning in this elegant waterfront venue battled against Sydney's lingering summer heat. The metropolitan beaches would be crowded with sleek, tanned bodies and sandy children. On the tangled city streets, traffic and exhaust fumes would still be thick, mingled with the blasts of restaurant smells evoking the cuisine of many nations. This was an attractive setting for a cocktail party, however, with its views over Darling Harbour, including a distant glimpse of the Harbour Bridge beyond the restored and remodeled shipping piers.

It was light-years away from the varied landscapes around Brant's, Dusty's and Callan's homes.

There had to be around fifty people in the room, Brant decided. They appeared to consist of twenty single outback men and twenty single urban women, as well as some journalists and photographers from the magazine and a handful of catering staff who were gliding around with drink trays and fiddly little morsels of fashionable food that looked way too scary to eat.

"Not *find* what he's looking for, find *out* what he's looking for, according to Nuala," he said to Dusty in clarification.

"Nuala, who has recently announced her engagement to a man she's known since she was, what, three?" Dusty pointed out. "Oh, yeah, she's a real expert on this relationship stuff."

"Getting Nuala's input on all this was your idea, I seem to recall. And she hasn't been going out with Chris since she was three," Brant said, in defense of his baby sister's credentials in the field. "She wouldn't look at him after she left school. She went to Europe for three years."

"She had boyfriends then?"

"Their names have been permanently blacked out of the Nuala Jane Smith archival records, she says, but, yeah, she had a few."

"So she really thinks—?"

"You want me to quote her?" Brant ticked his sister's arguments off on his fingers. "This will get Callan to focus on what he wants and what's missing from his life. It'll remind him that there are still some decent women in the world even without Liz in it. It'll show him he's not the only one whose heart is in—"

He stopped. *Pieces* he was going to say, but suddenly, they were no longer alone.

"Hi! Who do we have here? Dustin, right?" The overenthusiastic American woman discreetly consulted some notes on a clipboard, while a photographic flash went off in a man's hands, right next to her. Magazine people, both of them.

The flash made Dusty blink. If Dusty had been one of their own racehorses, Brant thought, the man would have shied and stepped a big hoof on the American's foot, including her spike heel. He would have broken several of her bones. "Call me Dusty," he said.

"Dusty…." The American beamed artificially. Her eyelids fluttered and she barely looked in his direction. She had sleek hair, a wide mouth and a distracted manner. Nice legs, too, Brant saw as he stepped back out of range. Owning racehorses gave a man a deep appreciation of good female legs.

Dusty gave them an interested glance, also. "Now, you're here to meet Mandy tonight, Dusty, and here she is!" the American said.

Ta-da!

Mandy stepped forward. She was around five foot four and her legs were pretty ordinary, but she had dark eyes and an eager smile. She was also totally thrilled with herself for correctly matching Dusty's personal details to his photograph and winning herself a place at the party tonight.

Dusty looked a little bewildered at her attitude, but when he answered the question she asked him and she listened with those big eyes fixed so intently on his face… Yeah, Brant thought he would probably have felt the ego stroke, too. It was nice when a woman was genuinely interested. He went in search of a drink, wondering with a faint stir of curiosity which of the as-yet-unpaired women in the room had been earmarked for him.

Passing Callan, he couldn't help but notice that his friend, the object of this whole outlandish exercise, was mentally miles away.

"Why am I here?" Jacinda Beale muttered to herself.

As always, she had reacted to this dressed-up, extravagant, city cocktail party like an animal caught in a searchlight. She didn't know a soul. She hadn't yet been introduced to the man she was supposed to meet.

The woman who was supposed to do the introducing—and who had introduced herself to Jacinda as Shay-from-the-magazine—flitted around looking almost as stressed out as most of the guests, many of whom were clearly too shy to mingle easily.

Why are you here, Jac?

Well, go ahead and pick an option, replied the cynical and panicky running commentary in Jacinda's brain. You're a scriptwriter, after all. Choosing between different character motivations is one of the skills of your trade.

There were several such options to choose from, some of which were more honest than others.

Because I gave in to an insane impulse and thought this might be fun…or, failing that, good for me.

Because Today's Woman *magazine is running a series of stories called "Wanted: Outback Wives," and I happened to a) guess correctly which Outback Wife-hunter's description of himself matched with which Outback Wife-hunter photo— it wasn't that hard!—and b) write a sufficiently appealing and correctly spelled letter outlining in three hundred words or less why I should get to meet him.*

Yes, believe it or not, an invitation to this cocktail party was meant to be a kind of prize.

Because I'm desperate, and I'll open any door that looks like it has a handle.

Because I'm a writer, so it's research.

That last one scared her, adding to the already powerful panicky feeling. Writers could claim that pretty much anything was research, and in the past for Jacinda, the claim had always been true. In the name of research, she'd tried on expensive jewellery, combed through a stranger's trash can, taken a ride on a seriously terrifying roller coaster, eaten in two or three of America's most famous restaurants… The list went on.

But was she really a writer anymore?

Heartbreak Hotel's head scriptwriter, Elaine Hutchison, still thought that she was.

"You're blocked, Jac," she'd said six weeks ago. "You have good reasons to be blocked, and you need a break. Take that gorgeous daughter of yours, cross an ocean, and don't come home for a month. By then, you'll be raring to go and I can give you Reece and Naomi's storyline because you are the *only* one I trust to make their dialogue remotely believable."

"Which ocean?" Jac had asked, because her initiative had also evaporated, along with her TV soap opera dialogue-writing skills.

"Any ocean, honey. Just make it a big one. Know what I'm saying? Know why I'm saying it?"

Elaine hadn't mentioned any names but, yes, Jac had known what she was saying, and why. She should put some distance between herself and Kurt until she was stronger, better equipped to move forward. She should recognize that despite Elaine's genuine friendship, she had divided loyalties because Kurt had the power to scuttle Elaine's own career as well as Jacinda's.

And the Pacific Ocean was the biggest ocean around—it conveniently washed ashore in California, too—so here she was on the far side of it, in Australia, at the bottom of the world, at the bottom of a glass, at a cocktail party she wasn't enjoying any better than she'd enjoyed all those dozens and dozens of cocktail parties with Kurt.

Even when she and Kurt had been in love.

Thud, went her heart.

Yes, she had been naive enough to love him once.

But their marriage had given her Carly, her precious daughter, so the news wasn't all bad.

"Jacinda?" said a woman's voice, in an American accent that matched Jac's own.

She turned to the energetic chestnut-haired magazine editor who'd greeted her on arrival. "Shay, hi…."

Introduction time.

There was a man hovering at Shay-from-the-magazine's elbow. Better looking than in his magazine photo, he appeared far less comfortable, however. The photo had shown him in his native element, with one long, jeans-clad leg

braced against a rust-red rock and his dusty felt hat silhou-
etted against a sky the color of tinted contact lenses. He'd had
his fingers laced in the fur of a big, tongue-lolling cattle
dog—also rust-red—and a smile that narrowed his brim-
shaded eyes so much you couldn't even see them.

Jac could see them now, however, and they were, oh, unbe-
lievable. Blue and deep and smoky with a whole lot of emotions
that thirty seconds ago she might have thought would be too
complex for a down-to-earth South Australian cattle rancher.

Yes, *Today's Woman* hadn't confused the issue by laying
any false clues. The outback sky, the cattle dog and the fierce-
looking lizard on the rock, which Jac's Australian friend Lucy
had identified as a bearded dragon, had strongly suggested that
the man was Callan Woods, cattle rancher, not Brian Snow,
opal miner, or Damian Peterson, oil rigger, or any of the other
seventeen Outback Wife-hunters, whose photos and biograph-
ical details had appeared in the February issue of the
magazine.

There were a lot of lonely outback men in Australia,
Today's Woman claimed. It was a big country, where such
men ran free in their far-flung and sometimes lonely occupations, but had trouble finding the right woman.

Jac wasn't going to be that, she knew.

Not for this man.

But now wasn't the time to tell him so.

"Callan, meet Jacinda," Shay-from-the-magazine said
brightly.

"Hi. Yeah," was all he said.

He didn't look happy to be here…which gave them one
thing in common, at least.

"Would you believe how Jacinda matched you with your
photo, Callan?" Shay gushed. "She actually identified the
species of lizard sitting on the rock! Can you believe that?"

"Yeah? The bearded dragon?" A stirring of interest

appeared in those incredible eyes as he belatedly reached out to shake Jac's hand. He had a firm, dry grip, which he let go of a little too soon, as if he really, seriously, didn't want her to get the wrong idea.

"The lizard was the reason I chose you as the one I wanted to meet," Jac confessed. "My daughter thought he looked so cute."

Too late, she realized that it wasn't a very tactful line. Callan was supposed to be the cute one, not the reptilian wildlife on his land.

But Callan didn't seem to care about her gaffe. Seemed relieved about it, in fact. "Yeah, my son Lockie loves them," he said, his eyes getting brighter as he mentioned his boy. "He had one for a pet, but then he couldn't stand to see it caged."

"So you have kids, too?" Jac asked. She grabbed on to the subject immediately, since it might be the only conversational lifeline they could come up with together. "My daughter is four."

Then she listened as Callan Woods told her, "I have two boys. Lockie's ten. Josh is eight. We lost…" He stopped and took a breath. "That is, my wife died four years ago. I'm sorry. I should tell you that up front." He lowered his voice and glanced at Shay, who was already moving on to her next introduction, as if tonight's schedule was impossibly tight.

"It's okay," Jac told him.

He might not even have heard her reassurance. "I'm not really a…what was it…Wild Heart Looking For Love." He parodied the words from the magazine so that Jac could almost see them spelled with capitals. "Couple of my mates wanted to take part in this and they roped me in, too, for a bit of support."

He glanced over his shoulder and caught sight of two tall men. One of them was looking down at a short brunette who had her hand pinned to his arm. Callan gestured at the two men for Jac's benefit. They were his "mates." She knew the Australian expression by this time. "I'm doing it for them," he said. "For Brant and Dusty. I'm not seriously looking for anyone. I should be up front with you about that."

The mates were staring this way.

At Callan.

Jac was good at character motivation. She saw the anxious frowns on their faces and the way they assessed both their friend and Jac herself, and she recognized the truth at once, now that this man had told her about his loss.

Callan was doing it for them?

No, it was the other way around. Brant and Dusty were doing it for him.

She heard him swear under his breath and understood the painful way his own words must be echoing in his head. *My wife died four years ago.* She hated saying it, too. *Kurt and I are divorced now.* It felt as if you were ripping open your clothing to show total strangers your surgical scars.

"It's okay," she repeated quickly to Callan Woods. "This is a very artificial situation, isn't it? Anyone would be crazy to hold out serious hopes of meeting the right person, no matter how much they were looking for it. But I don't think that makes it a pointless exercise. You know, just to get a bit of practice…or…or validation, maybe. I'm divorced. And it was a horrible divorce." *See, I have scars, too.* "I actually can't think when I last talked to a man I don't know, purely for the pleasure of making some contact."

He nodded, but didn't make a direct reply. Maybe he was better at talking to his rust-colored dog. After a few seconds of silence, he said, "You're not Australian."

"No. The accent's a giveaway, isn't it?" She smiled, but he didn't smile back.

"But you're living here?" he said.

"No, again. On vacation. Staying with an Australian friend

I met in California a few years ago. Lucy. She's great. She's babysitting my daughter tonight. She was the one who suggested I try that photo-matching thing in the magazine, just for fun. Most of them were pretty easy."

"I guess it made sense, added more interest, having the magazine turn it into a kind of contest."

"And, yes, it was fun," Jac agreed. "I'm not sorry I did it."

Oh.

Really?

Since when?

She'd spent the first twenty minutes of the cocktail party feeling deeply sorry that she'd given in to such an insane impulse at Lucy's prompting, but at some point very recently that had changed. The blue eyes? The lizard? The fact that Callan Woods wasn't serious about this, either?

"No," Callan agreed. "I wouldn't have done it, except for my mates, but, yeah, so far it's turned out not to be as bad as I thought."

Jac saw the expression in his eyes. Definitely relief. An after-the-dentist kind of relief that she understood and shared, and it felt nice to share the same emotion with a man again, even if it was a man she didn't know.

"When do you fly home?" he asked.

"Tuesday. Three days from now. We've been here a month, and I can't believe the time has flown so fast. I've loved all of it, and so has Carly."

"Tuesday." He relaxed a little more. "So you're obviously not serious about tonight, either."

"No."

"Thank heavens we got that established nice and early!"

They grinned at each other, grabbed a canapé each from a passing tray and somehow kept talking for the next two hours without quite noticing how quickly the party went by.

* * *

"Mine? A washout," Brant said over a state-of-the-art weekend urban café brunch the next morning, in answer to Dusty's question. "A total washout. She had a chip on her shoulder so big I'm surprised she could stand straight. When I told her that being single didn't bother me all that much, she acted as if I'd personally insulted her. She gave every one of my questions a one-syllable answer and couldn't come up with a single bit of small talk when it was her turn. Thank the Lord you didn't get her, Call."

"Why me?" Callan asked.

Brant frowned. "Why you, what?"

"Why is it good that I didn't get her? You think I'm particularly incapable of dealing with women with big shoulder chips and no small talk? Why?"

"Mine was great," Dusty cut in before Brant could answer, but not before he and Brant had exchanged a strange, uneasy, lightning-fast look. "A genuine, decent woman who knows what she wants and doesn't mind saying so. There's a good chance we'll stay in touch. I'm telling you, it was a heck of a lot better than I expected, the whole thing." He added quickly and awkwardly, "And, you know, I thought it was a promising idea from the start, so…"

Hang on a minute.

Dusty had a look on his face that Callan recognized. It spoke loudly of his awareness that he wasn't a very good liar, but what was he lying about?

Callan began slowly, putting the puzzle pieces in place as he spoke, "So *you* don't mind that you're single, Brant, and *you're* suddenly pretending you thought this was a promising way for an isolated outback cattleman to meet a future wife, Dusty, even though four seconds ago you pretty much stated the opposite…." He paused, watched the guilty expressions on his mates' faces. "Can one of you tell me the real reason we put ourselves through this?"

He wasn't stupid.

He didn't really need their answer.

Which was good, because they both stumbled through some garbled piece of bull dust and didn't actually give him one.

While the stumbling thing was still happening, he thought about whether he was angry with them—whether he wanted to be angry, whether he even had the energy.

Brant and Dusty had set him up in the worst way. They'd conspired behind his back. They'd conned him into putting his picture and his life story and his heartfelt feelings in a national women's magazine. Why? In the hope that he might meet someone? Or…or…start to believe in the possibility of someday meeting someone? Or…or…even just enjoy himself for a night and get a bit of an ego tickle from the bunch of eager women's letters the magazine had started sending him?

Angry about it?

To his own surprise he found himself grinning, after a moment. When all was said and done, they were his best friends. They meant well. They would never let him down. They were idiots, and he liked them.

"Serves you bloody right if yours was a washout, Branton Smith. Serves you right, Dustin Tanner, if you never hear from yours again. Me, like a prize con victim, thought I was helping you out, going along for the ride. Turns out I wasn't, and I'm not looking for anything beyond…yeah…keeping my boys happy, but I had a good time last night, talking to Jacinda."

He knew it couldn't go anywhere. He didn't want it to, and neither did she. That was probably the only reason they'd been able to talk to each other so freely in the first place—

because of the safety valve of her imminent departure and the glaring nature of his loss and her divorce.

She looked nothing like Liz, and that was a big plus, also. Where Liz had been compact and strong, Jacinda was long and willowy. She had big, luminous gray eyes, not twinkling, sensible green ones. She had wild dark hair, in contrast to Liz's neat, silky waterfall of medium blond, and an even, magnolia-olive skin tone, instead of fairness and freckles. Voices, accents, backgrounds, all of it was different and therefore much safer. Safe enough for him to feel as if Jacinda could be a friend, a new kind of friend, if he ever needed one.

This was how he saw her this morning—someone he might turn to, sometime in the future, for advice about his boys, or for a city woman's perspective.

He even had the address of Jacinda's friend Lucy in Sydney, and Jacinda's e-mail address back in America, and she had his, but he wasn't going to tell Brant and Dusty that. He just gave them another grin—a more teasing and evasive grin this time—and started talking about what they might do today, in each other's company, before heading out of Sydney and back to land and animals and family tomorrow.

And he felt better—easier in his heart—than he had in quite a while.

Jac honestly hadn't expected to see Callan again, even though they'd exchanged addresses.

His timing wasn't great. He showed up at seven in the evening, when she was in the middle of getting her daughter ready for bed. She and Carly had eaten, her friend Lucy was out tonight and now Carly was tired. She was tired enough to make a fuss about getting out of the bath even when her skin had gone wrinkly, so that Jac was wet all down her front when she encountered Callan at the apartment door. A minute or two later, Carly was suddenly *not* too tired to want to investigate the gift he'd brought for her immediately.

"It's just a little thing," Callan told Jac quietly, as Carly sat on the floor in her pink-stripes-and-teddy-bears pajamas and ripped at the bright paper. For Jac herself, Callan had brought flowers—a huge, gorgeous bunch of Australian things whose names she didn't know. "A paint-your-own-boomerang kit. Hope it's not more trouble than it's worth!"

"Could be, if she wants to sit down and paint it right now." She smiled to soften the statement. He had kids. He should understand. She added in a lower tone, "You didn't have to do this."

"I know, but I woke up this morning and—" He stopped and tried again. Came up with just three words. "I wanted to."

"You woke up this morning, but it's seven in the evening, now. Did it take you all day to make up your mind that you wanted to?" she teased. She'd decided last night that he had a sense of humor, but wanted to test this perception in a cooler light.

"Yep," he answered. "That's about right." His blue eyes glinted with amusement like sunshine on water. "Look, I guess it is getting late, but we could still eat somewhere, if you want."

So she had to tell him about Lucy being out, and Carly needing bed, and that she and her daughter had eaten already anyhow.

He nodded. "I should have called. You're right. I did leave it too late."

She thought about asking if he wanted coffee or a drink, but chickened out. Pick a character motivation. She didn't want to kiss him and discover she liked it—or discover she didn't. She didn't want to learn the hard way that they had nothing left to talk about, after those two easy hours last night. She definitely didn't want to send the wrong message about how lucky he might get by the end of this evening.

No!

"Thank you," she said instead. "The flowers are beautiful, and the gift for Carly. I really must get her into bed, now, or she'll be a mess tomorrow. She was up before six."

He looked at her wet front and her messy hair. She saw at once from his face that he'd read the situation correctly, and that he wasn't the kind of man to argue. Instead, he just gave her his courteous hope that she and Carly would have a good flight home, told her that if she ever needed anything—needed him, needed to write or phone—that she shouldn't hesitate.

"I mean that."

And Jac believed him. Didn't plan to put her trust in his words to the test, but found that the simple fact of believing him felt good—better, after Kurt, than she would have imagined possible.

Two days later, Jacinda and Carly's plane touched down at Los Angeles International Airport and reality kicked into their lives once more.

Jac had allowed herself and her daughter a day to get over the worst of their jet lag, but then Carly was back in full-day preschool, and Jac was back on the script-writing production line for her soap. The moment she walked into the writers' conferencing suite, a month on the opposite shore of the Pacific Ocean seemed to shrink to the size of a drop in that same ocean and she felt as if she'd never been away.

She didn't want to write.

She couldn't write.

Why the hell had she thought that she'd be able to write?

She'd picked up the mail held for her at the post office on her way in, and among the bills and credit card solicitations were two birthday cards from Kurt, one for herself and one for Carly, since they'd both been February babies and had celebrated while they'd been away. His handwriting on the envelopes, alone, would have been enough to paralyze her, let alone what he'd written to her inside.

Jacinda, sweetheart, don't spend Carly's birthday out of the country next year, please. Trust me, you can't afford that kind of statement. Emotionally, financially. You just can't, and you should know that. I'm going to be pretty busy this spring, and I'll need Carly in my life to give me some balance. The network is rethinking its programming, and I'll be micromanaging certain areas.

Don't make the mistake of thinking I'm too busy to catch my own shows, even when they're no longer my day-to-day concern. Reece and Naomi have some great scenes coming up—taut, edgy dialogue written while you were away by a young male writer who's incredibly fresh. Elaine will be taking a good look at them with me. She's been wanting to juggle the team for a while now.

Happy thirty-second birthday. Hope you've used the break as an opportunity to clarify your priorities.
Deepest regards,
Kurt.

This was what blocked her so badly. This kind of communication from Kurt. All the time. Phone calls, e-mails, letters from his lawyer, and even innocent comments from Carly after she'd spent an afternoon with him and his new wife. The threats were always so carefully veiled that they almost sounded like reassurances.

He changed his mind about what he wanted, and then the threats changed, as if to suggest that Jacinda should have been two steps ahead of his thinking all along. The reminders of his power and control, and his ability to wreak both personal and professional consequences pricked at Jacinda like poisoned barbs.

She had custody of Carly now, yes, because so far it had suited Kurt to utter lines such as, "All I want is my daughter's best interests," but she knew that if he wanted the situation to change, he'd stop at nothing to achieve his goal. She also knew that even if he had no intention of ever suing for custody of their child, he'd hang the possibility over her head like a sword on a fraying thread purely because of the power it gave him.

She read the card over again, to convince herself that the sinister tone was all in her head, but it didn't work. She knew Kurt. She'd been married to him for seven years. He'd risen higher and higher in the universe of network television, and yet she knew he would never be too big or too important to let go of any of the dozens of chains of control that he loved to yank. Her own chain, Carly's, Elaine's...

Jacinda saw Elaine's concerned look in her direction, and quickly brought up the Reece and Naomi file on her computer. She had a summary of the scene she was supposed to write this morning. "Reece and Naomi meet at their favorite restaurant and argue over whether to continue their affair."

She centered REECE near the top of the page, pressed Enter, then Tab, then typed the word *Hi*. She managed to get NAOMI to say hi, also, but for an hour after that, the screen stayed blank, while the words *taut, edgy* and *fresh*, in Kurt's spiky handwriting, floated in front of her eyes. She felt ill to the pit of her stomach, and when Elaine took her for a pep talk over lunch, she couldn't eat a bite.

Elaine didn't do much better. "I have to be honest with you, Jac," she said, sounding tense. "I can't run this kind of interference for you much longer. You know Kurt."

"Yes, I do."

"He has me walking on quicksand, and he knows it. We have the mortgage, we have school fees…"

There was an awkward pause, and Jac knew what she had to say.

So she said it. "Elaine, don't ruin your own career trying to protect mine." And she saw the relief in the senior writer's eyes.

When she got back to her computer, she discovered that there was an e-mail from Callan Woods waiting for her. Until she caught sight of her daughter's smile of greeting at pre-school three hours later, it was the only pleasurable, decent, *safe* moment in her entire day.

Chapter Three

The mail flight would get here at any time now.

Beside the packed red dirt of the airstrip, Callan sat in the driver's seat of his four-wheel-drive. He had the door open and the windows down to catch the breeze. In mid-April, the dry daytime heat in the North Flinders Ranges could still be fierce, even though it was technically autumn.

Lockie and Josh were back at the Arakeela Creek homestead doing their morning schoolwork via the Internet and the School of the Air. Sometimes when there was a visitor coming, Callan would give them a morning off so that they could come and meet the plane, but this time he'd said no.

He heard the buzz of the plane in the distance. It came in low with the arid yet beautiful backdrop of the mountains behind it, and he felt an odd lurch in his stomach as it got closer.

Was he looking forward to this arrival?

Like so many of his emotions since Liz's death, this one shifted back and forth, giving him no consistent answer.

Callan didn't know why Jacinda and her daughter were coming to Arakeela Creek, nor how long they wanted to stay, but he did know that Jacinda was a mess, that she wouldn't have asked if she'd felt she had any other choice, and that he couldn't even have considered turning down her desperate plea.

They'd been e-mailing each other for six weeks. A couple of times he'd thought about calling her, but the idea had panicked him too much. The e-mail correspondence was good. Nice. Unthreatening. A phone call would have been a stretching of boundaries that he wasn't ready for and didn't see the point in, since their lives were so far apart, in so many ways.

He honestly hadn't expected anything to come out of the magazine thing, and yet something had—a small, new window into a different world, a friendship at a safe distance. He was also in e-mail contact with two of the Australian women who'd written to him, via the magazine, but in contrast to what he'd developed with Jacinda, those exchanges so far didn't feel nearly as honest or as easy, and he suspected that either he or the women themselves would soon let them dwindle away. Meanwhile, letters from more women continued to arrive.

Why had his e-mails to and from Jacinda felt so much better?

Because she was a writer by profession, and her natural fluency smoothed their exchanges in both directions?

Maybe.

Sometimes, she hadn't been fluent at all.

Meanwhile, Dusty seemed pretty happy with his own outcome to the magazine story and the cocktail party. He and that small brunette, Mandy, were still in touch. He was even talking about flying back down to Sydney to meet up with her again, and had written polite notes to the other women who'd contacted him to tell them thanks, but I'm not looking anymore. Dusty was the same with horses—only ever bet on one in each race, and always bet to win.

Brant was a lot less happy. He'd been receiving way more letters than he wanted. More than Callan, apparently, and Callan had already received quite a few. Since Brant's property was closer to Sydney and Melbourne, where most of the letters came from, he'd met and been out with a couple of the women who'd written.

So far he hadn't been impressed.

Or hadn't admitted to being impressed.

Possibly because at heart he was perfectly happy as he was. The whole magazine campaign had been Brant's sister's idea, Callan had learned.

The plane skimmed the ground at the far end of the airstrip, bounced up for a moment or two, then bumped down harder, keeping its wheels in contact with planet earth this time. It careened along at speed, its wings rocking a little, but gradually slowed to a sedate taxi, propellers still roaring.

Callan climbed out of his vehicle. He didn't bother to shut the door or take the keys. Six weeks seemed, simultaneously, like a long time and like no time at all. Would Jacinda look the way he remembered?

It hadn't been her physical attributes that had drawn him, and yet the memories were all good. Big eyes, sparkly smile, an emotional warmth that showed in her whole body. Rose-colored spectacles, maybe? At a closer acquaintance, would a living, breathing, three-dimensional Jacinda Beale have anything in common with the woman who'd e-mailed him almost every day since they'd met?

Her e-mails had been far briefer over the past couple of weeks, he remembered. Stilted, almost. Cryptic, definitely. Not fluent at all. She'd said she didn't want to talk about it, that she couldn't talk about it, but that she was having some problems.

Then there had been total silence for several days. He'd even sent her a "Jacinda, are you okay?" message, which he'd regretted a split second after hitting Send.

Next thing, her phone call.

From Sydney.

Shaky voice, tense attempts at humor, nothing but stark honesty when she came to the point. "Would Carly and I be able to come stay with you for a little while? I can't think of anywhere else to go. Everything's a mess."

"Sheesh, Jacinda! What's the problem?"

"I—I can't talk about it yet. But I promise it's *not* because I'm, like, wanted for homicide in eleven jurisdictions, if that helps."

"It sets a person's mind at rest, yeah."

"Callan, I'm sorry to be doing this. I can't stay with Lucy. And I can't— You are the only person I know who feels… your ranch is the only place that feels safe, so far away. Just until I catch my breath? Just until then, Callan. I—I do know it's a huge thing to ask."

How could he have said no?

Even if, right at this moment, he wished she hadn't asked.

The plane had come to a halt in its usual spot less than fifty meters from his four-wheel-drive. A private outback airstrip didn't need a terminal building, or even a sealed blacktop runway. The dust thrown up by the aircraft was still hanging in the air like a tea-and-milk-colored curtain. It drifted slowly to the east as the plane's door opened and its steps folded down.

Rob, the pilot, helped Jacinda out and then reached for Carly. The little girl took her mother's hand, while Rob went to get their bags from the back storage hatch where they were stowed. He brought out a mailbag, too, Callan noticed. It looked bulkier than usual. It had looked bulkier than usual for the past two months, so maybe "usual" was due for a new definition.

The bulky mailbag weighed on him. Rob was holding it up, grinning. He knew the story by now.

More letters to answer. More women Callan didn't really want to meet.

Something squeezed tight inside him as he watched the woman and the little girl walk toward him. Carly looked neat and pretty and a little overwhelmed at finding herself in a place like this, so totally different from Sydney and L.A. Her mother moved awkwardly, her body appearing stiff in contrast to the unruly dark hair that whipped and undulated like fast-flowing stream water in the breeze.

Callan lifted his hand in greeting, but Jacinda didn't even say hello, just, "I'm sorry," the moment she reached him. It could have been *I'm sorry, I think I'm about to get sick,* because her face was stark-white and she could hardly move her dry lips, but he knew she was apologizing for a whole lot more than that.

He had to struggle to get his priorities worked out. Her nausea came top of the list right now.

"Take some deep breaths. Walk around." He grabbed a plastic bottle of ice water from the four-wheel-drive and unscrewed the cap, wishing he'd brought a tin mug or something. Little Carly would probably like a drink, also, although she didn't look anywhere near as ill as her mother.

Jacinda took the bottle and managed a few sips, then nodded. Yes, the water helped.

"You don't have to apologize for anything," he told her. "And you definitely don't have to talk."

"Carly?" She gave the water bottle to her daughter, even though Callan could see how much she still needed it for herself.

While Carly drank, Jacinda sucked and blew some careful air. Her gray eyes began to look less panic-stricken and her color was coming back. Callan tried to remember his impression of her the night they'd met, and again the next day when he'd made that impulsive visit to her friend's place with flowers and a child's gift.

She'd lost weight, he thought. She looked thin, now, rather than willowy. She wasn't wearing makeup, but then she probably didn't need it when she wasn't pale green. Those eyes were so big and those lashes so dark, and her mouth was already the kind of shape that some women tried to paint in place without reference to their natural lip line.

He tried to decide whether she was beautiful...attractive...pretty. Each of those words meant something slightly different, but he couldn't make up his mind if any of them fit.

Striking, maybe. That was the word for how she looked.

He felt as if he'd been struck.

By lightning.

By a sideways wall of wind.

By a blow to the head.

He hadn't expected to feel so protective toward her, nor so helpless himself. Suddenly, he was more aware of his own masculinity than he had been in...hell...how long? Years?

He felt that if he were clumsy with her, in words or actions or assumptions, he might break her like a dried-out twig. He also sensed that she could just as easily break him, without her even knowing it, without her even understanding her power or his vulnerability.

Well, gee, that all made sense!

"Tell me when you're ready for the drive," he said, his voice too gruff in its pitch.

Rob had brought three suitcases, an overnight bag and that bulky mailbag over to the four-wheel-drive. "You want these...?" In the back, his gesture finished the question.

Callan nodded at him and he opened the vehicle's rear door and lifted them inside, exaggerating his effort with the mailbag to suggest that it was almost too heavy to lift, full of all those women's letters. Callan couldn't help grinning, even though he shook his head at the man's antics. They knew each other the way outback people often did: five minutes of contact a handful of times a month could feel like real friendship.

"The drive?" Jacinda said, meanwhile. "Where? How far?"

"To the homestead. It's about five clicks." She wouldn't understand the Australian slang, and she probably didn't measure her distances in kilometers, anyhow. "Three miles or so," he translated for her.

"Right." She looked relieved.

"But it's bumpy. We'll wait a bit."

"I want to see the lizard," Carly said, looking up at Callan as if she knew him.

"Got a few more hops, so I'll say no to that beer," Rob came in, leaning his hand on the top of the vehicle.

"Next time, mate," Callan answered, as if beer had indeed been mentioned.

The lines were almost scripted, the kind of running joke that sustained male relationships out here. Rob never had a beer when he was flying, but the unstated offer—like an offer of help in times of trouble—was always there.

The two men waved at each other and Rob headed back to the plane. Jacinda managed to call, "Thank you!" in his direction and he waved again.

"Pick you two up on your way back," he said, but was tactful enough not to ask when that might be.

"Can I see the lizard?" Carly repeated.

"She loved painting the boomerang. She's talked about you quite a lot," Jac murmured. To Carly she added, "I'm not sure if there are lizards here at the airstrip, honey. Maybe we'll have time to look for one tomorrow. Can Mommy have the water again now, please?"

This time, she could take it in gulps, and when she'd had a long drink, she gave a grin of relief. "Never tasted so good!"

But he saw that her hands were shaking.

Carly had started to look hot and sweaty in the sun. She didn't have a hat. Jacinda pushed the fine semiblond hair back from her wide little forehead and frowned. "Are you feeling sick from the plane, honey?"

"Not now. I was only a little, before, not as sick as you, Mommy."

"So Callan wants to drive us to his house. Are you ready?"

"Where's his house?"

Good question. You couldn't see the homestead from here. It was set above a loop of Arakeela Creek, just under a kilometer from the line of white-trunked eucalyptus trees that marked the creek bed, on the far side of a low rise. "You'll see it soon, Carly," he told her. "Let's get you strapped in."

"You use seat belts out here? When there are no other cars around for miles?" Jacinda asked.

"They keep your head from hitting the ceiling on the bumps."

She thought he was joking.

He had enough expertise at the wheel not to need to shatter her illusions on that point today, on the relatively well-made track between the airstrip and the homestead, but if she did any more extensive driving with him around the property, she'd soon find out the truth.

Once again, he wondered how long she would need to stay, what he could possibly do to make her feel welcome and entertained, and what would happen to such a new and untested kind of friendship in the isolation of the outback.

Most importantly, why had she fled her life in Los Angeles? What was she running from? And what was she hoping for, when she'd told him in such a desperate voice that she needed to catch her breath?

He couldn't ask.

Not yet.

* * *

Callan stayed silent for the first few minutes of the drive.
Jacinda listened to the grind of the vehicle's engine and the
squeak of its bodywork and springs on the unsealed track.
The landscape they drove through was stark, yet she could
already understand why some people would find it beautiful. She found it beautiful, herself. It was like looking at the
very bones of the earth—bones that were colored clay red and
ocher yellow and chalky white. In the distance, near an arc
of eucalyptus trees, she saw a spreading herd of red-brown
cattle grazing, their big bodies dwarfed by the sheer scale of
ground and horizon and sky.

She knew she'd soon have to tell Callan why she was
here, but not yet. She needed to wait until she was a little
calmer and her blood sugar was a little higher, for a start. She
wanted him to believe her. She needed him to understand how
terrified she was and that her story wasn't the product of her
bitter feelings toward Kurt and her writer's imagination—
even if in some of her most paranoid, self-doubting moments,
she had wondered if it was.

…Because if he didn't believe her, and if she and Carly
weren't welcome here, she didn't know where else they could
go.

"There's the homestead," Callan finally said.

His bare, brown forearm and hand came into Jac's body
space, pointing strong and straight, across to the left of the
vehicle. She'd forgotten what a powerful, sturdy build he
had and, here in his natural element, the impression of
strength was emphasized all the more. What would he
look like on horseback, or wrestling with his cattle in a
branding yard?

The mental images were too vivid and far too appealing.
Kurt's strength had never been physical…or even emotional.
Instead, it was based purely on money and influence. Callan's

kind of strength would be so different, much simpler and more straightforward, and she needed that so much right now.

Right away she saw the cluster of buildings that he indicated, their forms and outlines growing clearer as the vehicle got closer. They had roofs painted a dark red that had faded to a dusty cherry color in the strong light and they were shaded by stands of willowy, small-leafed trees that she couldn't identify. Not eucalyptus. As a California resident, she knew those well. Some of the buildings were wooden, but the main house was made of sand-colored stone with a framing of reddish brick where walls met and windows opened.

She glimpsed something that looked like a vegetable garden. It contained a couple of short rows of orchard trees and was protected on two sides by walls made of some kind of dry brush, and on a third side by a screen of living shrubs. In a sparsely grassed field close to the house, several horses grazed or drank water from a metal trough, placed in the shade of some trees.

Several of the buildings had wide verandas, and all of them had metal water tanks hugging close on one side, to collect roof runoff when the rare rains came. Houses, storage sheds, barns, she didn't know what each building was for, but there was something very pretty and alluring about the grouping. It reminded her of circled wagons in an old-fashioned Western film, or a town in a desert oasis.

She had stretched a very new friendship by her desperate act of coming here, she knew, but at least she felt that she and Carly would be physically safe.

Far safer than she had felt they were in Los Angeles.

Safer than she'd felt at Lucy's after those phone calls had started coming at all hours—hang-ups, every one of them. They had to have been from Kurt.

"How big is your ranch?" she asked Callan.

"My station. We don't call them ranches here. It's around twenty-four hundred square kilometers."

"Wow!" It sounded like a satisfying number. "In acres, that would be…twice that? Four or five thousand?"

She was only guessing. Kurt had had a ranch around that size in eastern California. Six thousand acres. He used to spread his arms out and take a deep breath and tell everyone, "Man, this is a piece of land!"

But Callan laughed at her estimate. "Uh, a little bit bigger, actually. Nine hundred-odd square miles. In acres, six hundred thousand."

"Six *hundred* thousand? You're saying this is a *hundred* times bigger than my ex-husband's dude ranch?"

"It's a pretty small place compared to some in this country. Anna Creek, out west of Lake Eyre, is something like six million acres, the biggest pastoral lease in the world."

Jacinda didn't care about Anna Creek. "You own—heavens—*Rhode Island!*"

"Only I probably have a lot fewer cattle."

"How many? Don't tell me! More than the human population of the whole country?"

"Nowhere close. Again, around twenty-four hundred. One beast per square kilometer. It's arid, out here. The land just doesn't support more than that. Most of the time, they roam free, and they can be pretty hard to find when we want to round them up and send them to market."

She didn't care about the number of cattle, although she could well believe they were hard to locate in this vastness. Callan owned more land than the average European prince.

And a hundred times more land than Kurt.

Which probably shouldn't make her want to grin with pleasure, but it did.

"As far as the eye can see? It's all yours?"

"Yep." And though he said it quietly—lazily, almost—she could see the pride and satisfaction it gave him.

Soon they rumbled across a metal grid between two lines of fence, and a couple of hundred yards later, they'd reached the homestead. Callan parked the vehicle at a casual angle out front and switched off the engine. Two dogs raced around from the side of the house and greeted their human as if they hadn't seen him in a week. One was a black and white border collie and one was probably the red dog featured in Callan's magazine photo.

"Okay, Pippa," he said. "Okay, Flick. You like me. I get the message. But Jacinda and Carly don't need to get told the same thing, you hear? They're not used to wretches like you." He issued a couple of sharp commands and the dogs dashed over to sit in the shade of the house, pink tongues panting and lolling, attitudes repentant.

A screen door squeaked on its hinges and flapped back against the jamb, and three people materialized on the shaded veranda. They must have heard the vehicle's approach.

It wasn't hard to work out who they were—Callan's two boys and his mother, Kerry. All three of them had exactly his eyes—a glorious overload of piercing blue. He'd talked about them in his e-mails, and Jac knew that Kerry had been widowed by Callan's father's death eleven years ago and lived in a smaller cottage in this same grouping of buildings. That was probably it over there, about a minute's walk away. It was a smaller version of the main house, with the same faded red roof, the same brick-and-stone walls, and set beneath the same willowy trees.

"I can't get myself unstrapped, Mommy," came Carly's voice from the backseat.

Jacinda found that her own seat-belt catch was stiff, also. Thanks to its frequent exposure to dust, probably. She climbed out and opened the back door to help her daughter, aware that she was being stared at—in a welcoming way, but stared at all the same. Callan opened the four-wheel-drive's back door.

"Suitcases? I'll help," Kerry Woods said, coming down the stone steps that led from the veranda. "You're Jacinda and Carly, of course, and I'm Kerry." She patted Jac's shoulder and ruffled Carly's fine hair as Carly slid her little body down from the high vehicle to the ground. "Boys, don't just stand there, come and meet Carly. Someone to play with!"

"Does that mean we've finished school?"

"To play with *when* you've finished school, which is at lunchtime, as you well know, Lockie!"

It was now eleven-thirty, Jac saw when she looked at her watch. No, wait a minute, they were on central Australian time now, the pilot had said, which meant it was half an hour earlier here than it would be in Sydney.

"Did you have a good flight?" Kerry asked her.

"Yes, the view from the plane between Sydney and Broken Hill was fascinating. Um, I'm afraid between Broken Hill and here, though, I—"

"She looked pretty green when she landed," Callan cut in on a drawl.

Kerry made a sympathetic sound, and Carly asked her lizard question. The boys had gotten the dogs all excited again and they almost tripped Callan up as he reached the steps with the two heaviest suitcases. Josh ignored the lizard question and asked a jumbo-jet question of his own. Carly ignored that, but Lockie answered it in the derisive tone of an older brother. Kerry grabbed the third suitcase and mentioned tea and biscuits. The dogs said, *Yes, please!* Lockie and Josh protested about their schoolwork once more.

Chaos, all of it.

Fabulous, safe, friendly, normal, reassuring family chaos.

"I'd love some tea and biscuits," Jacinda said. She picked

up the bag that Rob-the-pilot had unloaded from the plane along with her luggage. "Should I bring this?"

"Uh, yeah, it's just the mail," Callan said.

"Wow! You get a lot of mail out here!"

"Not usually."

"More letters, Callan?" Kerry asked.

"I'm hoping most of it's other stuff."

"I think there are some books in here," Jacinda said and saw that he looked relieved.

She still felt shaky. The difficult flight, the remnants of jet lag following their trip from California four days ago, the fact that she hadn't been eating enough lately… Her blood sugar was down and she was stressed and emotionally stretched to the point where she thought she might snap like a perished elastic band.

Kerry must have seen at least a part of all this.

"Come inside," she said. "Boys, leave our visitors alone for a bit, until we get them settled. Callan, I made up both beds in the back corner room. It looks out on the garden, Jacinda, and there's a door opening to the back veranda. There's a bathroom just across the corridor, and I've forbidden the boys to use it while you're here. They can use Callan's. So if you want to freshen up, or if you want me to bring the tea to your room…"

Chaos.

Then peace.

Carly had already made friends with lizard-loving Lockie, if not yet with Josh, and wanted him to show her the garden. Inside the house, the air was pleasantly dim and cool in contrast to the bright light and heat outside. Along the corridor, Jac saw prize ribbons in different colors from various cattle shows tacked up on the wall. The three suitcases and the overnight bag sat in the middle of her new room, for when she felt ready to unpack. Callan's mailbag had disappeared somewhere, carried in his firm grip.

The guest room itself was spacious but modestly furnished—twin beds clothed in patchwork quilts, a ceiling fan, a freestanding varnished pine armoire, a matching chest of drawers with a mirror above, and a framed picture of a landscape that seemed to be made out of pieces of twig and leaf and bark.

Jacinda lay down on the bed and looked at the picture and at last felt truly safe. *At last.* She was far enough from Kurt, from his power and his contacts and his chains of influence and control. He wouldn't find Carly here, and even if he did, his power did not extend into this Rhode-Island-sized cattle kingdom.

She closed her eyes and her head still whirled, but at least her heart had stopped its skittering rhythm and had steadied to a regular beat. She couldn't stay here forever. Not more than a few weeks at most. Even in that time, she and Carly couldn't let themselves be a burden on Callan or his family. But for now, for now...

Twenty minutes later, as soon as she was sitting down with Kerry and Callan over their cookies and tea, she told them, "Please give me something to do. Anything. I mean that. I'd suggest something, only I don't know what you need. Dishwashing and cooking and vacuuming, obviously, but more than that. Don't treat me like a guest when I've dumped myself and my daughter on you like this."

She sounded sincere and almost pleading, Callan thought, and he knew it would be easier on all of them if he could find something for her to do. Mustering big, half-wild cattle on a dirty quad motorbike, maybe? Stretching wire on about four thousand meters of new fence? Harnessing herself to the faded red roofs and painting them?

Hmm. There was just a slight chance that in those areas, an ex–Los Angeles screenwriter wouldn't have the necessary skills. *Mum, help me on this....*

His mother had brought out a set of blocks for Carly to play with and she was happy with them out on the veranda, visible through the screen door. The boys were back at their school desks, Josh working on math problems and Lockie struggling with a book report.

They did their lessons via Internet and mail through the South Australian School of the Air. Callan had done the same thing up until the age of twelve, back when the Internet hadn't existed and his teacher was just a scratchy, indistinct voice on the high-frequency radio. In general, the boys enjoyed their schooling and it gave them a vital contact with other kids and the outside world, but Lockie wasn't a keen reader or writer. They'd all been suffering through the book report this week.

"School?" his mother mouthed at Callan.

He was about to shake his head. He knew why she'd suggested it. If she didn't have to supervise the boys, she'd be free to get more done in the garden. She worked too hard already, though, and had done since Dad's death. Callan didn't want to give her a way to work even harder.

But Mum didn't give him time to nix the idea. "Lockie would love some help with his book report," she told Jacinda. "Callan said you were a writer...."

Jacinda gave a tight little nod. She looked as if she'd suddenly felt demon fingers on the back of her neck.

Callan jumped in. "Mum, I don't think—I think that's like asking a doctor for free medical advice at a party."

"No, it's fine," Jacinda said. "Really."

Callan could see it wasn't fine.

Worse, Jacinda thought that Mum had meant right this minute, and she'd already stood up and gone into the office-cum-schoolroom adjacent to where they were sitting. Or rather, where Josh was huddled over his math book and

Lockie was staring morosely at an almost-blank computer screen. "What's the book, Lockie?"

What'sthebookLockiewhat'sthebookLockiewhat'sthebookLockie…

The words echoed in Jacinda's head like a dinning bell for several seconds after she spoke them.

I can do this, she thought.

It would be insane if I couldn't do this.

But she'd had trouble even filling in the passenger arrival card coming in to Sydney's airport on the plane. She'd bought some postcards three days ago—twelve hours before her frantic call to Callan—and she'd left them behind at Lucy's, unable to face what they did to her well-being. She'd picked up a pen at one point, on the day she'd bought them, stared at the rectangle of card and teetered on the edge of a full-fledged panic attack.

It was just like the panic attack that was boiling up inside her now, like thunder clouds boiling on a humid summer horizon. Only this time, there was no teetering on the edge. The panic attack descended and she had no power to fight it off.

The computer screen was so familiar. That slightly shimmery white space with its edging of Microsoft Word icons and line numbers, the bright royal blue band across the top, not much darker than the awesome blue sky above Callan's land.

BOOK REPORT Lockie had typed, centered on the page like the words REECE and NAOMI. The heading vibrated and blurred and shouted at her.

She couldn't breathe. Words tangled in her head, a nightmarish mix of dialogue lines from *Heartbreak Hotel* scenes she'd written months ago and lines that Kurt had delivered to her in person—those velvety threats, and pseudocaring pieces of advice and upside-down accusations. A black, cold, reasonless pit of fear and dread opened in her stomach and flight was the only possible response.

Out of here, out of here, out of here.

Dimly aware that Lockie was talking to her, answering her question about the book, she fled the room, out through the screen door, past a startled Carly, down the steps, out across the wide, hard-baked piece of red ground to a stand of trees grouped around a shiny metal windmill and an open water tank. She came to a halt, gasping, blood thundering in her ears.

The black pit inside her slowly closed over, leaving a powerful memory of her fear, but not the fear itself. She grasped one of the trailing branches of the willowy tree and felt a trickle of tiny, dusky pink spheres fall into her hand. Fruits? They were dry and papery on the outside and, when she rubbed them between her fingertips, they smelled like pepper.

A breeze made the top of the windmill turn. It was shaped like a child's drawing of a flower, with a circle of metal petals like oars, and it turned with just enough force to pump an erratic stream of water up from the ground and into the tank, whose tarnished sides felt cool and clean in the sliver of midday shade.

Jac began to breathe again, but she was still shaking.

"What happened, Jacinda?" Callan said behind her. She'd heard the screen door and his footsteps, but hadn't really taken in the sounds of his approach. "He wasn't rude, was he?"

"No, no, nothing like that." She turned away from the tank's cool side. "It was me. My fault, completely."

"So what happened?" He stepped closer—close enough to see the tiny, convulsive shudders that vibrated her body. "Hey…."

He touched her arm, closing his fingers around the bones

just above her wrist. His hand felt heavy and strong and warm, and before she knew it, she'd pulled her own hand around to grab him in the same place—a kind of monkey grip.

They stayed that way, too close to each other. He could easily have rested his jutting chin on the top of her bent head, could have hugged her or breathed in her ear.

"Lately I've been having panic attacks," she said. "Please apologize to Lockie. He was in the middle of telling me about the book and I just…left."

"Bit more dramatic than that, Jacinda."

"I can't even remember how I got out of the room." Without planning to, she pushed her forehead into Callan's shoulder, somehow needing to be in contact with his rocklike steadiness. She smelled hot cotton, and the natural fragrance of male hair and skin.

He held her gently and made shushing sounds, the kind he'd have made to a frightened animal—which was exactly what she was, she thought. There had certainly been no human rationality in her flood of fear.

When he made a movement, she thought he was letting her go, and the cry of protest escaped her lips instinctively. She wasn't ready yet. He felt too good, too *right*. The air between them had caught fire with shared awareness, sucking the oxygen from her lungs. Again, it was animal, primal, physical. Her body craved the contact, needed it like warmth or food. You couldn't explain it, plot out the steps that had led up to it; it was just suddenly there.

She could feel his breathing, sense his response and his wariness. Grabbing on to his hands and kneading them with her own, she gabbled something that was part apology, part explanation, and didn't make much sense at all. Then she felt him push her away more firmly.

"Carly's worried about you," he murmured on a note of

warning. "She's coming down the steps now. And Mum's behind her."

"I'm sorry."

"No. Will you stop that? The apologizing?"

"You can let me go, now. I'm fine."

"Not sure if Mum's going to stop Carly from coming over here. This must look pretty, um, private."

He'd felt it, too. The awareness. She knew he had.

But he didn't like it any more than she did.

"Yes," she said. "Okay. Yes. Let me talk to them."

"Wait, though. Listen, I don't want to push, but I really can't afford…don't want…for my mother to get the wrong idea." He stepped back, making it clear what kind of wrong idea he meant. "Jacinda, when you can, as soon as you can, please, you have to give me some idea of why you're here."

Chapter Four

"Mum's giving the kids some lunch," Callan reported. "I've told her you and I needed to talk."

"Thanks. We do. I don't want to keep you in the dark about what's been going on."

"Sit on the bench. No hurry. Are you hungry? Thirsty?"

"I'm fine. I can wait."

He'd brought her out to the garden, and it was beautiful. She'd never realized herbs and vegetables could look so pretty. There were borders of rosemary and lavender and thyme, beds of young, fist-size lettuces set out in patterns of pale green alternating with dark greenish-red, orange-flowered marigolds like sentinels at the end of each row. Shade cloth stretched overhead protected some of the beds from the harshness of the midday sun, while brushwood screens kept out the dusty wind.

The soil looked rich and dark, nothing like the red- and ocher-hued earth of the surrounding country, so it must have been trucked in from elsewhere. Beyond the garden there was a chicken run, and she could see several rusty-brown and glossy black birds scratching happily, watched over by a magnificent rooster. Carly would love a newly-laid egg each morning.

Jac whooshed out a preparatory breath, knowing she couldn't spend the next hour admiring plants and hens. "Where to begin," she said.

"You had a bad divorce," Callan prompted. "But I thought that was over. Property settlement, custody, all set."

"So did I, but Kurt has other ideas. He wants Carly." Did he really? She still wasn't sure what game he was playing. "Or he wants to terrorize me with the idea that he wants Carly," she revised. "Which is working, by the way. I'm terrorized. His actions have gone beyond industry power games."

Kurt had always loved to play those, too.

"Yeah?" Callan studied her face for a moment with his piercing blue gaze, then seemed to realize it might be easier if they both looked away, that she wouldn't want her emotions under a microscope while she talked. He picked up some bits of gravel from under the bench and started tossing them lazily, as if they both had all the time in the world for this. Somewhere overhead, a crow cawed.

"Can I copy you with the rock-throwing thing?" Jac asked, and he grinned and deposited half his handful into her open palm. They threw gravel together for a minute in silence before she could work out how to begin. Decided in the end just to tell the story as straight as she could. "Last week, a woman that Carly didn't know, a complete stranger, tried to collect her from preschool. And she looked just like me."

The memory was still very fresh, and the words came tumbling out as she told Callan the full story. She'd seen the woman herself. Hadn't thought anything of it, had just idly registered that a slender female with long dark hair was getting into the same make, model and color of car as her own, fifty yards down the block from the preschool gate.

Maybe, yes, she'd had some idea in the back of her mind that Kurt himself might try to pick up Carly one day, even though he wasn't supposed to and the preschool staff knew it. She'd started coming ten minutes earlier than usual because of her suspicion, but she hadn't imagined a strategy as devious as this.

She had gone inside and found the head teacher, Helen Franz, sitting at her desk pale and shaking and unable to pick up the phone to call the police. The stranger had known Carly's name, her best friend's name, the teachers' names.

"This woman, this...this...*me* look-alike, comes past Helen toward Carly," Jac told Callan. "She says to Helen, 'Hi, Mrs. Franz, I'm a touch early, I signed her out on my way through,' and Helen says that's fine—because, you know, I have been coming early, the past few weeks—and that Carly is right here. 'Here's your mom, honey.' And she doesn't really look closely at this woman, but she has no suspicions at all and she's all set to let Carly go. That was what made Helen start shaking, afterward, when she realized what she'd almost done. I started shaking, too, as soon as she started telling me. So Helen's actually ready to let Carly go. 'That's fine, Jacinda,' she tells this woman. No suspicions.

"Except that Carly knows it's not me. She won't budge. Digs in her heels. Throws a tantrum, which isn't like her. The woman says, 'Sweetheart, you don't have time to finish your game.' And she has my mannerisms. My voice. Carly starts screaming. Helen comes closer to see what the problem is. Carly screams out, 'That's not my real mommy. It's an alien!' She's terrified. Completely terrified. Partly because the deception is so neat and close. It would have been less frightening for her, I think, if the woman hadn't looked anything like me at all."

"I can understand that," Callan muttered. He stretched his

arm along the garden bench. He'd finished with the gravel. He looked skeptical, but interested. "Yeah, that makes a lot of sense. It's…yeah…scary if someone looks right and wrong at the same time. It really gets to you."

"Meanwhile, Helen's still one step behind, at this stage. She looks up to find the woman heading out of there, just quietly slipping away. But fast. As if she's been given instructions to abort the mission the moment she's seriously challenged. She had my style of sunglasses, an outfit like one of mine, my hairstyle. She was really well rehearsed. *Coached,* Callan."

He looked at her, eyes narrowed in the bright light, and she saw the doubt still in place. Dropped her bits of gravel. Grabbed his arm with dusty fingers. "Yes, I know it sounds paranoid…crazy. But my ex-husband is a big-time TV producer. He has access to desperate actresses, expert makeup artists, wardrobe people, acting and movement coaches. He could pull it off like *that.*" She snapped her fingers. "I can put you in touch with Helen Franz if you want to hear it from her. We never called the police, in the end, because nothing actually happened, but she wrote up a full report. There were two other teachers in the room who witnessed the whole thing from a distance. It did happen, Callan!"

"I—I guess I'm not doubting it. But who would have gone along with something like that? It was a kidnapping attempt!"

"Kurt wouldn't have called it that when he hired the actress. He would have called it a reality TV show with hidden cameras, or a method-acting audition for a big movie role. He would have paid in five figures. And he's Kurt Beale. So people listen. Desperate actresses sure listen! They listen to anything! And they believe him. And they do what he says. He has the power, he has the control. He loves to use it. He's Kurt Beale," she repeated.

"Yeah?" Callan said. Then he gave a slow grin. "Well, I've never heard of him."

She closed her eyes. "I know. That's exactly why I'm here."

She told him about not being able to write anymore, about being scared the inspiration might never come back, about resigning from *Heartbreak Hotel* for Elaine's sake, about fleeing to Sydney and getting all those hang-up calls at Lucy's.

"And panicking," she added. "I know I'm panicking. I do know it. Overreacting, obsessing over worst-case scenarios. Do you know what a curse it can be, a writer's imagination? But there's no place I can draw the line, Callan. If you seriously asked me, is Kurt capable of taking Carly and hiding her somewhere so I'd never see her again? Is he capable of stalking me in the entertainment industry so that I'll never write again? Is he capable of murder, that kind of if-I-can't-have-her-then-no-one-can awful thing that some men do? There's no place I could draw the line and say, "No, I know Kurt, and I know he wouldn't do that." He *could* do it. Any of it. I know it."

"Hey…hey."

"Yeah, enough about me, right?" she tried to joke. "You look like you're thinking six hundred thousand acres isn't going to be big enough for both of us."

"No, no, the opposite. I wanted to tell you that six hundred thousand acres *is* big. We're isolated. You're safe here. For— well, for—"

He wanted the bottom line. How long did she want to stay?

"A month, okay?" she told him quickly. "Our return flight is in a month. I'll have something worked out by then."

I'll know if there's a chance I can ever go back to writing.

I'll decide on somewhere Carly and I can safely live. Texas, maybe. Vermont, or Maine. Somewhere like this, where there's space and air, and where Kurt has no power.

I'll have talked myself out of the panic attacks, and Carly won't sleepwalk anymore.

"Carly sleepwalks," she blurted out.

"Does she?"

"Yes, I should tell you, and the boys, and your mom. It started a couple of months ago, before we came to Sydney that first time. The doctor thought it might be the stress of the divorce and all the conflict, Kurt's games. She doesn't do it every night. Maybe once or twice a week."

"Is it dangerous?"

"No, but it's unpredictable, and she can get upset if she's woken up in the wrong place or the wrong way. I've been sleeping pretty lightly, though, so I always hear her getting up. If she's handled gently and not startled in any way, I can just lead her back to bed."

"I can't think how it would be a problem from our end. The boys are pretty sound sleepers. And Mum's in the other house."

"Yes, it's probably fine, but I thought you should know." They both sat silently for a moment, then she added, "You say *Mum,* not *Mom.*" She imitated the clipped sound of the word, compared to the longer American vowel.

"Yep. Short and sweet."

"I like it. What should I call her, by the way, your mom?"

"Just Kerry."

"And Carly?"

"I'd say keep on calling her Carly." He nodded thoughtfully. "Might confuse her if you changed it to Goldilocks, at this stage."

Jac laughed. "Well, Goldilocks is in fact her middle name, but I take your point." The moment of silly humor was nice. Unexpected. "No, I meant—"

"I know what you meant. What should Carly call Mum? Just Kerry. Or Gran, like the boys do. She won't mind either way."

"Thanks. Thank you from the bottom of my heart for this, Callan."

For seeming so relaxed about it.

For making her laugh when she wasn't expecting to.

For not being Kurt.

"Does she have any grandmothers of her own, your Carly?" he asked.

"No, she doesn't. Kurt's mother died just before he and I met. Mine, when I was twelve. My dad lives back east." She stood up, didn't want to talk about any of that, right now. "I love those chickens." She walked toward the wire mesh that separated them from the vegetable garden and called back, "I never realized their feathers would be so beautiful. The black ones are almost iridescent on their breasts."

"And they're good layers, too." His tone poked fun at her, just a little. Iridescent feathers? These birds weren't for decoration. They had a job to do!

"Is egg collecting something Carly and I could handle? She'd love it, I think."

"Sure." He stood up and came over, and they looked at the chickens side by side.

"Do they…like…bite? I'm good with horses. Kurt and I used to ride on his ranch."

If you could call six thousand acres a ranch.

She had, once.

But she'd seen Callan's place, now.

"But chickens…" She spread her hands. She didn't know anything about chickens. They hadn't fit with Kurt's image.

"They'll peck at anything that looks like it could be something to eat," Callan said. "Shoelaces, rings. But they'll stop when it doesn't taste good. And they're not aggressive. You can pet 'em and feed 'em out of your hand." He pulled some leafy sprigs of parsley from a garden bed and gave half of them to her, then bent down to hen level and stuck his parsley through the wire. A red-brown bird came peck-peck-pecking at once. "See? Try it."

She squatted. "Well, hi there, Little Red Hen."

"The boys have names for them. They can introduce you and Carly properly after lunch."

"Her ex-husband was stalking her," Callan told his mother. "Professionally and personally. She needed somewhere safe, and far."

"Well, Arakeela should be both," his mother said.

They stood on the veranda, watching the two female figures in the chook run—the adult and the little girl. Their clothing was bright in the midafternoon light and their hair glinted where the sun hit, one head dark and the other blond. Lockie and Josh had introduced Carly and her mum to the rooster, Darth Vader, and the hens, Furious, Gollum, Frodo, Shrek, Donkey, Princess and Hen.

Carly thought those names were great. Callan and Kerry could both hear her little voice saying, "Tell me which one's Frodo, again, Mommy?"

"Well, I know it was one of the black ones…."

The boys had gone, now, having shown Jacinda and Carly the chooks' favorite laying places. They were working on the quad-wheeled motorbikes in the shed, changing the oil. Most outback kids of their age got to ride quad bikes around the property when they helped with the cattle, but Callan was pretty strict about it. If Lockie and Josh were going to ride, they had to know how to take care of the bikes and they never rode one unless he was there.

"How long are they staying?" Kerry asked.

"Their return flight is a month from now, she said. I don't know how it's going to work out, Mum, to be honest, but I couldn't say no."

"Of course you couldn't! Do you think I'm suggesting it?"

"You seemed a bit doubtful."

"I could tell something was wrong, that's all. That she wasn't just a tourist friend wanting an outback stay."

"She's been having panic attacks. That was what happened with Lockie's book report before lunch. She doesn't know what she'll do for an income instead of writing, if the…you know…drive and hunger and inspiration never come back."

He knew nothing about writing. Couldn't imagine. How did you create a plot and action out of thin air? How did you dream up people who seemed so real that they jumped off the page or out of a TV screen like best friends? How did you string the words together, one by one, so that they added up to a story?

And yet he understood something about how she felt. He knew the same fear that the drive might never come back. He knew the huge sense of loss and failure, now that the hunger was gone. He had the same instinctive belief that without this certain special pool inside you, you were physically incomplete, even though the pool wasn't something tangible and solid like a limb.

"She probably just needs to rest her spirit," Kerry said. "Take the pressure off and forgive herself."

"I guess," he answered, not believing it could be that simple. Not in his own case.

Take the pressure off? Rest the spirit? Forgive yourself? Was that all it took?

His mother didn't know.

Hell, of course she didn't! And Callan would never tell her.

He hadn't breathed a word about the freckled blonde at the Birdsville Races three years ago. When he'd gone down to chat to the Scandinavian backpacker camping at the water hole a few months later, Mum had thought he was only protecting their land. He'd reported that he'd told the young woman about where it was safe to light a campfire and where best to photograph the wildlife that came to drink at the water hole at dusk.

Mum had no idea that he'd seen a phantom similarity to

Liz in both those women, and that the women themselves had picked up on the vibe. As Jacinda had said before lunch, however, when she'd told him about the woman at Carly's preschool, it was more terrifying to confront the differences when someone bore a passing resemblance to the person you loved.

They hadn't been Liz's freckles, her kind of blond, her skin, her body, her voice.

Why had he gone looking for something that he could never find?

No one, but no one—not Brant or Dusty, *no one*—had known about the Danish girl's open-eyed seduction attempt, or Callan's failure. No one ever would.

"We got eggs!" Carly shrieked out, coming out of the hen run. "Look, guys, we got eggs! Six! Mommy has four and I have two because my hands are too little. I have one brown one with white speckles and one brown one with brown speckles."

"Carly? Don't run so fast, honey," said her mum, coming up behind her, "because if you trip and fall, they'll break."

"But I want to show 'em to Callan and—" She slowed and looked back at her mother for guidance, asking in a stage whisper, "What's the lady's name?"

Jacinda looked at Callan and shrugged, asking a question with her face. Kerry or Gran? They'd discussed it—that joke about Goldilocks—but Jacinda clearly didn't know what to say. She had that vulnerable look about her again—the loss of grace, the slight slouch to her shoulders. It made her look thinner. And it made him want to give her promises about how he'd look after her that she would be bound to read the wrong way.

Before he could answer, Kerry stepped off the veranda.

"It's Gran, love," she said, in her usual plainspoken way. As she spoke, she leaned down to admire the eggs that had made Carly so excited. "You can call me Gran."

* * *

Jet lag crept up on Jacinda and Carly a short while after the evening meal. Jac tried to hide her yawns and droopiness, but Carly wasn't so polite. "Mommeee! I'm so tired! I wanna go to bed right now!" They were both fast asleep before eight o'clock.

At midnight, according to the clock on the table beside the bed, Jac woke up again. At first she couldn't work out why, then she saw the pale child-size shadow moving near the door. Carly was sleepwalking, and subconsciously she'd heard her daughter's familiar sounds.

She caught up to her in the corridor and tried to steer her back to bed. Carly wouldn't come. "Honey? This way… Come on, sweetheart."

"Butter banana on the machine in the morning." She talked in her sleep, too, and it never made any sense.

"Let's turn around and come back to bed," Jac repeated.

Carly's eyes were open, but she wasn't awake. She had a plan. She wanted something. And as always when sleep-walking, she was hard to dissuade. "I'm coming in the morn-ing up," she said, pushing at Jac with firm little hands.

"Well, let's not, honey."

"No!" Carly said. "Up in the, in the out."

Maybe it was best to let her walk it off. The doctor had said that it wasn't dangerous to waken her, contrary to pop-ular myth, but it did always end with Carly crying and talking about bad dreams that she would have forgotten by morning if Jac could get her back to bed while she was still asleep.

"Okay, Carly, want to show me?" She took her daughter's hand and let her lead the way.

They crept along the corridor, through the big, comfort-able living room and out of the front door, first the solid wooden one and then the squeaky one with the insect-proof mesh. Oh, that squeak was loud! Would it wake Callan and the boys? Jac tried to close it quietly behind her.

Carly looked blindly around the yard, while Jacinda waited for her next move. An almost full moon shone high in the sky, a little flat on one side. It didn't look quite right, because it was upside-down in this country. Even with the moon so bright, the stars were incredible, thousands of pinpoints of light against a backdrop of solid ink. No city haze.

Carly went toward the steps leading down from the veranda, and Jac held her hand more tightly. She didn't stand as steady on her feet when she was asleep, even with her eyes open. She could easily trip and fall. At the last moment, she turned. Not going down the steps after all. There was a saggy old cane couch farther along the veranda, with a padded seat, recently recovered in a summery floral fabric with plenty of matching pillows, and she headed for that.

Jac thought, *Okay, honey, we can sit here for a while.* There was a mohair blanket draped over the back of it.

Carly nestled against her on the couch. "Yogurt, no yogurt," she said very distinctly. Then her face softened and she closed her eyes.

"No yogurt. I'll carry you back to bed in a minute," Jac whispered.

She unfolded the blanket and spread it over them both because the night had chilled considerably from the moment the sun had dropped out of sight. The blanket was hand-knitted in bright, alternating squares of pink and blue, and it was warm and soft. No hurry in getting back to bed. So nice to sit here with Carly and feel safe.

Callan found them there several minutes later. He'd heard that screen door, had guessed it was probably Jacinda, unable to sleep. They didn't lock doors around here at night. If anyone showed up with intentions good or bad, you'd hear their vehicle a mile off and the dogs would bark like crazy.

Still, after thinking about it and feeling himself grow more and more awake, something made him get up to check that everything was all right.

Yeah, it was fine. The two of them were dead to the world, snuggled together under the blanket. The fuzz of the fabric tickled Carly's nose and she pushed at it with her hand in her sleep. He moved to go back to bed himself, but the old board under his foot creaked and, coupled with Carly's movement, it disturbed Jacinda and she opened her eyes.

"Was she sleepwalking?" he asked.

"Yes, and we ended up here. I didn't mean to fall asleep myself. Did we waken you?" She looked down his body, then back up. He wore his usual white cotton T-shirt and navy blue pajama pants—respectable, Dad-type nightwear that couldn't possibly send the wrong message.

"I heard the screen door," he confessed.

She was wearing pink pajamas, herself, in kind of a plaid pattern on a cream background, and her dark hair fell over her shoulders like water falling over rock. Her skin looked shadowy inside the V of the pajama front, and even when she smiled, her lips stayed soft and full.

"Why does your mother sleep over at the little cottage?" she asked.

"Oh…uh…" He had no idea why her thoughts would have gone in that direction. "Just to give the two of us some space. She moved in there when I married Liz." Newlyweds…privacy…he didn't want to go there in his thoughts, and continued quickly, "She'll sleep in the main house if I'm away, of course, but she works pretty hard around here and sometimes she needs a break from the boys."

"Right. Of course."

"Why did you ask?"

She blinked. "I don't know. Gosh, I don't know!" She looked stricken and uncomfortable.

They stared at each other and she made a movement, shifting over for him, finding him a piece of the blanket. Without saying anything, he sat down and took the corner of the blanket. Its edges made two sides of a triangle, across his chest and back across his knees. A wave of warmth and sweetness hit him—clean hair and body heat and good laundering.

The old cane of the couch was a little saggy in the center, and his weight pushed Jacinda's thigh against his. Carly stretched in her sleep and began to encroach on his space, which stopped the contact between himself and her mom from becoming too intimate. This felt safe, even though it shouldn't have.

"Well, you know, ask anything you like," he told her. "I didn't mean you had to feel it wasn't your business."

Silence.

"It's so quiet," she murmured.

"Is it spooking you?"

"A little. I guess it's not quiet, really. The house creaks, and there are rustlings outside. Just now I heard…I think it was a frog. I'm hoping it was a frog."

"You mean as opposed to the notorious Greerson's death bat with its toxic venom and ability to chew through wire window screens to get to its human victims?"

"That one, yes."

"Well, their mating cries are very similar to a frog's, but Greerson's death bats don't usually come so close to the house except in summer."

She laughed. "You're terrible!"

"We do have some nice snakes, however, with a great line in nerve toxins."

"In the house?"

He sighed at this. "I really want to say no, Jacinda, but I'd be lying. Once in a while, in the really hot weather, snakes have been known to get into the house. And especially under the house."

She thought about this for a moment, and he waited for her to demand the next flight out of here, back to nice, safe Kurt and his power games in L.A. "So what should I tell Carly about snakes?" she finally asked.

"Not to go under the veranda. Not to play on the pile of fence posts by the big shed. If she sees one in the open, just stand still and let it get away, because it's more scared than she is. If she gets bitten—or thinks she might have been, because snake bites usually don't hurt—tell someone, stay calm and stay still."

"If she gets bitten, what happens?"

"She won't get bitten. I've lived on this land my whole life, apart from boarding school, and I never have."

"But if she does?"

"We put on a pressure bandage, keep her lying quiet and call the flying doctor."

"Which I'm hoping is not the same as the School of the Air, because I'm not sure what a doctor on a computer screen could do about snake bite."

"The flying doctor comes in an actual airplane, with a real nurse and real equipment and real snake antivenin."

"And takes her away to a real hospital, with me holding her hand the whole way, and she's fine."

"That's right. But the pressure bandage is pretty important. I'll show you where we keep them in the morning. And I'll show you how to put one on, just in case."

She nodded. "Got it. Thanks. So you've done some first-aid training?"

"A couple of different courses, yeah. So has Mum. Seems the sensible thing, out here."

"And is that how you run your land and your cattle, too? Sensibly?"

"Try to."

They kept talking. He was wide, wide awake and so was she. The moon drifted through its high arc toward the west, slowly shifting the deep blue shadows over the silver landscape. It was so warm under the blanket, against the chill of the desert night. Carly shifted occasionally, her body getting more and more relaxed, encroaching farther into his space.

Jacinda was a good listener, interested enough to ask the right questions, making him laugh, drawing out detail along with a few things he hadn't expected to say—like the way he still missed Dad, but thought his father would be proud of some of the changes he'd made at Arakeela, such as the land-care program and the low-stress stock-handling methods.

Callan thought he'd probably spooked Jacinda more than she'd admitted to regarding the snakes, but she hadn't panicked about it, she'd just asked for the practical detail. If it happened, what should she and Carly do?

And the fact that she hadn't panicked made Callan think more about her panic over Kurt. The last piece of his skepticism dried up like a mud puddle in the sun, replaced with trust. Whatever she was afraid of from her ex-husband, it had to be real or she would never have come this far, landed on him like this. She wasn't crazy or hysterical. She needed him, and even though he didn't know her that well yet, he wasn't going to let her down.

"Do you have any idea of the time?" she asked eventually. She hid a yawn behind her hand. "Has to be pretty late."

"By where the moon is, I'd say around three."

"Three? You mean we've been sitting here for three hours? Oh, Callan, I'm so sorry! You have work to do in the morning. I'm a guest with jet lag, I should never have kept you up like this."

"Have I been edging toward the door?"

"No, because Carly has both feet across your knees!"

"True, and who would think she'd have such bony heels?"

The little girl must have heard her name. Her eyelids flickered and her limbs twitched. Callan and Jacinda both held their breath. She seemed to settle, but then her chest started pumping up and down, her breathing shallow.

"I think she's having a bad dream," Jacinda murmured. Carly broke into crying and thrashing, and had to be woken up to chase the dream away. "It's okay, sweetheart, it wasn't real, it was a dream, just a bad dream. Open your eyes and look at me. Mommy's here, see? We're sitting on the porch. The moon is all bright. Callan is here. Everything's fine." In an aside to Callan, she added, "I'm going to take her to the bathroom and get her back to bed, but you go ahead."

She stood up, struggling to gather Carly into her arms at the same time.

"You're carrying her?"

"She'll get too wide awake if I let her walk."

"She looks heavy for you. Would she come to me?"

"It's fine." She smiled. "There's nothing builds upper-arm strength as effectively as having a child, right? Better than an expensive gym. Thanks for sitting up with me, Callan."

"No problem."

For some reason, they both looked back at the couch, where the mohair blanket had half-fallen to the veranda floor, then they looked at each other. And suddenly Callan knew why she'd asked that question about his mother sleeping in the cottage, three hours ago, even if Jacinda herself still didn't.

She'd unconsciously imagined how it would have looked to Mum if she'd happened to waken and find them sitting there together, under the same blanket, sharing the warm weight of Jacinda's sleeping child.

His mother had given him a particular kind of privacy

when he and Liz had been married, moving over to the cottage. When Liz had died, Mum hadn't moved back. Somewhere in her heart, although she never spoke about it, she must hope he'd someday need that kind of privacy again.

He should tell her gently not to hold her breath about it.

Chapter Five

"Saturdays and Sundays we don't have school," Lockie told Jac. He added, "It's the weekend," as if maybe Americans didn't know what weekends were.

His explanation covered the wilder-than-usual behavior of both boys this morning, which Carly had latched on to within minutes of waking at six. They kept early hours at Arakeela Downs. This was Jac's fourth awakening on the vast cattle station, and she had discovered that the dawns here were magical.

And chilly.

There was something satisfying about it. She would beat the predawn bite in the air by scrambling into layers of clothes, along with Carly, and head straight for the smell of coffee luring her toward the kitchen. Lockie, Josh and Callan would already be there, making a big, hot breakfast. Toast, bacon and fresh eggs with their lush orange yolks, or oatmeal and brown sugar, with hot apple or berry sauce.

They'd start eating just as the sun slid up over the horizon, and the colors of the rugged hills Jac could see from the kitchen windows would almost make her gasp. She and Carly would go out into the day as soon as they could. "To feed the chooks" was the excuse—Carly constantly referred to the hens as chooks, now; she'd be speaking a whole different language by the time they got back to the U.S.—but in reality, Jac just couldn't bear to miss the beauty of this part of the day.

The bare, ancient rock glowed like fire, slowly softening into browns and rusts and purples as the sun climbed higher. Dew drenched the yellow grass, the vegetable garden, the fruit trees, and made spiderwebs look like strings of diamonds. Flocks of birds in pastel pinks and whites and grays, or bright yellows, reds and greens, rose from the big eucalyptus trees in the wide creek bed and wheeled around calling their morning cries. The air was so fresh, she felt as if simply breathing it in would be enough to make her fly.

When Lockie had managed to sit down at the table, after teasing the dogs along with Carly and Josh at the back door, Jac asked him, "So what happens at weekends?"

"We get to go out with Dad. Riding boundary, checking the animals and the water."

Callan was listening. "Except today it's not work, it's a picnic," he said. "We're going to show Jacinda and Carly the water hole."

"Can we swim?" Lockie asked. "Can we get yabbies?"

"Yeah!" Josh's face lit up, too.

"Yabbies? What kind of a disease is that?" Jac asked the boys, grinning. It did sound like a disease, but from their eagerness she knew it couldn't be.

"A really nasty one!" Lockie grinned back. "Don't you have yabbies in America?"

"We're pretty advanced over there. Doctors have already found a cure."

"Yabbies you catch in the water hole and you cook them and eat them," Josh said. He was a little more serious than his big brother, a little more prickly and slower to warm to the American visitors, with their accents that belonged on TV and their ignorance regarding such obvious things as yabbies.

"Like big prawns," Callan said.

Setting silverware on the table, Jac looked up at him. "Shrimp?"

"Big freshwater ones." He poured the coffee into two big mugs and added a generous two inches of hot milk to each. The two of them liked their coffee the same way. It was one of the simple, reassuring things they had in common. Not important, you wouldn't think, but nice. "Yes, guys, we can swim and fish for yabbies," he said. "If you and Carly want to go on a picnic, Jacinda, that is."

He looked for her approval, courteous as always. They'd been over-the-top polite to each other since Tuesday night, and over-the-top careful about respecting each other's space. Which was dumb, really, because space hadn't been trespassed upon in any major way during those hours of moonlit talking on the veranda.

"If that's not interfering with your routine." Jac whacked the politeness ball right back over the net at him. She didn't know quite why they were both doing it. For safety, obviously, but she didn't really understand the source of the danger. "We'd love it."

Carly was nodding and clapping her hands.

"Doing something different on a Saturday *is* our routine," Callan said. "I like to check the water holes pretty often. Sometimes you get tourists leaving garbage, and you don't want that, or a dead animal fouling the water. Good drinking water's too important for the cattle and the wildlife out here."

"That makes sense." She found it interesting when he told

her this kind of stuff, but also suspected that when he slipped into the tour-guide routine, it was another safety valve.

"So we'll ride there, give the horses some serious exercise, take lunch, yabby nets, the whole kaboodle, light a fire, make a day of it. I'll see if Mum wants to come, but she'll probably stay at home."

"She's pretty amazing, your mom."

"Yeah, and I spend half my time trying to get her to be less amazing." He grinned, and relaxed. "Last flying doctor clinic we went to, that's what the doc told her. You need to cut down on the amazing, Mrs. Woods, it's pushing your blood pressure too high."

The kitchen timer beeped, which meant their boiled eggs were ready, and the five of them sat down to breakfast.

Like a family, Jacinda decided.

No, she *guessed* it, really.

She'd never been part of a family in that way.

Callan somehow read this information like a teleprompter, directly from her forehead, because as they ate he asked her, over a background of kid noise, "So where did you grow up? Where is your family from? Did you live your whole life in L.A.?"

"No, New Jersey, until I was twelve. Very different from L.A. but just as urban. I've never been in a place like this." She deliberately chose to focus on the geographical element of his questions, ignored the mention of family.

It didn't work.

"Why did you move?" Callan asked next.

Uhh… "When my mom died."

"Your dad didn't want the memories in New Jersey?"

"No, Dad stayed. I was the one who moved."

Okay, she was going to have to talk about it now, after giving him that revealing answer. It wasn't so terrible. She believed in honesty and didn't know why she was always so reluctant to unload this stuff. Because it made her sound too much like a stray mongrel puppy who'd never found the right home?

She hadn't thought of it quite like this before, but it made a connection.

Kurt had treated her like a stray puppy. He'd scooped her up, after they'd met at a script-writing seminar when she was still incredibly naive and raw. He'd had her professionally groomed, house-trained her himself, put a diamond collar round her neck, spoiled her rotten.... And then he'd lost interest when she still didn't perform like a pedigreed Best in Show.

Callan was waiting for her explanation.

"Dad didn't believe he could raise a teenage daughter on his own, you see," she said. "I have two brothers, but they're much older. They were eighteen and sixteen when I was born. Dad's seventy-eight now, and lives in a retirement home near my oldest brother, Andy."

She'd had a very solitary childhood. Her parents had both been in their forties when she was born, unprepared for their accidental return to diapers, night feeds, noisy play and bedtime stories. They'd expected her to entertain herself and she'd mostly eaten on her own, in front of a book. And then Mom had died....

"So Dad sent me to Mom's younger sister, because she had daughters and he thought she would know what to do." She pitched her voice quietly. Carly wasn't ready to hear about her mom's lonely childhood yet. Fortunately, she and the boys were keeping each other well entertained, vying for who could make the weirdest faces as they chewed.

Seated to Jac's left, around the corner of the table, Callan looked at her. He took a gulp of his coffee. She liked the way he held his mug, wrapping both hands around it in appreciation of the warmth. "But he was wrong about that? Your aunt didn't know what to do?"

"I was a bit different," Jac admitted. "I mean, don't go imagining Cinderella and her wicked stepmother, or anything. She tried very hard. And my cousins tried…only not quite so hard. They were three and five years older than me, beautiful, blonde and busy, both of them. They were into parties and dates and modeling assignments and dance classes. They had a whole…oh…family style that I had to slot into and mesh with. Frantic pace. Drive-through breakfasts and take-out dinners in front of TV, or on the run. Modeling portfolios and salon appointments and endless hours stuck in traffic on the way from one class to another. And I just didn't. Mesh with it, I mean. I'd grown up almost as an only child, with a very quiet life. I liked to read and think and imagine. I dreamed about horses and learning to ride. I was the polar opposite of cool. And even after the four years of ballet I took with my cousins, you would not want to see me dance!"

He nodded and stayed silent for a moment, then added with a tease in his voice, "But I'd like to see you ride."

She smiled at him, happy that he'd dropped the subject of family. "It'll be great to ride. But what will we do about Carly? She's been on a three-foot-tall Shetland pony a handful of times at Kurt's ranch, around and around on a flat piece of grass with someone holding the pony on a rope. She couldn't ride a horse of her own out here."

"We'll work something out."

"She can ride with me," Lockie said. "I'll show you how to gallop, Carlz. I'll show you Tammy's tricks. You wait!"

"Carlz" looked up at him, round-eyed and awestruck. "Yeah?" she breathed.

"Uh, Lockie, let's save the galloping and tricks for another time, okay?" Callan said. He got a glint in his eye when he saw how relieved Jac looked, then he dropped his voice and said to her, "Nice little friendship going between those two, though."

"Yes, and I think it's really good for her, Callan. I appreciate it."

Carly hadn't sleepwalked since that first night. Possibly because with all the activity generated by boys and dogs and chooks, horses to feed, gates to swing on, trees to climb and a million places to hide, by bedtime she was just too worn out to stir. This morning, as soon as she'd eaten her breakfast, she was off with the boys, who'd been dispatched to catch the horses, bring them to the feed shed where their tack was stored and get them ready.

"But Carly stays outside the paddock and outside the shed, okay?" Callan said, as all three kids fought to be the first one out the door. "She's too little, she doesn't know horses and they could kick if she spooks them."

"Will they remember?" Jac asked.

"Yep. They're good kids."

Jac liked his confidence, and after almost four days here, she trusted it. Given more responsibility and physical freedom than any child she'd ever met…let alone the child she'd once been, herself…the boys knew their boundaries and stayed within them. They understood the dangers in their world, and respected the rules Callan gave them to keep them safe. They'd keep Carly safe, also.

"…while we get the rest of the gear together," Callan said.

By the time they were ready to leave, the temperature had begun to climb, in tandem with the sun's climb through that heavenly, soaring sky. It would probably hit eighty or even ninety degrees by midafternoon, Jacinda knew. Everyone had swim gear under their clothes, and water bottles and towels in their saddlebags, as well as their share of picnic supplies. On a pair of medium-size, sturdy horses whose breed Jac didn't know, the boys also had yabby nets, bits of string and lumps of meat for bait.

Kerry was staying home, and Carly was riding right in

front of Callan on his big chestnut mare, Moss, her little pink backpack pressing against his stomach. She looked quite comfortable and happy up there. Her mommy was a little nervous about it, but Josh's old riding helmet and Callan's relaxed attitude helped a lot.

It was a wonderful ride. The dogs were wildly jealous, but Kerry wanted them at home with her for company. Their barks chased after the four horses and five humans for several minutes until the trail that followed the fence line cut down toward the dry creek bed and the hill between creek and homestead cut off the sound, at which point, "They can bark all they want but we don't have to hear," Callan said.

He let the boys lead the way and brought up the rear himself, with Jacinda in the middle. It felt good to know that he was behind her, that he would see right away if something went wrong and he'd know what to do about it.

Not that you could imagine anything going wrong on a day like today. A breeze tempered the sun's heat, and the stately river gums spread lacy patterns of shade over the rapidly warming earth. They startled a mob of red-coated kangaroos who'd been sleeping in some dry vegetation and the 'roos bounded away, over the smooth-worn rocks and deep sand of the creek bed. On the far side of the creek, there were cattle grazing on coarse yellow grass. Some of them looked up at the sound of the horses, but soon returned to browsing the ground.

"When does the creek actually flow?" Jacinda asked, craning around to Callan in her saddle. It was a different style from the ones on Kurt's ranch, not so high in front. "In winter?"

"Only when we've just had rain," Callan answered. He nudged Moss forward to close the distance between them a little. Carly sat there, so high. Her little body rocked with the motion of the horse's gait like she was born to it, and her helmet looked like a dusty white mushroom on top of her head. "It doesn't stay running for long. A couple of days. Enough to top up the water holes. Fortunately we have a string of good deep spring-fed ones in the gorge, and a couple more downstream."

"Does the creek water ever get to the sea?"

"Nope. It drains into Lake Frome, east of here."

"Which is dry, too, most of the time, right? A salt pan?" She'd been looking at a map and some books with Carly while the boys did schoolwork during the week.

"That's right. Salt and clay. Flat, as far as the eye can see. I like these mountains better."

"Well, yeah, because you own these mountains."

She couldn't keep the satisfaction out of her voice, and he picked up on it. "You really like that, don't you?"

Yes.

A lot.

The safety of it.

The strength.

"Almost as much as you do, Callan Woods."

He didn't answer, just did that lazy, open grin of his, which she could barely see beneath his brimmed stockman's hat. Correction—she could see the mouth, but not the eyes. Didn't matter. She already knew what the eyes looked like. Kept seeing them in her mind when she twisted back the right way in her saddle, bluer than this sky, brighter than sun on water.

It was midmorning when they reached the deep water hole lodged in the mouth of the red rock gorge. Callan and the boys led the horses down to drink, then tethered them in the shade on the creek bank, where they found tufts of coarse grass to chew on.

"Swim first?" he said.

"Is it really safe?"

"If you're sensible."

"So you mean it's not safe?" She imagined crocodiles.

"It's deep in parts, and it's cold."

"But no crocodiles?"

He laughed. "Not a one. But it's colder than you would think, especially once you go a few feet below the surface. Keep Carly in the shallows. See, it's like a beach. The sand's coarser than beach sand but it shelves down nice and easy."

"Mmm, okay." She could see for herself the way the water darkened from pale iced tea to syrupy cola. "Why is it that color?" she asked.

"It gets stained from the eucalyptus leaves. In some lights, it looks greener. The boys and I like to jump and dive in a couple of spots off the ledge on the far side, there, but we always check the places out first. I've been swimming in this water hole my whole life, but you can get tree branches wedged in the rocks that you can't see from the surface, and you don't want to get caught or hit your head."

"I'll stick with Carly in the shallows."

He was right. It was cold. Enough to make her gasp when she stepped into it from the warm sand. And it had a fresh, peaty kind of smell that she liked. Carly splashed and ducked and laughed, while Jac watched the boys and their dad swimming across an expanse of water that looked black from this angle, toward the rock ledge. They trod water back and forth, scoping out the depths for hidden dangers, then having determined that it was safe, no hidden snags, they hauled themselves out onto the rock, climbed to the high point, gave themselves a good long run-up and started to jump.

After fifteen minutes, Carly's teeth began to chatter. She lay on a towel in the sun for a short while, but soon warmed up again, put a T-shirt over her semidry swimsuit and was ready to make canal systems and miniature gardens in the sand. Lockie had had enough of the water, also. He swam back to the beach to get his towel, but Callan and Josh were still jumping and whooping, their voices echoing off the rock walls of the gorge behind them, the only human sound for miles around.

"Swim over and give it a go," Callan called out to Jacinda. He stood at the edge of the highest part of the ledge, a good twelve feet above the waterline.

Not in a million years, Jac thought.

"I'm watching Carly," she called back.

"Lockie's with her now. She's dressed. She'll be fine."

"No, really…"

"I'm going back to the sand, Dad," Josh said. He and Callan did one last whooping jump from the ledge together, with legs kicking wildly in the air and arms turning like windmills, then they swam toward the stretch of beach.

"She'll be fine with the boys," Callan repeated when he approached Jacinda, as if there'd been no break to the conversation. "She'd have to go in pretty far to get out of her depth here."

He touched bottom and stood waist-deep, then began to stride toward the beach, the water streaming from his body as he got closer and shallower. He reached Jacinda, his skin glistening and his dark, baggy swim shorts hanging low on his hips. He wasn't self-conscious about his body, just took it for granted.

Jac didn't. She saw hard bands and blocks of muscle, a shading from tan to pale halfway down his upper arm, a neat pattern of hair across his chest, and the way the cold and wet made every inch of his skin taut.

Standing calf-deep, he gestured behind him. "See, there's about six meters of sand all the way along this side, before it starts to shelve down. She's safe without you. And you'd be safe, too, if you came for a jump off the ledge. It's so much fun, Jac."

He used the same tone that some men might reserve for attempting to get a woman into bed, and it was the first time he'd called her Jac, even though she'd asked him to three days ago.

"Mmm…"

That's not an answer, she realized. *I can't believe I'm even considering this.*

"Hey?" he cajoled. "Thinking about it? The rush as you race forward and hit the air? It's so good. And you have to yell, that's a requirement. Lockie first did it when he was five. Promise you'll yell?"

Live a little, said his eyes. There was a contained eagerness coming from him. He was like Carly about to give Mommy a special piece of artwork from preschool. How could you not respond just exactly the way those eyes begged you to?

"Callan, I'm not even promising to—"

"You need a reason to yell in life, sometimes, and this is the best one I know."

"Yeah?"

I don't believe this.

I am considering it.

I'm seriously thinking about it.

The yelling idea is incredibly attractive.

Her heart started beating faster. She could smell horse on her body, dust in the air, creek water in Carly's wet hair. She was eight thousand miles from the place she called home, on six hundred thousand acres of land.

And she was seriously wondering if she might be brave enough to run and jump, while yelling, into a deep, creepy water hole.

Just do it.

"Gotta earn those yabbies." Callan held out his hand, ready to pull her up. Behind him, Lockie had started putting lumps of meat inside old stocking feet and tying them with string. Under his direction, Josh was searching for good long sticks of eucalyptus to act as fishing poles.

"This is way outside of my comfort zone!" Jacinda warned as Callan's grip locked with hers.

A moment later, she reached a standing position and they came face-to-face, confronting Jac with something else that was way outside of her comfort zone. His hard, wet body, his slightly quickened breathing, his exhilarated grin. All of it was too close and too real when they stood just inches apart like this.

Feeling it, too, and clearly not liking it, he let her go and told her in an awkward way, "Strip, before you chicken out."

She was only wearing a T-shirt over her two-piece tank-style animal print swimsuit. She crossed her arms, peeled the T-shirt over her head and dropped it on a patch of dry sand safely distant from the kids' messy play. She discovered Callan looking over at the kids. His lean, strong neck looked too tight and twisted. It wasn't a natural angle. He'd been— what?—*averting his eyes* while she stripped?

In her animal print, she felt like Jane to his Tarzan. But had Tarzan been that much of a gentleman?

"I'm coming as far as the ledge, but I don't promise to jump," she said.

His head turned again, back to her, and a frown dropped away, replaced with a twinkle in the depths of those eyes. "We'll see," he drawled.

He grabbed her hand and galloped her into the water. Getting deeper in two seconds than she'd gone with Carly in fifteen minutes, she gasped again. He was right, the deeper you went, the colder it got. "Let me go!"

"Swim," he said, and struck off ahead of her with a powerful stroke.

She followed, terrified. The water felt so different to California pool water or salty ocean. So smooth. *Sooo* deep. How far down did it go? She had to fight away images of creatures lurking down there.

Before her imagination got out of control, they reached the

lower part of the ledge and she hauled herself up onto the warm rock, copying Callan's fluid movement with a more awkward one of her own. Her body tingled all over and she panted for breath.

"You did great," he told her. "You're a good fast swimmer."

"Only because things were chasing me."

"Bunyips?"

"Wha-a-at? There *is* something down there! I knew it! What the heck are bunyips? Oh sheesh, I'll never get back to the beach, now! I'll have to go the long way around, over the rocks."

Which didn't look easy.

"Don't panic. Bunyips are mythical. Kind of an Australian version of the Loch Ness monster."

"You know, Callan, there are people who don't think the Loch Ness monster is just mythical. I don't think these things should be dismissed. I've read articles about it, and there's also that in-some-ways-quite-credible urban myth about alligators in the New York—"

He wasn't listening. He'd somehow gotten hold of her hand again and they were climbing to the higher part of the ledge, over the rough shelves of rock that acted like steps. At the top, he turned away from the water and led her back into the shade of the gorge's overhanging sides. He had her in a kind of monkey grip now. He was holding her forearm in the circle of his fingers, and she held his forearm the same way. It was so strongly muscled that her fingers went barely halfway around.

"Repeat after me, Jac," he said. "Bunyips are mythical."

"Bunyips are mythical. But I have a very powerful imagination, I'm telling you."

"Okay, louder. Bunyips—are—mythical."

"Bunyips—are—mythical. And if they're not, you know how to scare them away, right?"

"Bunyips are mythical. And plus they're very friendly."

"Callan…"

"Right, now, let's go, but this time we'll yell it. Ready?" He didn't give her a chance to tell him she wasn't. Hand in hand, they sprinted forward, with Callan yelling at the top of his lungs. "Bunyips…are…"

Jac joined him on the last word, screaming it, whooping it, as they came to the end of the ledge and hit the air, legs still working wildly, arms flung high but still joined. *"Mythical!"* The word echoed off the gorge walls, bouncing like a ball, and she heard it come back to them while they were in midflight. Their voices seemed to claim this whole place.

She whooped again.

Felt a surge of utter exhilaration.

Hit the water.

Callan still had her hand. They went down, down into the icy darkness and she kicked frantically to bring herself back up, just as he was doing. She broke the surface gasping and laughing. "Get me out of here! I *know* there's a bunyip down there!"

"Wanna do it again?"

"Unnhh," she whimpered. "Unnhh!"

Do I?

Could I?

"Yes!"

They jumped together four more times, whooping and yelling and laughing, until Lockie complained, "Dad, you're scaring the yabbies! We haven't caught a single one."

"Try for them in that reach of water behind the rocks where it gets muddy," he called back to his son. "Are we done, Jacinda?"

"I think so," she said, breathless and starting to shiver.

The contrast between the cold water and the hot sun on the rocks felt wonderful with each jump and climb, but she'd had enough, and Carly must be getting hungry. They were cooking sausages and lamb chops for a midday barbecue, and Callan still had to light the fire. They swam back, side by side, no bunyips in sight, nothing nipping at her toes.

Walking through the shallows, she confessed, "I was so scared, Callan, you have no idea!"

"It's a healthy kind of scared, though, isn't it? You push the fear back with yelling, and then you feel great."

"How would you know? You said you'd been doing it your whole life. You can't ever have been scared here."

"I haven't been scared *of* here—of the water hole."

"Or bunyips."

"Or bunyips." He paused. "But I've been here, scared." Paused again. "I've come here a few times to try and yell it away, and it's always worked."

"Scared of what, then, if not the water hole?" She said it before she thought, shouldn't have needed to ask.

"After Liz died." His voice went quiet and his body went still, reluctant and stiff. "Scared of—"

"I'm sorry, I'm sorry. You don't need to spell it out. I understand."

He gave a short nod. "Yeah, there was nothing unique about it."

"I'm sorry," she said again, but she didn't show that he'd heard.

"I got given some, you know, brochures at the hospital in Port Augusta," he said. "Information leaflets. About bereavement. And they had lists of things I might be feeling, and I was. Feeling those things. All of them. It's stupid. I hated having my whole gutful of emotions put onto a bloody list. There were lists of things you could do about the emotions, too. Ways of getting help, ways to help get yourself through it."

"But those lists didn't have yelling and jumping into the water hole?"

"Nope."

And that was good, Jac understood, so Callan had jumped into the water hole a lot.

She felt privileged, sincerely privileged, that he'd wanted to push her to do it, and very glad that she had. She was pretty sure he didn't offer the same opportunity for terror and yelling to just anyone. She was very sure he was right to think that she needed it.

Bunyips were mythical.

And Kurt's power games were a long way away.

"Got one! Got one! Got one!" Josh shrieked out.

About twenty seconds later, Carly screamed, "Mommy, I got one, too!"

"Let Lockie put it in the bucket for you, Carlz," Callan warned her quickly. "It might nip you with its claw if you touch it. Lockie—?"

"I'm helping her, Dad, it's okay."

"Let's get that fire going."

He grabbed his towel and dried himself with the vigor of a dog shaking its wet coat, then dragged his T-shirt and jeans over his still-damp body, hauled on his sturdy riding boots and went to work unpacking backpacks and saddlebags, while Jac was slower to cover her damp swimsuit with her clothes. She couldn't help watching Callan as she dressed.

There was a circle of big river stones in the shade near the creek bank. The remnants of charcoal within it, as well as the blackened sides of the stones themselves, told Jac that the circle was another detail to this place that Callan had known his whole life.

"Want to find some bark and sticks?" he said.

She gathered what he'd asked for, while he broke thicker wood into short lengths with a downward jerk of his foot. He had a fire going within minutes, with water heating in a tin pot that he called a billycan. Out here in the middle of the day, the light was so bright you could barely see the flames, but you could feel the heat and the water was soon steaming.

Jac checked on the yabby tally. The kids had twelve in their red plastic bucket, but the yield seemed to be slowing and interest had waned. "The bait meat's losing its flavor," Josh said.

"And yabbies aren't stupid. They're on to us," Lockie decided. "Twelve'll have to be enough." He stood up, leaving the bucket behind, and wandered in the direction of the horses.

"They're our appetizer," Jac said, without thinking.

"We're going to eat them?" Carly wailed. "We can't *eat* them!"

They were kind of cute, in a large, shrimpy sort of way, Jac conceded, with blue and black and green markings that would turn red and pink when they were cooked. Too cute to eat?

"Nah, it's okay. They won't know it's even happening," Josh told Carly in a matter-of-fact voice.

"How come they won't know?" she asked.

Over by the fire, Callan called out, "Lockie, can you grab the tea bags while you're there?" Lockie was still with the horses, looking for something in a saddlebag.

"Dad drops them into the boiling water and they don't even have time to feel it. If I was a yabby, I'd way, *way* rather be eaten by a human than anything else."

"Why, Josh?" Carly asked seriously.

"Because anything else would be eating me alive."

"Eww! Yeah! Alive! Are you listening, yabbies?" Carly spoke seriously to the scrabbling contents of the red bucket. "We're nice, kind humans. We're not going to eat you alive."

Which seemed to deal with the whole *too cute* issue, thank goodness.

Ten minutes later, Carly was eating a hot yabby sandwich, with butter, pepper and salt.

Jac ate one, too, and it sure tasted good. "This is one of those moments when I blink and shake my head and can't believe I'm here," she told Callan, hard on the heels of the last mouthful, her lips still tasting of butter and salt.

"Yeah?" Callan waved pungent blue smoke away from his face.

He had a blackened and very rickety wire grill balanced on the stones over a heap of coals. It looked as if someone had fashioned it out of old fencing wire, but it held the lamb chops and sausages just fine, and they smelled even better than the yabby sandwich had tasted.

In a little pan, also blackened, he had onions frying in the froth from half a can of beer. The other half of the can he drank in occasional satisfied gulps, while Jacinda sipped on a mug of hot tea.

"I've just eaten something that a week ago I'd never even heard of," she said. "I've swum in terrifying water, chock-full of bunyips. I've let you tell me about snakes in the house without screaming."

"I noticed you didn't scream." He gave her his usual grin. "I was impressed."

"Thank you. Meanwhile, there's a road faintly visible over there that you claim leads eventually to Adelaide, but there hasn't been a car on it since we got here, what, an hour ago? In fact, have I seen or heard a car since Tuesday? I don't think so."

"There have been cars."

"I haven't noticed them. I've been too busy. It's incredible here. Carly is—Carly will—I hope Carly never forgets this. It's going to change who she is."

And "Carly" is code for "Carly and me."

It's going to change who I am, even more, but there are limits to my new yelling-and-jumping-induced bravery, and I'm not prepared to say that out loud.

"Wouldn't be surprised if it changes the boys, too," Callan answered.

He flipped a couple of lamb chops with a pair of tarnished tongs, drained the last of the beer and looked at her with those steady blue eyes, and she suspected...decided...hoped...that "the boys" was code, also.

Chapter Six

"Dad?" Through a fog of steam, the bathroom door clicked shut behind the new arrival.

"What's up, Lockie?"

"Can I talk to you for a sec?" The tone was reluctant, yet confiding.

"Can't it wait until I'm done in the shower?" Callan had been caught this way by Lockie before.

His evening shower was one of the few intervals in his day that was both relaxing and private, and maybe that was why Lockie came looking for him here. He knew the two of them wouldn't be disturbed by Josh or Gran or the dogs or, tonight, Carly or her mother.

The shower ran on bore water from deep in the ground, which meant it was as hard as nails but hot and steamy and in plentiful supply. Conserving water was deeply bred into anyone who lived beyond Australia's coastal fringe, but four minutes of steamy peace per day was, surely, not too much to ask.

Apparently, yes.

"Well, you see, the thing is…" Lockie trailed off. The reluctance had increased.

Callan sighed and surrendered his peace, realizing he wasn't dealing with a mere request for homework intervention or a new computer game, here. "Go ahead, spit it out."

"You know when we were at the water hole today?"

"I have a faint memory of something like that, yes, even though it's been a whole four hours since we left the place."

Out it came in a sudden rush. "I left my Game Boy behind on a rock."

"You what?" Callan shut off the water and reached around the edge of the shower curtain for his towel. "You brought your Game Boy down there? Why?"

"In case I got bored."

"But you didn't get bored. I didn't even see you with it."

"I got it out after we stopped yabbying, but then we had lunch and I forgot about it and I left it and I only remembered it now."

"Right."

"Sorry, Dad."

"What do you think we should do about it?" He wrapped the towel around his waist and slid the shower curtain aside, confronting his son.

He was strict about this kind of thing, and Lockie knew it. The boys were good, usually. Callan had trained them that way. They always left a gate the way they found it. They did a job, then put their tools away. They didn't leave feed bags open to attract vermin, or riding gear lying around to get its leather cracked in the sun.

"I think I should go back first thing in the morning and get it," Lockie said. "Like, very, very first thing."

"I think you're right," Callan said. "And I think you know I'm not happy about this. How long did you have to save up your pocket money to buy that thing? A year?"

"I'm not happy about it, either."

It was almost fully dark out, now, and they were just about to eat. Mum had cooked something special, the way she often did on a Saturday or Sunday. Smelled like lasagna and garlic bread, and the kids had already discovered and reported that there would be hot peach cake and ice cream for dessert.

Callan was hungry. He'd been up since five-thirty this morning. He didn't want to have to stir from the house again tonight.

"Is it going to be safe on a rock all night?" Lockie asked him.

"Yeah, that's what I'm wondering. What do you think?"

"If dew gets in it, or a 'roo knocks it off, or a cow steps on it, it could get destroyed."

"All those things are possible."

"So maybe I should go now," Lockie said.

"No, Lockie." Callan sighed. He wasn't going to send a ten-year-old out alone on horseback or a quad bike after dark, on the tail of a long day. "We'll eat, and then I'll go."

"I can come with you."

"Nope." Lockie looked yawning and droopy-eyed already. He'd helped with the horses, done various yard chores. He didn't need to come. "You can watch some TV, then read in bed for a bit and go to sleep."

"I can pay you my pocket money for the next couple of months, like, for your time."

Callan laughed. "No, you can just not do it ever again."

"Thanks, Dad."

He told Mum about the problem as he helped her serve out the meal, which was indeed lasagna, and he felt hungry enough to eat a whole trayful.

"Take Jacinda with you," she said at once. "You won't ride, will you? You'll take the four-wheel-drive?"

"Seems best. Although it's rough, getting to that spot in a vehicle, especially in the dark."

"You can walk the last few hundred meters. But you must take Jacinda. Two pairs of eyes. Even if Lockie thinks he can describe to you exactly which rock it's on."

Which Lockie couldn't.

"If Jacinda wants to come," Callan said.

"Of course I'll come," Jac told him.

They'd just eaten Kerry's fabulous meal, all appetites sharp after the day spent outdoors. She felt deliciously sated, and she felt exhausted. It was very tempting to pick up on the various outs he'd offered her and let him go alone. If she was too tired, if she didn't think Carly would settle to sleep without her, if a rough ride in a four-wheel-drive held no appeal…

But she'd vowed earlier in the week to jump at any chance to help around here. Searching a creek bed with a flashlight in the dark was definitely something she could do.

"So Gran will put me to bed?" Carly wanted to know.

"That's right, ducks," Kerry said cheerfully.

"Yes," Jac agreed, wondering how many new nicknames her daughter would have at the end of four weeks. She already answered quite happily to Carlz and ducks. "And I'll creep in and kiss you as soon as I get back, beautiful."

"Kiss me now, too."

"Of course."

A few minutes later, Jac had a not-very-suitable pink angora sweater over her T-shirt, and two flashlights in her lap, and she was seated next to Callan in the four-wheel-drive, ready to leave.

He hadn't exaggerated about the rough ride. "Problem is,"

he half yelled above the engine noise, as they bounced and lurched along, "there's a track, but you tend to lose it in the dark."

"Because it's not much of a track, if it's what we rode along today."

"You have a point."

"Ow! And I'm going to have some bruises!" Her shoulder bumped the door.

"Sorry, I should have insisted that this would be way too much fun for you in one day."

"After the fun of the bunyip jumping?"

"But you did like the horse riding and the barbecue, right?"

"I liked the bunyip jumping, too, Callan."

Instinctively, they turned to look at each other at the same moment. His face was shadowed and indistinct in the darkness, but she could see that grin. And she could feel the awareness, the way she'd been feeling it at certain moments for the past four days.

They were both so cautious about it, so full of doubt. It was still only a hint in the air, like the smell of approaching rain or the sound of a church bell across city rooftops. Distant. You had to strain to catch it. The rain might pass over different terrain and never fall. The wind might carry the sound of the bells away.

And they might very easily never act on this…this little zing, this recognition. They might let it go. Smile and move on. It might fade as they got to know each other better, if what they saw on the surface wasn't reflected deeper within.

Or they might get too scared, because things like this rarely stayed simple for long.

For now, it made Jacinda's heart beat faster sometimes, it made her stomach go wobbly, and she watched these things happening in her body and didn't know what to think.

The vehicle lurched again, throwing her in his direction, this time. They jarred against each other, one solid, the other soft. He reached and clamped an arm around her shoulder, working the wheel with one hand. "Going to stop under that tree, and we'll walk the rest."

The awareness hit again, stronger in her because she'd felt his body against hers, harder to resist. It made her breathing go shallow. It started her wondering.

The tree he'd mentioned loomed in the headlights, its trunk the same grayish white as the horse Jac had ridden today. After a couple more lurches and the screech of protesting suspension, Callan braked beneath it, switched off the engine and jumped out.

Jacinda followed him, handing him a flashlight.

"See that moon?" he said. "We hardly need these." He tossed it up in his hand and caught it. "We can leave them switched off until we're searching the rocks." Lockie's description of the Game Boy's location had been vague.

They tramped along in the dark, surrounded by the same magical blue and silver shadows and shapes that Jacinda had noticed the other night. They didn't talk. Callan had said as they drove that there might still be wildlife at the water hole at this hour. They always came down at dawn and dusk to drink. "And if we're quiet, we can take a look."

It was good not to talk. Good just to walk along, listening to the sound of their feet on rock and sand, listening to the way Callan's boots creaked, aware of the way he moved with such sure-footed balance and such economy.

In Los Angeles, everyone seemed to talk all the time. They were chained to their cell phones, locked in meetings, constantly updating arrangements, passing messages through secretaries. There was a whole, ever-shifting hierarchy regarding who Kurt would speak to directly, who he'd call back right away, who he'd fob off on an assistant and who he wouldn't call back at all.

There was a standard repertoire of lies and evasions. *I love the script. This is so fresh. We're in contract negotiations right now. Our marriage is rock solid.* Jacinda had believed way too many of those statements for way too long—believed them when she'd heard them from Kurt, from his staff, from his so-called friends.

She'd had a solitary childhood. Too much silence. First, her parents' quiet, immaculate home, and then her own protective silences, withdrawing to the inner kingdom of her imagination, as she sat squashed into the corner seat in the back of the car while Aunt Peggy drove her cousins around.

When Kurt had brought her into his world, fresh from taking her college degree in English and creative writing, she'd loved the opening of new horizons; she'd loved all the talk, meeting other writers, traveling to Europe, adventures on yachts and ski slopes and horseback. She'd wanted to talk and hadn't needed silence, at first.

But then she'd hit overload, and had discovered that her distant, reluctant parents had given her a positive legacy, after all. Silence could be good sometimes. It could be necessary. It didn't mean that communication disappeared. Sometimes you could understand more about a person when you left some space between all the words.

"We should start looking for the wretched thing," Callan finally said. His voice sounded a little rusty, as if he hadn't wanted to break into the rhythm of their walking. "Here's the water hole just ahead."

"Can we check for kangaroos first?" she asked him on a whisper.

"They're much less scary than bunyips, I promise."

"No, I want to see them drinking. You said we might."

He looked at her, gave a quick nod, grabbed her hand and they crept toward the water hole. It looked still and beautiful, but they crouched behind a rock, waiting and watching for several minutes, and there were no animals there.

Only the two of them.

Jac didn't feel quite human tonight, alone with Callan in the desert. Watching the water hole for signs of movement, she heard his breathing, felt his body like a flannel-and-denim-covered magnet just inches away. A man like this gave masculinity a whole new meaning, reminded a woman that human beings were animals, too.

"We were a bit late for them, I guess," he said, as they walked back toward the ring of barbecue stones in the creek bed. "It's better when there's still some daylight. We'll make a special trip one day. You can bring your camera."

She'd forgotten it on their picnic, today. "That would be great. Could we get up extra early and come at dawn? I just love the light and the air then."

"We can climb Mount Hindley, watch the sunrise, make breakfast over the fire in the creek. Would that be good?"

"Oh, it would be wonderful!"

He gave her a look. They still hadn't switched their flashlights on. "You sure you're from L.A.?"

"Last time I checked."

"You're supposed to like shopping malls better than water holes, aren't you?"

"I like new things." She thought about it for a moment. "No, that's not right. That sounds like I am talking shopping malls." She tried again. "I like being made to see things in a new way. Like dawn."

"Dawn is new?"

"It's new for me. In L.A. dawn means you stayed out late at a party, or you had to set the alarm early for a flight. If you do see the sunrise, you only see it through glass. You don't smell it, or feel the dew falling on your skin. Here, dawn is…yes, new. It notches my senses up higher, makes me aware. And writers need that. Writers—" She stopped.

There was an old, fallen eucalyptus tree lying on the creek

bed at this point. Its trunk was as big as a concrete culvert pipe, as hard and smooth as iron. Without taking his eyes from her face, Callan leaned his lower back against the curved wood as if the two of them had all the time in the world. He put his flashlight down on the tree trunk beside him, tested its balance for a moment, then let it go.

"Tell me about writers," he prompted.

But Jacinda shook her head and closed her eyes against the idea. "Doesn't matter."

"No, it was important," Callan insisted. "I was interested. Say it."

She faced him, ignoring the invitation in his body language that told her to lean against the horizontal trunk, too. Those bells of awareness weren't so distant or so faint, now. The breeze had carried the sound this way and it was clearer, much closer. But she still had the freedom to ignore the bells, if she wanted.

"I don't know if I'm a writer anymore, that's all," she said. "I think it's gone. Was it ever really there, I wonder?"

"Hey, you made a living at it."

"I had an ear for dialogue, and I could make those crazy soap-opera plot twists semibelievable when I put the right words into the characters' mouths. Was it ever more than that? If it was, I can't remember." She laughed, moved a little closer to him, although she was barely aware of it, and reached her hand out to the tree trunk. It wasn't white or gray, it was silver, and scoured to satin by years of sun and wind. "I have this novel somewhere," she confessed. "Not finished. Miles from finished. A few early chapters and some notes, and snatches of dialogue from a couple of big scenes later on."

"Was it any good?"

"Listen to you, asking me something like that!" She laughed and leaned her hip against the wood. They were like two strangers propped at a bar, trading life stories with loosened tongues.

"It's a really naive question, isn't it?" he said. "Sorry."

"No, no, it's not naive. Well, I guess it is. But it's good naive. No one in L.A. would ever ask that question because of course I'm going to say it's good. I'm trying to sell it, aren't I? I'm going to put the right spin on it, package it into a sound bite. Do you know there are people in the industry there who can talk up a project so well that they get development money for script after script even when they've never actually written a word?"

"They're the ones who sound like they're not writers."

"Truth is, Callan, I have no idea if my novel is any good. I have no idea if it's important. Finishable. Remotely saleable. I just have no idea."

"But you must have known, once."

"I think it's been dying inside me for a long time."

"But you think dawn in the North Flinders Ranges might bring it back."

She shook her head again.

"Yes." He rolled his body ninety degrees so that they faced each other. "Because that's where this started. You were telling me why you loved our dawn, and why you needed to see new things. Because you're a writer."

"Let's find Lockie's Game Boy."

"You hope you can get it back. Being a writer, I mean." He put his hand on her arm. "You really want to get it back. It's important to you."

"It's not your problem, Callan."

"No, but I can understand—" He stopped suddenly. "No, you're right, it's not my problem."

She knew there was more he wanted to say. Or didn't want to say, but could have said. The words stayed locked inside him, powerful and important in some way.

Stuck.

Too scary.

Her thigh was pushing lightly against his. They weren't pretending anymore. He held her softly, weighing their options as he weighed her in his arms. *Let each other go, or pull tighter? Hey, Jac? What do you want? The same as me? Yes, I know what you want....*

She looked up into his face.

New.

She hadn't known him at all two months ago, and even after the magazine article and the cocktail party, this face had only existed in her memory like a few snapshots and video clips. E-mailing him, she had remembered the first smile of relief he'd given her when he'd realized she wasn't serious about the Outback Wives thing, either, and his quiet good manners the following evening when he'd brought her and Carly the gift and the flowers.

She'd kept his picture from the magazine and, to be honest, she'd looked at it a couple of times. Learned it by heart, along with all the things the picture said about him.

New, but fascinating.

He wasn't smiling. His mouth was flat and closed and smooth. She liked its shape. She loved his eyes, and the lines of his brows and jaw. Above his mouth, she found a small stretch of skin that he'd missed this morning when he'd shaved. She brushed it with the ball of her thumb, the way she'd have brushed a streak of dirt from Carly's face, and it felt rough.

She waited for him to make the next move—it sounded too clinical and cold, putting it like that—but he didn't. He didn't let her go, either, just kept that light hold, and watched her watching him. She could still feel the roughness of the beard stubble on her thumb, long after she'd taken her hand away. The tension built and became unbearable. He bent his head, suddenly, and pushed his forehead against her neck, whooshing out a breath into the soft angora of her sweater.

"Oh, Lord, Jacinda!"

"I want to kiss you," she blurted out, because *someone* had to say it, someone had to take some action.

"I want to kiss you, too."

"So do it. Please?"

He was so tense, she could feel it, every muscle knotted tight enough to hurt. He breathed against her neck this time, then touched his mouth to her skin there, the movement dry and soft. He made a sound deep in his chest, imprinted his lips on her skin once again. They were so warm.

She waited.

For more.

Oh, Lord, this was unbearable.

Wonderful and unbearable.

Why didn't he move?

You might have thought he was holding a grenade with the pin already pulled. They both stood turned to stone…except that stone was never as warm and alive as his body. She couldn't hold on to this any longer; she wanted to force that mouth to move on her neck, to come and find her.

Tilting her jaw, she rubbed her face against him like a cat. She tightened the press of her body, rocked her hips a little. He was aroused. She could feel it. Finally—*finally!*—he moved to find her lips, only brushing them at first, then softening his mouth, tasting her.

"Yes," she said. The word was part of the kiss. "Like this."

It was such a relief to get there at last, such a release. She wrapped her arms around his neck, parted her lips, felt the pleasure spinning through her, tasted the faint notes of peach and vanilla in his mouth. He wanted this, so she didn't disguise her own need, deepened the contact until they were drinking each other and tangling their tongues. She gave him everything with her kiss—thanks and hunger and happiness and hope.

That was what you had to do, at some point. You just had to give yourself to it and wait until afterward to see how it felt, what you wanted next, what the repercussions might be.

Yes, she and Carly were leaving in three and a half weeks, going back to Sydney. Two days after that, they'd fly out of the country, to a future she hadn't begun to work out yet. But none of that was enough of a reason never to kiss this man, never to give or to explore.

She gave some more, slid her hands around and ran them down his back, over the tight curve of his denim-clad backside. She pulled him closer. Mmm. Their legs pressed harder together, and she knew he would feel her breasts, too, not Hollywood huge but neat and nice and female.

Mmm, Callan.

She let the hot mound at the top of her thighs squash against his hardness, the denim of two pairs of jeans diluting the intimacy. Oh, but she wished the denim wasn't there! She wanted his fingers dragging aside the lace edge of her underwear, wanted everything he could do to her, wanted the words he would say, and the convulsive tensing of his whole body.

It was like jumping into the water hole. You started, you ran, you yelled, and you didn't want to stop. She just hadn't expected the idea of stopping to feel so impossible and wrong. She didn't care that the air had started to chill, that the sand would be hard and scratchy and cold, that they might get spied on by mythical bunyips, she just *wanted*.

Him.

The escape.

The heat.

The newness.

How long did it take her to understand that he hadn't traveled toward the same place?

Too long.

He had to drag his mouth and his legs away before she realized, before she sensed the change in him—she could practically hear the squeal of the brakes—and then she felt foolish...and a little too naked...because the zing in the air was more like a force field now. It pushed her away, didn't draw her closer, and he'd already started to apologize before she had a chance to draw her first breath of non-Callan-tasting air.

"I'm sorry. I'm sorry," he said. "I'm so sorry!"

"For what?" She blinked.

"This... I shouldn't have done this." He'd half turned back to the fallen log in a gesture of self-protection, and every angle in his body screamed regret. What didn't he want her to see or know? She already knew he was aroused. So was she. Her body throbbed, her mouth tingled, and she was hot and moist and swollen. It shouldn't be a source of shame for either of them. It was human...normal...wonderful.

"Why, Callan?" She felt too bewildered to keep it from showing. "It was—it was good, wasn't it? Real nice."

Real nice? Sheesh, no wonder she didn't dare call herself a writer anymore! *Real nice* bore as much connection to what she'd felt in his arms as cheap hamburger meat bore to sirloin steak.

"It—it— Yes, it was nice. But it sets up—I shouldn't have done it." He circled around, his actions restless, erratic and unpredictable, like a freshly filled balloon escaping from somebody's grip before they'd knotted the opening. Whoosh. All over the place.

"Kissed me?" she said. "What does it set up? It doesn't set up anything."

In her confusion, she came across as indignant to the point of anger, and way too aggressive. The whole atmosphere between them jarred her spirit. How could the physical connection have simply...evaporated?

"Not anything bad, anyhow," she went on, trying to speak more reasonably. "Please don't think I'm expecting—" She made some vague circles with her hand, not wanting to put her expectations or lack of them into concrete phrasing. She was only here for a few weeks. She hadn't been thinking ahead, nailing down a prescribed pathway.

"I'm sorry," he said again. "I'm not saying you're responsible for any of this."

Any of what?

"I don't know what the problem is, Callan." She said it gently because he looked so troubled.

"Yeah, neither do I." The words came out on a growl. "But whatever it is, it's mine, not yours. Okay?"

"Okay," she echoed obediently. "Um, in that case, thanks for a fabulous kiss. Shall we leave it at that?"

He nodded, but didn't look grateful that she'd let him off the hook. "Best to." His circles around the creek bed grew wider. "We have to find that damned Game Boy," he muttered. "They're going to wonder what's happened to us, up at the house."

I'm wondering what's happened to us, too, Jacinda thought. *And I'm not up at the house. I'm right here. I'm looking right at you, Callan, and I have no idea.*

She didn't join in his search. Or not wholeheartedly, anyway. She was still too confused, didn't know whether she should be burning with mortification, angry with him, or whether all of that would have been an overreaction. He looked as if he felt all of those same emotions on her behalf anyhow. He didn't look happy with himself. Didn't look happy with the entire universe.

He muttered something about Lockie's carelessness…stupid electronic toys…shouldn't ever have let him buy the thing in the first place…kids got spoiled with that stuff.

Then he found it, sitting in what was probably the first

place they should have tried, on a rock near where the horses had stood in the shade. He expressed his relief in a profanity and headed directly for the four-wheel-drive, his strong shoulders hunched as if to keep Jacinda safely away.

They drove back to the homestead, the jolting of the vehicle echoing her jarred confidence. He'd said it wasn't her fault, but that was such a classic line. *It's not you, it's me.* Did anyone ever mean it when they said that?

Wheeling around in the front yard, he eyed the lit-up house with a bull-like glowering stare. "Looks like Mum's still getting the kids to bed."

"Carly gets overtired sometimes, after a long day, and it's hard to settle her down. I hope Kerry's not having trouble with her."

"We're all tired. So please, just forget this ever happened. All of it." He sounded angry, and she didn't understand.

"Do you want us to leave, Callan?"

"What?" His eyes narrowed. "No! Heck, no! That would be even worse." He struggled with himself and she decided that if he was angry, he wasn't angry with her, which made her shaky with relief because the memories of Kurt's veiled, terrorizing anger were still too strong. "Please stay," he said. "If you can. If you can forget tonight."

"I'll try." Then something made her add, touching him on the arm, "But no, Callan, I don't want to forget it. It was—"

"But I do," he cut in.

She didn't have time to cut off her final words. "—so good."

He didn't say anything. Didn't look at her. Just opened the creaky door and climbed out of the vehicle.

Chapter Seven

That night, Jacinda couldn't sleep for thinking about it... thinking about him. The way he'd kissed her. The way he'd turned his back.

It must have been after one in the morning by the time the memories released her body from its prison of sensual awareness, and her mind from circular questions. Even then, she had a restless night and was shocked to see how bright the morning light had grown when she woke up.

Eight-thirty, already?

Carly was long gone. Jac could hear her outside with the boys. Dressing, she heard a car, also, its engine missing some beats as the sound dropped to idling level in the front yard. She could make out an adult male voice that didn't sound like Callan's.

"Oh, that's Pete," Kerry told her a few minutes later, in the kitchen. She stood at the sink, washing fresh eggs and vegetables. "He's one of our local North Flinders people, the

Adnyamathanha. He used to be a stockman here, but he lives at the settlement at Nepabunna, now. He still drops over pretty often to help Callan out."

"Drops over?" Jacinda repeated. "How far is Nepabunna from here?" Callan had mentioned the place, she thought, but she'd gotten the impression it wasn't very near.

Kerry grinned, the same open, wicked grin that genetics had also given to her son. "Just a hop. Around a hundred and fifty kays. Ninety miles to you."

"It's okay. I'm learning to translate distances. And a hundred and fifty kilometers is just a hop?"

"It's practically next door."

"Well, so I've learned a new definition for *next door*, too."

"And it's handy for us that he is that close, because some things are a bit much for me, these days. We take on a couple of seasonals when we're doing a big muster, but when they're not around, it's just Callan and Pete. They're driving out to Springer's Well today, working on a new mustering yard Callan's been wanting to put up, and doing some tagging. Lockie's going with them, I think."

"Oh. Right. Carly will miss him."

Carly and *him* being code for *I* and *Callan*.

He's avoiding me, she decided, *because of last night at the water hole.*

Or else I'm kidding myself to think our kiss was that important to him, even in a negative, let's-forget-it-ever-happened way, and he's just building a mustering yard.

Whatever that was.

Going outside to find Carly several minutes later, she saw that Lockie and the two men were ready to leave. They were taking the chunky four-wheel-drive truck that Jac had seen garaged in a shed, and its rear tray was filled with the pile of heavy fence posts that Callan had warned Jac and Carly away from last week because of the snakes that might be living underneath.

Callan stood on top of the posts, tanned legs braced and broad shoulders working loosely as he casually caught the tools that Pete tossed up to him. He wore sturdy work gloves— possibly as a concession to the snakes—khaki shorts that came halfway down his thighs, heavy boots and the ever-present hat.

He looked so gorgeous like that—so physical, so strong, so much in his element—it made her ache.

Last night made her ache.

He waved at her and she waved back, starting to smile.

Then he turned away.

She stood like a marble statue, rocked by the strength of her response to the sight of him, stomach dropping at the brevity of that wave, hoping none of it showed. He was saying something to Pete, whose full head of white hair contrasted in the sunlight with skin that looked like hot chocolate fudge, dark and shiny.

Callan was definitely avoiding her.

Leaping down from the rear tray, he went around to the driver's side of the vehicle and climbed in, calling Lockie at the same time. "We need to get going, mate." Lockie scrambled into the middle of the front seat, Pete climbed in after him and Callan revved up the engine.

The truck circled out of the yard in the usual boiling mass of dust, bouncing its cargo of fence posts noisily up and down. Pippa and Flick stood in the back like sentinels and barked at the rush of air that increased as the vehicle picked up speed. Carly and Josh ran from the dust, shrieking as if pretending it was chasing them like a monster, up the veranda and into the house.

Callan waved at Jacinda again through the dry, choking curtain. Lockie and Pete did the same, and then they disappeared from sight heading down the track that headed toward the alleged road to Adelaide.

Jacinda's breathing went sharp in her chest and she was shocked at how vulnerable she felt. Because of one kiss? Because it hadn't ended with the promise of more? Because Callan's wave and turn told her he'd meant what he'd said, last night, and the fact that he hadn't stopped to introduce her to Pete only served to emphasize his state of mind?

Or just because she wasn't going to see him all day?

"I'm too emotional. It's just stupid," she muttered, moving aimlessly around the yard as she listened to the ebbing sound of the engine.

But she'd always been this way. She knew it. Could manage to pep talk herself out of it sometimes, if she was really careful about it. Today it might be tough, because there was so much going on inside her. Yesterday, she'd felt so alive. Exhilarated. Proud of herself. She'd jumped into that water hole. She'd heard the echo of her voice thrown back from the rocks like a battle cry.

All of that was still there in this potent mix of feelings, but she didn't know what to do with it, how to match it against Callan and his apparent rejection.

There was more to his reaction than met the eye. She felt sure of it. With time, she would understand and it would be all right.

Give it time, just give it time.

Turning to go back inside the house, the sudden certainty calmed her spirit, gave her direction, but then she hit the shade of the veranda and the certainty ebbed just as suddenly as it had come, the emotional transition as sharp as the physical one between heat and shade.

Callan wasn't Kurt.

Kurt was the king of complex, incomprehensible reactions, shifting layers that you had to peel back and pick apart. Callan was probably as simple and uncomplicated as he seemed. He'd kissed her. He'd defeated that initial impulse of curiosity and chemistry between them. He'd decided that any kind of involvement was a mistake. He'd stopped. He didn't want it to happen again, and he'd told her so.

Get a grip, Jacinda.

In the kitchen, Kerry was kneading bread dough, while Carly and Josh bickered over LEGO in the next room. Josh still acted more protective of his territory than Lockie did. He wasn't quite convinced that Carly's presence at Arakeela Creek was a plus. "I need all the curved bits for my tower," Jac heard him say.

"But I'm making a tower, too."

"I started making my tower, first. You're not old enough for LEGO. Your fingers aren't good enough."

"Yes, they are."

"They're not, and anyway, I started my tower, first."

Kerry and Jac looked at each other, wondering about intervention. "Give it another minute?" Kerry suggested.

"Can you teach me what to do with the bread, while we listen and hold our breath?"

Kerry laughed. "That's about right, isn't it, holding our breath?"

"I wonder why Carly and Lockie do so much better together. He's that much older, I guess, and she's less of a threat to his space."

"More than that." Kerry paused for thought and thumped away at the elastic ball of dough, flinging it with some violence onto a floured wooden board. The nearest store was several hours away, so if you wanted fresh bread out here, you made it yourself. When Jac smelled it baking, every second day, she practically drooled.

"Josh is like Callan, I think," Kerry said after a moment. "He works hard to get his life just the way he wants it, and then he doesn't like it to change."

"That's Callan?"

"It's a part of Callan." Kerry paused in her thumping and

began to knead, pushing the dough away from herself so that it stretched into an oval, then folding it toward herself again and rotating it ninety degrees. The fluid efficiency of the movement said that she'd done this thousands of times before. "Which makes him sound too rigid, doesn't it?" she added, shooting a sharp look at Jac.

"I wouldn't say he was rigid, from what I've seen of him," she answered carefully.

"No, he's not. I'm glad you can see that. He just…needs time with some things."

They were both silent for a moment, and the air felt a little too heavy, too full of meaning. Kerry seemed extra alert to nuances today, watchful somehow.

Watchful of me. Watchful of Callan and me, and the way I react to his name.

Jac didn't know if that was a good thing, or not. What had Kerry thought about the two of them taking so long to retrieve Lockie's Game Boy last night? What had she sensed in the air between them?

"Want to have a go at this, then?" the older woman said eventually.

"Can I? Will I ruin it? I've never made bread before. Should I thump, or knead?"

"I've done enough thumping. It releases the gluten in the flour, makes the bread lighter and more elastic. And it's good for working out your aggression."

On cue, they heard Carly's voice rise in an angry scream. "You did that on purpose!"

"Somebody else is working out some aggression, I think," Kerry drawled. She strode out to the children, the firm rhythm of her feet signaling a no-nonsense approach. "Joshie, we need to work this out," Jacinda heard.

She began tentatively kneading, thinking that Kerry was probably the best equipped to handle the situation, in this instance. Kneading bread dough was tougher than it looked, however.

Push, fold, quarter turn. Push, fold, quarter turn. Tougher than it looked, but it felt good. The dough was like a baby's skin, satiny smooth and warm from its first rising. The dusting of flour slipped across it like talcum powder on that same baby's tush. Push, fold, quarter turn. Physical, creative, satisfying. Human beings had been doing it for thousands of years.

Kerry and Josh discussed LEGO towers in the next room—the possibility of two towers, of coordinated efforts to make a whole village of towers, square ones as well as curved, of Carly being the assistant and Josh helping her with bits that were too fiddly for her fingers. Eventually hurt feelings were soothed and territorial impulses reined in.

"We'll see how long it lasts," Kerry drawled again when she returned.

"And that's what Callan was like?" She couldn't help talking about him, despite what Kerry might think.

"Actually, no, he was pretty good at sharing," the older woman answered. "They're close in age, him and his sister. Nicky's only fifteen months younger, so he never had to adjust to her as something new. As far as he was concerned, she was always there."

"And she lives in Adelaide, now? Is that right?"

"A couple of hours north of there, the Clare Valley. She studied agriculture and married a farmer, but he has vineyards, not cattle."

"You must have found it hard when she moved so far away."

"To be honest, Clare was better than I'd hoped. I was afraid she might end up in Sydney or Perth!"

"Still, is it hard to keep in close touch?"

"Not with a bit of effort. We e-mail a lot, and take turns

to phone each other every week. Sundays usually. Tonight it's my turn. I send her drawings from the boys and she sends me magazine articles and newspaper clippings and we gossip about those. Silly things like celebrity marriages. We're big fans of Prince Frederik and Princess Mary! But I'd communicate with Nicky by carrier pigeon if I had to. I don't think it really matters what you talk about, either, if it helps you stay close. And I'm getting my first grand-daughter in two months! I'll be going down to stay with them, then."

"That's wonderful."

Except that Jacinda was a little regretful that she'd nudged the conversation away from Callan. She had an itchy, secret urge to talk about him that she couldn't remember feeling since her teens, when telling her friends, "I don't even *like* Matt Walker," had given her the delectable excuse to say a certain male classmate's name out loud.

"If Callan doesn't like change, we're probably imposing on you even more than I'd realized, with our visit," she said after another moment of silence.

"I shouldn't have said it. I'm not putting it the right way." Another pause. "I'm thinking about Liz, not about you and Carly." The words came out in a rush, as if Kerry might regret anything she said too slowly.

"Oh, okay."

Kerry divided the ball of dough in two and began shaping each piece into a log, ready for the greased loaf tins she had waiting on the countertop. "You see, thinking about the future, about the boys, about how lonely Callan must some-times feel—how lonely I *know* he feels—I worry that any woman who's not Liz is going to scare him too much. He's never been any good at asking for help. Which means he's going to have to get past the fear on his own, and I'm not sure how he'll do it. Or if he can."

She opened the oven door and it squeaked. After putting the tins on a lower shelf, she spread a damp dish towel on the top shelf. Jacinda knew that in the moist, tepid space of the oven, the loaves would rise to a high dome shape over the next hour. Squeak went the oven door as Kerry closed it again. Neither she nor Jacinda had spoken.

It's my turn, though.

Talking like this, in the middle of routine household chores, made it easier to tackle tough subjects, she decided. When you were silent as you gathered the right words, other activity was still going on and the silence didn't seem so difficult.

"I think…I wonder if…" she tried after a moment. "I think he's stronger than that, Kerry." She thought about what he'd said yesterday about yelling and jumping to get rid of the fear. He had his own strategies. They might not be the ones suggested in the hospital leaflets—he didn't *want* them to be the ones in the hospital leaflets—but they were strategies, all the same.

Kerry looked eager, as if she itched to talk about Callan, too. "Has he said something to you? Has he talked much about Liz?"

"Not much. A little. He's said—"

"No, please!" She warded off Jac's words with her hands. "Don't tell me what he said. I'm not asking for that. But I do worry."

"Of course you do." Jacinda was a mother, just as Kerry was. She knew. "But I think Callan at least does know what he's fighting in himself." He'd talked about the *fear,* and this made more sense now. The fear of change. The fear, if Kerry was right, of there being no one in the whole world to match Liz. "And you know, Kerry, when you understand the enemy, that's always an advantage."

"True. He is a fighter. In his own way. *Always* in his own way!" She laughed, and ran water into the electric jug, which she then placed on the countertop and plugged in.

"Yeah, I've noticed that, too."

"The boys do him a lot of good. Lockie, now that he's getting older."

"It's funny," Jac said. "Before I had Carly, I always assumed I'd be the big influence on her. That I'd make her who she was. And of course I am doing that. But I think she's changed me more than I've changed her. I never realized that would happen, that kids had such, oh, *influence*. Kerry, does that make sense?"

"It does."

They talked about it a little more—kids and change, Callan and Liz. Nothing earth-shattering. Some of it a little tentative, still. But nice.

"Are you having coffee?" Kerry asked. "It'll only be instant." The electric jug was about to boil.

"Instant is fine. I'd love a cup." Jac got the coffee down from the shelf while Kerry found two mugs and poured the boiling water in, leaving plenty of room for Jacinda's big dollop of milk. Kerry had filled the jug just an inch or two higher than she needed, and rather than waste the precious water, she poured it in to soak the mixing bowl she'd used for the bread dough. Jac made a mental note to take more care with saving water from now on. Her shower, this morning, for example…

"Is it a pain in the butt, doing that?" she asked suddenly.

Kerry looked surprised. "Doing what?"

"Thinking about saving water all the time. Every drop. Pouring the dregs from the electric jug into the dough bowl. Piping the shower and laundry water out to the garden so it gets used twice."

"I guess I don't think about it, it's such second nature. It's part of living here, and I love living here."

"Teach me, won't you? Don't let me do the wrong thing, here, without thinking. Make sure you teach me." All at once, for some reason, the words meant more. She wasn't just talking about saving water. She was talking about Callan.

Teach me about Callan.

Don't let me do the wrong thing with Callan.

If Kerry understood, she didn't refer to the fact directly. Instead, she poured milk into the two mugs, gave Jacinda's the extra zap in the microwave that she liked. Handing Jac the hot mug, she took a big breath.

"Callan and Liz were too alike," she said, at the faster pace she seemed to use when she wasn't quite comfortable with what she was saying. Her voice had dropped, too, in case there was any chance of Josh listening in the other room. "I don't want to say that, because it sounds critical. I loved Liz. I was so happy that Callan had found someone like her, someone who belonged here and belonged in his life. If I could have, I would have gone in her place. People say that. But I really would have gone in her place."

"I know you would."

"They were the kind of couple that grows together. Like two trees, the way trees shape each other sometimes. They would even have looked alike, after fifty years. She was the kind of wife a man should have for fifty years. She was so safe for him, though. It made it even harder when she died." She looked across the top of her coffee mug, her expression appealing for Jac to understand. "Does that make any sense at all?"

"You mean, if their marriage had been more of a challenge…?"

"Yes. Callan would have been equal to a more challenging marriage. And it might have left him…" She slowed and stopped, stuck for the right words. "Better prepared." She shook her head impatiently. "It still sounds wrong. I can't put it right. I can't say it without it sounding like I'm criticizing him, or her, or their marriage."

"No, but I understand."

And I wonder what it is that you're not saying. I'm not

used to this, Kerry. I haven't had a woman like you in my life before, to talk to. I lost my mother too soon, and I was never close enough to my aunt, so, no, I'm not used to this.

Are you telling me that I could be good for Callan, even if I'm nothing like Liz? Because I'm nothing like Liz? Do you want me to be a part of his awakening from grief, Kerry? Or are you warning me away because I could never truly belong? I'm only here a few more weeks….

Despite her best hopes, despite the creative act of helping with the bread, despite playing with Carly and Josh, and working in the garden, Jac stayed restless and uncertain and churned up inside all day.

At four, she needed more air and space than the homestead and its garden could provide. "I thought I'd go for a walk down to the creek, Kerry, if that's all right with you," she told Callan's mother. "I'll take Carly with me."

"Leave her if you'd rather," Kerry answered. "She's quite happy with her drawing, and I'm making them a snack in a minute."

"Thanks. All right, then. I will leave her."

Not knowing how long it would take her to walk this restlessness away, Jac was happy that Kerry had suggested leaving Carly behind. She really wanted to stride, breathe, think uninterrupted thoughts. She drank a big glass of water, found her hat and sunglasses and set out, following the fence line down to the wide swathe of dry creek bed, the same way they had gone yesterday on horseback.

When she reached the creek, however, she turned north along it instead of south, wanting to explore some new ground. Keeping to the creek bed itself, she covered the distance slowly because the sand was deep in some places, uneven in others, and there were stretches of rock and smoothly worn river stones as well.

The late afternoon was pleasantly still—cool in the shade

and hot in the sun. She heard birds overhead, and disturbed a couple of lizards. If there were snakes, they had sensed the vibration of her footfalls and disappeared before she caught sight of them, as Callan had said they would.

She didn't want to think about Callan.

"Five days down, twenty-three to go," she said aloud to the eucalyptus trees. She had to make some decisions about the future. At least examine the possibilities.

It was frightening how little pull she felt toward home. Pull? More like dread. Running through a mental list of California friends as she'd done many times before, she couldn't think of a single one who would risk alienating Kurt by taking her side, or by helping her in any way. They'd support her with lip service as they'd done since her separation from Carly's father, but nothing more.

Lip service wasn't enough.

And who did she have farther afield?

She thought about her two brothers, and her father, back east, and knew she'd let those relationships slide more than she should have done. She could have phoned or e-mailed more often, over the past few years. She should have made more of an effort to see her brothers for holidays.

It wasn't enough of an excuse to say that they hadn't met her halfway, even though it was true. If she'd worked harder at it, kept pushing, giving something to the relationship, they surely would have seen some value in getting closer to their little sister after a while. Their kids were almost grown, but teenagers might have loved a cute baby cousin.

She thought about the way Callan and Kerry had stayed so close yet still managed to give each other space, thought about the love in Kerry's voice when she'd talked about Nicky hundreds of miles away, her coming baby, all the ways they found to communicate, and the determination when Kerry had said that she would contact Nicky by carrier pigeon if there was no other way. Families didn't just chug along like magic, maintenance-free engines. They had to be worked at like anything else.

Jacinda had never made a conscious decision that working on her relationship with her brothers was important to her but she could make that decision now.

Was it too late?

If she'd had a pen and some postcards in her pocket, she would have scribbled greetings to her brothers on the spot. If she'd had a car, she would have jumped into it and zipped to the nearest—

Store.

What "nearest store"?

It was well over a hundred miles away.

Still, the idea of making contact, even with such a trivial, tentative first step as an e-mail or a postcard from outback Australia, stayed with her and felt important. She'd have to ask Callan. Maybe he or Kerry had some cards. Or maybe they were planning a trip into Leigh Creek soon—they did that fairly often, she thought—so she could buy some, to replace the ones she'd left in Sydney in a panic. She felt more confident about being able to write postcards, now.

But how did the mail plane work? Where did you get the postage stamps? Definitely, she needed to talk to Callan.

And it was probably about time to turn around and start heading back.

The journey back along the creek bed seemed farther than she would have thought, and she realized that she'd lost track of time while she'd been thinking about her future and her family. The color of the sky had begun to change. If she didn't soon reach the line of fence marching at right angles into and across the creek, she might miss it in the fading light.

No, here it was, at last, just visible. In the distance, as she climbed through it and up out of the creek bed, she saw one of those familiar trails of dust. It marked the track that led from the main road to the homestead, which meant it had to be Callan, Lockie and Pete returning from their long day's work just in time for a good wash before the evening meal.

Her heart lifted and lurched at the same time.

Callan.

Who'd kissed her last night and then turned away.

Callan, who got his life the way he wanted, and then resisted change, which was pretty much the opposite of what Jac needed to do. Her life wasn't the way she wanted it, right now, but changing it was easier said than done.

Thinking about this and not about where she was going— it was getting hard to see the detail of the terrain, despite the huge yellow full moon rising—she tripped on a loose rock and instinctively grabbed the top line of fence wire for support.

It was barbed.

In the front seat of the truck, Lockie slept, his head lolling onto Pete's shoulder. At some point, Pete had lifted the head gently and placed his own felt bushman's hat there for a makeshift pillow. Callan himself was tired enough to consider that the squashed hat looked darned comfortable. The dogs were flung out on the now-empty rear tray sleeping, too, and when Pete lowered Lockie's head back down, he didn't even stir. He'd worked well today, and he'd learned some new skills.

At the wheel, Callan blinked several times to keep himself alert. His eyes felt gritty from the dust and his head ached from squinting in the bright light for hours, even though he'd worn sunglasses. They'd made some good progress on the new mustering yard, but they'd need several more days yet. Pete wasn't as strong or quick as he used to be. And they might run out of supplies before they were done. He had a new shipment to pick up sometime this week in Leigh Creek.

Turning in front of the homestead, he felt a surge of well-being at the sight of the lights, and his aching muscles began to relax. There would be dinner waiting. He might have a beer with the meal. Jacinda could cook, he'd discovered. Maybe she would have convinced Mum to let her do so today and they'd get to taste some new California creation or an Asian stir-fry. His stomach growled in anticipation, and he knew a shower would feel pretty good, too.

Even better than the meal and hot, clean water, there would be people. Mum, Josh, Carly…and Jac. His treacherous heart jumped sideways as he thought about her, but he couldn't dwell on the reaction right now. Pete was pushing his big hand against Lockie's slumped shoulder.

"Wake up, little mate," Pete said. "Dinner's up."

"You staying for it, Pete?" Callan asked him, as Lockie opened bleary eyes.

The older man shook his head. "Headin' home."

"Come in for a bit."

"Do that, I won't get goin' again. Have to stay all night."

"I already told you to do that."

Pete shook his head again. "Gettin' home. Got some things to check up on."

"Well, bring your gear tomorrow and stay tomorrow night."

"Maybe." He was already heading for his car, with around two hours of nighttime driving still ahead of him, and the return trip first thing in the morning. He was a tough one.

Lockie had woken up. "I'm starving!"

"Let's see what's cooking."

Pippa and Flick followed them onto the veranda and found the fresh food and water Callan's mother had already put out for them.

Inside the house, there was a fabulous aroma coming from the kitchen, but no sign of food on the table, which surprised Callan a little. Mum would have heard the truck. She would have known how ready they'd be for the meal. Josh and Carly had had baths and were prowling around in their nightwear, looking almost as hungry as Callan felt. His mother appeared with bathwater damp on her shirt and he asked, "Should I set the table?"

"I'm getting worried, Callan. Jacinda's not back."

"Not back?" His heart did another of those weird lurches that risked becoming a habit. "Where did she go?"

"For a walk, two and a half hours ago. Longer."

"What did she take? How long was she planning to be gone? It's almost dark out there!"

"I know. I thought she'd be gone half an hour. I'm not even sure she had water with her."

"Feed the kids," he said, energy surging back into him and hunger forgotten. "I'll get the dogs, and we'll head to the creek on foot to look for her. I'm not going to treat this as a crisis just yet."

"I'll do that for you!" his mother answered. "I like Jacinda a lot, and she's no fool…." She touched his arm, as if it was important that he know how she felt about Jacinda.

"No, she's not," he agreed.

And I've lived here all my life. I'm not going to panic because a grown woman is an hour late back to the house.

"But, Callan, she has no idea what this country can do to people who make mistakes."

"I know. Listen, if I'm not back in half an hour, get Moss saddled for me."

In the space of two minutes, he'd packed water and a couple of snacks into a backpack, as well as the jacket he'd found hanging in her room. He'd also packed the first-aid kit and a long roll of bandage.

Watching as he dropped it into the backpack, little pajama-clad Carly got a stricken look on her face. On top of hunger, fatigue and his own lurking fear, her frightened reaction didn't help.

"Where is Mommy? Why isn't she back?" she said.

Chapter Eight

The barbed wire had pierced and torn the skin on Jacinda's palm in four places. It stung and throbbed, and the remaining half mile to the homestead felt like ten times that distance as she thought about taking each cautious step in the dark. She didn't want to trip again. She needed better shoes. Proper hiking boots or something. And she shouldn't have stayed out so long, even though she'd needed all that time to think.

I'll try e-mailing Andy and Tom tonight, on Callan's computer, she decided as she started walking again. She then spent the next five minutes of carefully trod distance trying to work out when she'd last done so. Could it really be more than two years?

The dogs started barking when she still had two hundred yards of fence to follow. They sounded overexcited and ready for action, but surely they didn't think she was a stranger?

Someone must have let them through the gate because they came at her out of the darkness with a speed that frightened her, still letting out high, urgent sounds. She saw a circle of light behind them, bouncing in time to someone's stride, then heard Callan's voice.

"Jac, is that you?" He raised the flashlight in her direction.

"Yes, and please tell Pippa and Flick that I'm friendly!"

He whistled at the dogs as he came closer and they ran to heel beside him, panting and turning their faces up to him as if they expected a reward. "Yes, guys, well done, you found her," he told them.

"Found me?" Jac reached them, while Callan was still bending down to the dogs.

"Please don't scare us like that again, okay?" He pointed the flashlight beam away from her and toward the ground, but it had already shone into her face and dazzled her vision and she had spots before her eyes.

"Scare you?" She blinked, covered her closed eyes with her hand for a moment, but her vision was slow to clear and, when she opened them again, she could still barely see him. She could sense him, though. That big body, that aura of dust and hard work. "Callan, I wasn't lost or anything." She peered at him. It was the first time they'd talked all day. "Were you worried?"

Stupid question. He didn't look worried, she saw at last as the spots faded. He looked angry, slapping the flashlight in a slow rhythm against his hard, denim-clad thigh and narrowing his eyes. "How much water did you have with you?" he demanded.

"I had a big drink before I left."

"And did you take a jacket? Even a cotton sweater?"

"I only went for a quick breath of fresh air." She began to guess that these weren't adequate answers.

"And you were gone nearly three hours."

"I know. I was thinking about a few things. Time got away from me a bit, and I didn't turn back along the creek as soon as

I should have. I was a bit shocked to see that the light was going." Instinctively, she touched the sunglasses on top of her head, useless now. She had her baseball cap folded and stuffed into the back pocket of her jeans, equally useless once the sun went.

"Sunglasses aren't a survival kit."

He poked at them with a rigid finger, pushing them farther back into her hair—a gesture that could have been tender in other circumstances, but wasn't this time. It brought him closer, though, and she remembered with every sense and every nerve ending how she'd felt in his arms last night.

"If you'd twisted your ankle on a tree root and had to sit there all night until we found you," he went on, "you would have been happy in short sleeves without a drop to drink or a morsel of food, with the temperature dropping into the forties, is that right?"

"Well…"

"People who get lost or hurt out here…people who don't have the right gear…people whose engines break down and they go looking for help instead of staying with their vehicle…they die, Jacinda, and it doesn't take that long, either." His voice rasped and dropped deeper. "This country doesn't forgive mistakes."

"Shoot, I didn't think, did I?" she realized aloud.

He whooshed out a sigh, bent down once again to Pippa and gave her a rough pat, his strong hand splayed out in her thick fur. The way he marshaled his emotions was almost palpable. His shoulder muscles moved under his shirt. "I guess I never spelled it out to you," he said, after a moment. "Too busy giving you a crash course in snake behavior."

"Which I very much appreciated!" She took a breath. "You're right, I should have taken water and a jacket. Shouldn't have needed a crash course in that kind of basic common sense. And I did grab on to the barbed wire, just now, so common sense has definitely deserted me this evening."

"We've both been a bit...yeah...off beam today," he growled, and she knew he was thinking about last night.

"See, I've spiked my hand." She blurted out, then grabbed the flashlight from him, pointed the beam at her palm and showed him.

"We'll need to take care of that as soon as we get back to the house. Are you up to date on your tetanus shot?"

"Lord, I have no idea! No, wait a minute." She remembered that she'd had one when Carly was a baby, as part of a routine health check with her doctor. "Yes, I would be." Thank goodness, one area in which she could impress him as faintly sensible. "Have I upset Kerry, too?" she added, thinking about her earlier conversation with Callan's mother.

Liz would never have let something like this happen. Gone off without water, food or clothing? Never!

She had belonged here, body and soul.

And yet Kerry considered this to have been a mixed blessing.

"She was pretty concerned when Pete and Lockie and I got back before you did," Callan said. "She couldn't tell me what you'd taken with you." He was silent for a moment. "Sorry I was angry. We didn't know where to start looking, didn't want to worry Carly."

"Is she worried?"

"Mum's with her," he hedged. "Dinner's on the table."

"She *is* worried. Oh, hell!" She began to stride back to the house, and Callan and the dogs went with her.

"Best way for you to learn, I guess," Callan said.

"You're right. I'll know next time."

"Forget it. Forget that I was angry, please. It didn't help."

"We're both tired."

And what's the bet that Carly has a sleepwalking episode tonight? Jac added to herself inwardly.

Carly rushed into her arms back at the homestead, as soon as they saw each other. "Mommy, I thought a snake bit you. I thought you were lost."

"It was my fault, sweetheart. I was fine, but I should have let Kerry know exactly where I'd be, and I should have turned back sooner. I won't make that mistake again."

"Gran was worried about you."

"I know she was."

Pressed against Carly's warm little back, Jac's injured palm throbbed. The decision to contact Andy and Tom felt like less of a positive step than it had seemed a short while ago, and when she asked after dinner if she could use Callan's computer to send some e-mails, she sat in front of a blank screen for too long before anything would come.

Finally, with her left hand crisscrossed in fresh Band-Aids and still smarting after the run-in with the barbed-wire fence, she typed, Hi, Andy! Guess what? I'm in Australia! Visiting a friend at a place called Arakeela Creek. With Carly, of course. Don't run to get a map. It won't be marked. Even though it's the size of Rhode Island. How are the kids? How's Dad? You can reach me at this e-mail address until May 13. Let me know how you're doing. Your sister, Jacinda.

Just in case he'd forgotten her name?

She looked at the words on the screen. She thought about all the other things she could have said. Talked about Kurt? Apologized for not keeping in better contact? At least re-drafted it into some slightly more complex and grammatical sentences? *With Carly, of course* had no verb.

A familiar feeling of panic and dread began to flutter inside her, making Kerry's fabulous chicken casserole sit uneasily in her stomach, and she knew that for now, these few stilted phrases would have to be enough. She hit Send and Receive, then copied the sent message and pasted it into a new one addressed to Tom, cut the *How's Dad?* sentence and replaced it with Any special news?

"And I used to call myself a writer," she muttered.

When she hit Send and Receive again, she got a system message telling her that the message to Andy had bounced. Checking again after a wait of less than a minute, she was told that Tom's had bounced, also. In the long interval since she'd last made contact this way, both her brothers' e-mail addresses had changed.

Coming in to his office to see if she needed any help with his computer and e-mail system, Callan could see her disappointment, she knew, even though she tried to hide it.

"Do you want to try calling them instead?" he asked. He looked to be fresh out of the shower. The ends of his hair were still wet against his neck and his tanned skin looked smooth. He smelled of soap and steam.

She thought about the time difference, and said, "Too early in the morning there." It was eight in the evening here and Carly was already asleep, which meant six-thirty in the morning on the U.S. east coast. Then she added more honestly, "And anyway, over the phone I don't think I'd know what to say."

"That's too bad." He looked sincerely disappointed.

In her?

For her?

In her brothers?

Either way, it made her determined not to give up so easily. "But would you have any postcards, or something?" she asked. "I'd like Andy and Tom to at least know where I am, in case…well, they don't often get in touch, but you never know."

"I have to head into Leigh Creek later in the week to pick up some supplies. You can get postcards there, and anything else you need. Have a think about it. Your own brand of shampoo, or any food that Carly likes that we don't have. We'll bring her with us. It's a bit of a drive, but we can have some stops along the way."

"Thanks," she said. "That'd be great."

And if Carly was with them, Jac surely wouldn't spend the whole drive remembering how it felt to kiss him, the way she was doing now….

They didn't quite know what to do or say next, how to end the conversation. Callan picked up some unopened letters from a big pile on the corner of the desk and let them drop back down. Was he planning to apologize again for getting angry at her about her poorly planned walk? She didn't want that. Nor did she want any more awkward references to last night.

It was gone, finished, done with.

She had to keep telling herself that.

"You've got quite a pile of mail there," she said quickly, to deflect the subject onto something…anything…safer.

"Forwarded from the magazine," he answered, and only then did she realize what the letters were.

From women.

Hoping Callan was "sincerely looking for an Outback Wife."

Looking closer, she saw that all of them were still sealed. "You haven't opened them?"

"I've opened a ton of 'em. And I've replied. I was e-mailing a couple of them for a while, but that's tailed off. These are just the letters from the past two mail flights, which I…uh…haven't gotten to, yet."

"My goodness! You need a secretary!"

He grinned, and some of that easy, familiar humor between them came creeping back. "Are you applying for the position?"

So they looked at the letters together, and she helped him with his replies. Kerry brought them each a mug of tea and offered her opinion of a woman who stressed the importance of Callan being "visually literate."

"Whatever that means! Give her a discouraging answer!"

"Want to draft some replies, Mum?" Callan offered.

"Oh, no, thank you! I'll leave you to it!" She quickly disappeared.

In the next letter they opened, a woman announced that if she and Callan became involved, she was "prepared to live in the wilderness for up to two years before we renegotiate a move to a more urban environment."

This one received one of the polite "Thanks for your interest, but I'm not looking for anything right now" replies that Callan had become impressively fluent with by now.

A few letters later, a girl called Tracey "hadn't had much luck with men, because I'm shy, which I know is my fault. I have a good family—two brothers and a sister, my mum and dad—and we're close, but I'd move away from Ballarat for the right man. I'd want to take things slow, though. I think marriage, or any relationship, is too important to get wrong because you haven't thought it through."

"She sounds nice," Jacinda said. "You should write her a good letter."

"She looks nice, too," answered Callan, showing her a simple snapshot of a slightly chunky woman of around twenty-five or so, with a tomboy smile and light brown hair.

Jac leaned closer to see the picture better, and her arm brushed Callan's. Turning instinctively, she found him looking at her and could read his face like a book.

She looks nice, but right now you're the woman I want. It's too complicated so I'm not going to give in to it, but you're definitely the woman I want.

"Maybe we've done enough secretarial work for tonight," he said on an uncomfortable growl. "I'll write something back to her tomorrow."

Jac nodded. "This is more words than I've strung together in—well, a while."

Frustrated, she knew she needed something more, something other than drafting polite lines to people that neither she nor Callan really knew—and, yes, she included her brothers in that. A need was building inside her, demanding release and expression. It made her scared and it made her twitchy, and she'd only ever known one way to get the feeling under control.

She needed to…really, genuinely, seriously…write.

"I'm going to check on Carly," she told him, even though she knew Carly was asleep. She wanted to see if by some faint chance she had writing materials in a forgotten outer sleeve of one of her suitcases.

"Callan, would you have a legal pad or a notebook I could use?" Jacinda looked a little tense about asking the question.

A lot tense, in fact. Meeting in front of the waistband of her jeans, her fingers zipped back and forth as she rubbed her nails together, making a buzzing, clicking sort of sound that gave out way too much of a clue as to her state of mind. She didn't seem to notice that she was doing it.

"Even just some scrap paper?" she added, as if she only had a shopping list to write.

"One of the boys' old school notebooks?" Callan suggested. He pretended he hadn't noticed the tension, or the sound and movement of the fingernails, even though his gaze kept pulling in that direction. "They get a new set every year and some of the ones from last year still have a lot of blank pages. Would that work?"

"It'd be great."

She looked relieved that she'd managed to ask the question, that he hadn't asked too many questions of his own in response, and that she'd gotten an easy answer. Her hands dropped to her sides, but the thick denim waistband of the jeans stood out a little from her tightly drawn in stomach, showing the weight she must have lost in recent months, and Callan kept looking there, at the place where the clicking fingernails had been, for just a second or two too long.

"Let me dig one out," he said, dragging his eyes upward, trying to forget how clearly he'd pictured himself seated in a squashy armchair. He would have grabbed her as she went by. He would have wrapped his arms around that willowy waist of hers, and hugged the tension out of those drawn-in stomach muscles.

He wanted to tell her to put the weight back on so that she filled out the lean lines of the jeans. He wanted to apologize again about coming down too hard on her tonight about going for a walk with no water. He hadn't exaggerated the potential danger in this country, but he could have skipped the anger, because the anger was far more about…something else.

He wanted to thank her for helping him with the letters. He knew it must have been hard at first, despite the way she'd relaxed into it. Yes, and he wanted to tell her exactly how he came to understand so much regarding her tension and fear about the whole writing thing, even though he'd hadn't tried to write a poem or a story since high school.

"I'm sorry, if it's too much trouble at this hour it can wait until morning," she said quickly, ready to backtrack on the whole writing idea at the slightest excuse.

"It's fine."

True, he was about to head off for bed. It already felt overdue after the long day working on the new mustering yard with Lockie and Pete, and the heart-pumping but mercifully short-lived interval when he'd feared that Jacinda might be lost. But he was still racked with guilt and regret about what had happened down at the water hole last night.

They should have simply been tracking down Lockie's Game Boy and getting the hell out of there, instead of watching for wildlife and exchanging life stories and—

Yeah.

Guilt and regret and awareness rushed through him, none of it helped by having sat with her in his office writing polite rejection letters to other women for almost an hour.

It wasn't Jacinda's fault.

It was totally, utterly him.

Had he managed to get that across to her? Could finding an old schoolbook of Lockie's for her, without asking her what she wanted to use it for, in any way make up for the way he'd turned away from her down at the creek, and then again back at the house? Make up for the way he'd barely been able to look at her this morning, hadn't introduced her to Pete, and was almost sinfully grateful that she'd slept in so that they hadn't needed to confront each other over breakfast? For the way he'd been angry at her tonight, the moment that first flood of relief at her safety had ebbed away?

Why the heck had he let last night's kiss happen at all? He'd known it would end that way.

Only maybe he hadn't known.

Maybe he'd been kidding himself all along.

In his office, he dug out the cardboard file box where he kept the boys' old schoolbooks. He didn't know why he hung on to them. Because it was easier than throwing them out? He wouldn't have said he was the nostalgic type, and yet he did have a problem with change, didn't he?

Mum had talked about it a couple of times since Liz's death. Mum's attitude had been helpful rather than accusing, but there'd been the hint of criticism all the same. He'd never wanted to go away to school, as a twelve-year-old, and it had taken him months—had taken hooking up with Dusty and Brant—for him to settle into Cliffside.

And now here were these stupid schoolbooks he put away every year like a pack rat, because something inside him wouldn't allow them to get thrown away.

He took out a stack of them and flipped through, finding worksheets about the ocean and weather, and words with *sh* in them that gave him a little twist inside because of the fact that Liz, who would have been so proud and so interested, had never seen them.

Was that why he kept them? Some stupid, illogical, subconscious, impossible belief that if he kept them long enough, her benign spirit would pay a visit and take a look?

Brrr, shake it off, Callan.

How much working space did Jacinda need? He didn't want to slight her writing ability with just three pages, or scare her with a whole blank book. He thought he understood too much about her fears.

Jacinda looked nothing like Liz. He'd told himself lately that he'd been looking too hard for Liz in those other two women, three years ago, and maybe he'd seriously believed last night, down at the creek, that with her long dark hair and olive skin, Jacinda looked different enough to cure the problem.

The Problem.

A cure?

Maybe it was only getting worse. A man hit his sexual peak by twenty. At thirty-four, things could easily have started to slide. The level of need. The frequency. Had losing Liz pushed him so far away from his natural potency that he'd never claw back the lost ground?

Everything had been fine…fantastic…powerful…intense…while he and Jacinda had kissed last night. The chemistry between them was huge, not something you could explain or trace to its source but something animal and instinctive. Water on a thirsty day. A completion. She had tasted so good.

He loved the way she moved. Loved how at first she'd been happy just to wait and feel those motionless, paralyzed lips of his against her neck while he gathered his courage and gloried in his unexpected and almost shocking need.

Oh hell, he'd wanted her so badly and it had felt so good to rediscover how that felt. A little later, he'd loved her moments of hunger and impatience, too. How could a man's ego not be gratified by that? She wanted him, and she hadn't kept it a secret.

But then the pressure of her needs and her expectations had hit. He'd felt her heat against him, telling him she wanted more, insisting it with warm, full pressure, and he'd panicked and…oh, hell…deflated and pulled away—*hopefully* before she could have noticed.

He hadn't compared her to Liz. He hadn't—was this wrong?—even thought about Liz while he was kissing Jacinda. Not for a second. And when he'd panicked, it had been about the other women, the two very different blondes, and the excruciating awkwardness that had played out both times when his performance had fizzled.

He could still remember it in painful detail. The girl at the races, with her disinterested *Whatever…* when he'd stumbled through an apology and hinted at an explanation. *After my wife…* If the girl had noticed his raspy throat and horrible struggle for words, she hadn't reacted. She'd already been putting on her clothes, miffed at her disappointing night.

The other woman, the backpacker, had soothed him like a baby at first. He'd felt foolish, so uncomfortable at her sickly reassurance. It was the way you talked to a three-year-old who couldn't get his pants on the right way around.

Never mind, sweetheart, we'll keep working on it and you'll do better next time.

She'd turned the whole thing into a personal challenge. Dr. Birgit, Scandinavian Erotic Therapist, to the rescue. He'd felt as if they were writing a new chapter in a sex manual, full of strenuous gymnastic positions and clinical efforts at stimulation.

None of which had worked.

Oh, jeez!

Stop thinking about it!

Here. How about this book? He flipped through Joshie's "Journal Writing" notebook from three years ago and saw several pages of painstaking numbers showing the date, and labored sentences summarizing his day. "We wnt to the crek. I rod Sam. His sadel sliped. I staid on. Dad fixded it up tite agen."

The book had about twenty spare pages left at the end of it. If Jacinda could fill those, she might not feel so tense and uncomfortable about asking him for more.

He hoped she did fill them, because he could tell it was important to her.

He put the file box away, closed his office door and took the notebook along the corridor to where she waited for him in the kitchen. Her hands still didn't seem to know what to do with themselves. She hugged herself, finger-combed her hair, picked up a cleaning sponge and wiped down the countertop even though it was clean already.

"Oh, you found something?" she said, when she saw the book in his grip. She smiled eagerly, but dropped the smile too soon, as if she didn't want him to guess that this remotely mattered to her.

Too late for that.

Handing it over, he hid the depth of his understanding and told her, "Just let me know when you need another one."

"Thanks," was all she said.

After asking Callan so impatiently for paper to write on, Jacinda left Josh's old notebook blank that night. She looked at it for a while, standing alone in the kitchen after Callan had gone, fingers and brain tingling to begin, but then fatigue overtook her.

And doubt.

What would she write in it, anyhow?

What was the point?

The simple act of having to ask Callan for it seemed to have doubled the pressure. Even though she'd tried to play it down, he wasn't stupid. He was a practical man. He'd expect results. He had no idea about writing. He'd want to see six new chapters of her long-gone novel by tomorrow night.

Why had she brought the subject up? She could probably write down all the words left inside her on the inside of her wrist or the palm of her hand. She should have asked for a Post-it note.

Carly did sleepwalk at midnight that night, after her earlier fear about Mommy's safety out in the dark. Or was it because she'd picked up on Jac's own tension over—well, various things? Carly's emotional radar was scary, sometimes, and Jac wondered how much Kurt's behavior during the separation and divorce had affected her daughter deep inside where it might never clearly show.

During her nighttime escapade, Carly had a drink of water in the kitchen, went to the bathroom and checked on the dogs sleeping on the veranda, all of it in her sleep. Then, fortunately, she seemed happy to be led back to bed. Jacinda slid gratefully between her own sheets and didn't lie awake for another hour as she'd feared she might.

And when she awoke the next morning to the sound of Darth Vader crowing in the chook run, heralding first light, the second thing that came into her head after looking across at her beautiful and safely sleeping daughter was the notebook Callan had given her, and its blank pages.

She wanted to fill them.

She did.

It was a hunger that postcards could never satisfy.

Even though every scrap of the doubt was still there, the need was stronger, and wouldn't go away. She craved the physical act of holding a pen in her hand and moving it across the paper. She *needed* to think about words, much better words than just, "How're you doing?" and "Thank you for your letter." Dressing quickly, she grabbed the book, found the pen she'd taken last night from a jar on the kitchen benchtop and went out to the veranda.

No one else was up. No sounds of movement came from Callan's room farther along. No light was visible in Kerry's little cottage across the dusty front yard. It was the coldest hour of the day. Jacinda sat on the cane couch, spread the mohair blanket over her legs and pulled it up over her shoulders. She thought about coffee but decided to wait, not wanting to risk disturbing Callan if he was having a rare lie-in.

She opened the notebook and found the first empty page. The lines on one side were widely spaced, suitable for a child's first efforts at literacy, and on the opposite side, the paper was completely blank, ready to be filled by a stick figure and a clumsy tree.

Five minutes went by, but nothing happened. She was tempted to doodle. Her fingers tended to make all these elaborate curly patterns and shapes without her even thinking about it on the rare occasions when she wrote by hand. But she resisted the doodling. She wanted to wait for words.

And finally they came.

"I'm sitting here," she wrote, "watching light seep upward into the sky like the curtain rising on a Broadway show."

It didn't rank with classical literature's great opening sentences, but she told herself not to care. *It doesn't matter,*

Jacinda. Just keep going. There doesn't have to be a story, or a direction, or a logical sequence. Not yet. Not ever. You're not selling this. You're not showing it to a soul. No, not to Callan, if he asks. So just keep writing.

Her hand had begun to ache and she'd penned four pages when Callan found her. The light was on over at Kerry's, and she could hear the boys in the kitchen. She must have been sitting here almost an hour.

"Want coffee?" Callan offered.

He stood beside the wicker couch, looking too tall, and she had to fight the need to cover her page because he had a bird's-eye view and could have read it if he'd wanted to. As it happened, he wasn't looking at the page, he was looking at her face.

"I'll come inside in a minute," she told him, twisting toward him and leaning her elbow over the paper as if it were just a casual, accidental movement.

"No, I can bring it out for you," he said. "You're busy."

"No, I'm— That rooster of yours doesn't like visitors to sleep in, does he?" she joked lamely. "I'm only filling in time till Carly wakes up."

"Well, she has."

So you're not buying my excuses, Callan?

Could you pretend, at least?

"Oh, does she want me?" She shifted, started to close the book.

"She's with the boys. She's fine." He leaned down and flipped the pages open again, and their fingers touched. He pulled his hand away. "Keep going, and I'll bring the coffee."

"No, no, I'm finished. I'm done. It's okay."

"You looked like you were still working on it."

"It's not work. It's nothing."

"Still, keep going and I'll bring your coffee out," he repeated stubbornly, for the third time.

"Okay. Thanks." She didn't want to argue anymore, because if she argued, he'd have questions about what she'd written, and she didn't want questions.

He didn't seem in a hurry to get the coffee he'd offered, however. He just stood there, leaning against the open doorway, making her skin itch and ripple with awareness. His body was magnetic. She wanted to grab his hip or push her face into his chest and smell his shirt.

Finally, mercifully—after probably a whole six seconds had elapsed—he asked, "Did I give you enough? I mean, are there enough pages left in the notebook? Because there are a couple more I can give you. And I have printer paper, too. Or if you want to use the computer again…"

"For the moment, I'm fine with this." She laid her hand across the half-filled page.

It was, seriously, years since she'd written this much by hand, and yet she hadn't even considered Callan's computer, she realized. Somehow, this was the method that felt right for now, this filling of white paper with blue scrawl. She liked the physical act of scribbling out a wrong word, or jetting an arrow across the page toward a sentence added in after further thought.

Callan still hadn't left.

"I'm guessing you don't plan to show me right this minute." He smiled, but she wasn't in the mood to get teased on this.

"No."

"No?"

She covered the page protectively with her arm once more. "It's nothing. It's terrible. It's just— It's not a story, or anything. It's just little snatches. Impressions."

"Like a poem."

"Not even that. Sort of like a poem." *Unnh!* "I might turn some of it into a poem later."

"And then you can show me." He gave her a sly look, and there was the promise of a grin hovering on his face.

"No! Please don't... *Please* don't treat this like a joke, Callan, or like tasting a batch of cookies I've made. It's not like that. I couldn't—I'm sorry, I don't have a sense of humor about it, and I can't explain that, I can't explain why it's important, I just—"

"Hey...hey."

Oh crud, now he'd sat down, frowning and concerned. Now she'd really turned this into something. She should have fobbed him off, just agreed that, yes, it was a poem and that, sure, yes, she'd show it to him when it was done, and hope that the whole thing would drop from his mind because surely he had better things to think about.

"I'm not treating it like a joke, Jac," he said.

His blue eyes were fixed on her, as motionless as the surface of the water hole at night, as deep and bright as the midday outback sky. The old, sagging couch pushed them closer together, the way it had on her first night here, as shameless as a professional matchmaker. *Go on,* it said, *feel his thigh pressed against yours. Don't fight it. You like it.*

"I'm not laughing at you about this." His voice had a husky note in it. "I wouldn't. I know it's important."

"It's not important." She pushed her hand against his upper arm and tried to shimmy her butt sideways so the matchmaking couch didn't get its wicked way. Callan leaned back, respecting her need for space, still watching her. "It's stupid," she said. "Writing really doesn't matter. If I never wrote another word in my life, the universe would not be a poorer place."

"You don't believe that."

She laughed. "No, I don't, but I should! Because it doesn't make sense that it's so important. I'm not expecting you to understand any of this."

"Give me some credit."

"No, I didn't mean that you're not smart or— You're not a writer, that's all."

"Do I have to be? Isn't there only one thing I need to understand? Without it, you're incomplete," he said simply.

She nodded silently, stunned at the words.

Yes.

She'd never heard it put so plainly.

Without it she was incomplete.

"You just said it," she stammered. "Y-you're so right. How—?"

"Everyone has things like that. Their kids, their work, their land. Their gardening, their guitar playing, their sport." His tone had changed, sounded more distant and defensive, like a lecture. But then he couldn't sustain it, and seemed to give up the attempt. His voice dropped again, the pitch low and personal. "You don't need to ask yourself or anyone else why writing is important, Jacinda. You just need to know— I have to have this in my life to feel complete. That's okay. That's no big deal. The bad, impossible part is that if something takes it away, it kills you, doesn't it? It cripples you, torments you, until you find a way to get it back."

"How did you know that?" It was almost a whisper. Barely aware of her action, she grabbed his hand, let the couch lean her in closer to him. "Just hearing you say it is…great, such a relief…thank you. For taking it seriously. For saying it. But how did you know about the torment?"

His body sagged. His eye contact dropped as if the thread of communication between them had been sliced through. He looked as if he was talking to the floorboards or to his shoes, not to her.

"Hell, Jacinda! D'you honestly think you're the only one it's ever happened to?" he muttered.

Chapter Nine

Callan wouldn't follow through.

Jacinda didn't push or demand, but she wanted to understand what he meant. How had it happened to him? Where was he incomplete? He couldn't be talking about the loss of Liz, because there was grief in that, yes, but no shame and she was certain that she'd seen shame in him when he'd said those words.

D'you honestly think you're the only one it's ever happened to?

Shame? Why?

They had common ground, it wasn't a source of shame, and she thought they should grab at it and make use of it, but he clammed up and wouldn't talk about it, said it wasn't important, he couldn't explain, she should just forget it. Carly's arrival on the veranda a moment or two later gave him an easy way out that he snatched up as shamelessly as a serial dater might claim, "I lost your phone number."

"Woo-hoo, Carlz!" he said. "Ready for another big day?"

Knowing how much she didn't want to feel pressured about her writing and therefore not wanting to pressure Callan in return, Jac let it go for the time being. Instead, she hugged Carly, closed Lockie's old notebook and took it into the house. Four pages was enough for now. Four pages was good. Even a sentence would have been good, so four pages was actually great.

Three days later, she'd written fifteen.

They still weren't a part of anything. Too disjointed and personal for a story. Too poetic for a diary. Not jazzy and chatty enough for a blog on the Net.

She wrote about the colors of her favorite hen's feathers in the sun, about the feel of bread dough in her hands, and the words that Kerry had used when she'd taught the recipe and the technique. She wrote two pages of stuff she imagined herself yelling at Kurt, not in his huge executive office or out front of Carly's preschool, but the things she would have yelled if she'd been standing on the rock ledge at the water hole about to jump in, while Kurt was down on the sand— and okay, admittedly, since this was a fantasy, *cowering* there.

She wrote out the words *six hundred thousand acres* and they looked really good on the page, much better than just the numbers. They looked so good that she found out some other numbers from Callan—the distance around the perimeter of Lake Frome, the length of all the fences on his land, the height above sea level of Mount Hindley and Mount Fitton and Mount Neil—and wrote those down in words, also.

She wrote about all the new things Carly did, and the new discoveries she made.

Including a snake.

Yep, bit of a shock, that. She and Carly had gone out to collect eggs before lunch on Tuesday and hadn't even seen the huge, silent thing coiled against the shade cloth at the side of the chook house until they were close enough to touch.

Oh…dear…Lord.

Her heart had felt like it had stopped, but Carly's scream was more one of surprise than fear. Kerry had come running from her vegetable garden and had quickly been able to tell them it was only a carpet python.

Right.

Only.

Harmless, Kerry had said. Really. Wouldn't even squeeze you to death, which had been Jac's second theory, once she'd abandoned the toxic venom idea.

"Take a look at it, Carly," Kerry had invited, and Carly had looked.

From a little farther away, so had Jac.

They'd seen the markings and Kerry had told Carly her version of an Australian aboriginal myth about a lizard and a snake who had taken turns to paint markings on each other's backs, which had kept both Carly and Jacinda looking at the python long enough to really see its beauty.

Because it was beautiful. The markings were like the neat stitches in a knitting pattern, with subtle variations of creams and yellows on a background of brownish gray—gorgeous and neat and intricate. Jacinda was discovering so much that was beautiful on Callan's land, and Callan watched her doing it, knew she was writing about it, and seemed to be happy with that, even though he didn't say very much.

On Thursday, they drove for three hours with Carly to Leigh Creek in the truck, and picked up fence posts and post-cards, among other supplies. The town was modern and neat and pretty, with young, white-trunked eucalyptus trees and drought-tolerant shrubs flowering pink, yellow and red. For lunch they stopped in a tiny and much older railway town called Copley just a few miles to the north of Leigh Creek and ate at Tulloch's Bush Bakery and Quandong Café—well-known in the area, apparently, as well as a popular tourist stop.

"You have to taste a quandong pie for dessert," Callan decreed, so the three of them ate the wild peach treats, which tasted deliciously tangy and tart, something like rhubarb, inside a shortcrust pastry with crumbly German-style streusel on top.

Jac sat in the café for a little longer and wrote her postcards, while Callan entertained Carly by taking her for a wander around the quiet little town. The postcards were tough, and there were lots of places where her pen hovered over an uncompleted line while she searched for words. But she managed to fill the space in the end, and included Callan's e-mail address. "I'd love to hear from you, if you get a chance," she told both her brothers, hoping they would realize that she meant it, hoping they'd care enough to respond.

On the long journey home, Carly fell asleep in the seat between them, and with her sweet-scented little head on Jac's shoulder, Jac got sleepy as well. They'd left pretty early this morning, and Callan had even let her drive for part of the journey. In a truck of this size, on outback roads, it had been a challenge but she couldn't have chickened out. It seemed important, right now, to push herself in new ways, to prove her own strength—to herself, more than to anyone else.

Proving yourself did definitely leave you sleepy, though.

The smooth gravel of the road hummed and hissed beneath the wheels, and even the sight of a group of kangaroos bounding away across the red ground didn't do more than make her eyes widen again for a few moments.

Callan teased her when she woke up again. "You had a good nap, there, judging by the size of the wet patch on your shirt."

"Oh! Was I—?"

Drooling? True, Carly sometimes did, in her sleep.

Without speaking, he handed Jac a tissue, but there was no wet patch that she could find. She wadded the tissue up and pelted him with it. "I was not!"

"Snoring, muttering, reciting Shakespeare and your bank account number. Kept me awake, so thanks."

"I was not! Pass me another tissue!" Even though it wasn't a very effective weapon.

"Okay, I won't mention any of the other things you do in your sleep."

"I snoozed lightly. For about ten minutes."

"Forty-five, actually."

"You mean we're nearly back?" Taking a better look at the surrounding country, she recognized Mount Hindley approaching to the right. She knew its distinctive silhouette, now. "Oh, we are! I really did sleep!"

"Yeah, my conversation was that interesting."

"You didn't say a word!"

They grinned at each other over Carly's head and it just felt good.

On Friday evening, he asked her, "Do you still want to see the animals drinking, down at the water?"

"I'd love to."

"Because we could do it tomorrow, if you want."

Apart from Thursday's trip into town, he'd been working hard since Sunday to get the new mustering yard completed, going out to Springer's Well with Pete first thing every morning and not returning until late in the afternoon, leaving Lockie behind after that first day because of School of the Air. The mustering yard was almost completed now, Jacinda knew, ready for the next roundup of cattle for trucking to the sales down south.

Pete had had enough of the twice-daily drive between

Arakeela Downs and Nepabunna by Monday afternoon, on top of the even rougher trip out to Springer's Well, so he'd stayed at the homestead overnight on Monday and Tuesday nights to give them longer working days.

He had slept on the front veranda, wrapped in a sleeping bag laid on top of the ancient canvas of an army camp stretcher. He'd been an easy guest. Didn't talk too much. Didn't make a mess. Ate whatever was put in front of him.

And he'd told Carly stories about the mythical Akurra serpent, whose activities explained the existence of the water holes and gorges all over this region, as well as the existence of Lake Frome. "Big rocks in the creek, Akurra's eggs. Belly rumbles 'cos he drank too much saltwater, and you can feel it under your feet. You feel one day, Carly, if the earth ever shakes a bit, that's Akurra."

Mythical serpents, real carpet pythons, yabby sandwiches...Carly took it all in stride. But her little legs probably weren't yet equal to a dawn climb up Mount Hindley, so Callan suggested that this time they leave all the kids and Kerry behind. He packed breakfast and hiking supplies that evening, and suggested that Jac bring a day pack, too.

"For water and sunscreen, your towel, your camera, and somewhere to put your sweatshirt once the sun gets higher."

Packing these items, Jac thought about the second schoolwork notebook that Callan had given her today—"In case you're in danger of filling up the first one," he'd said, and she dropped that in, also, along with a pen. She thought she was probably just giving herself unnecessary extra weight.

If he hadn't made that rash promise about a dawn hike to Jacinda down at the water hole last Saturday night, he wouldn't be doing this, Callan knew. He set the alarm for five-thirty because they wanted to get to the top of Mount Hindley to see the sun's first rays, but he didn't need its jangling sound to rouse him. He'd already been lying awake since four forty-five, locked in a whole slew of illogical feelings.

The thought of several glorious early morning hours alone with Jac made him heat up way too much.

He just liked her.

A lot.

Her company. Her outlook. Her smile.

And he was a man, so liking channeled itself into predictable pathways.

Physical ones.

He knew that his mood changed when he walked into the house and she was there. His spirits lifted, floating his energy levels up along with them the way empty fuel cans used to float the scrappy wooden rafts he and Nicky had hammered together to ferry around the water hole as kids.

Who noticed?

Someone had to.

Mum wasn't blind, and her hearing was pretty sharp, too. Could she hear the way his voice changed? He got more talkative, louder. He laughed more. He threw Carly up in the air, wrestled with Josh, told bad jokes to Lockie, got all three kids overexcited before bedtime just because he was too keyed up himself and couldn't keep it dammed back.

And Jacinda reacted the same way.

He could see it and hear it and feel it because all of it echoed exactly what was happening inside him.

Their eyes met too often. They found too many reasons to share a smile. The smallest scraps of conversation took on a richer meaning. Shared coffee in the mornings was cozier. Jokes were funnier. It took him longer to wind down enough to sleep at night.

Sometimes he felt so exhilarated by it, as if he were suddenly equipped to rule the world. Or his corner of it, anyhow—those six hundred thousand acres that impressed her so much.

The new mustering yard was great, structured to minimize stress and injury to the cattle. His yield and his prices were definitely going to improve. The long-range weather forecast held the hope of rain, and he'd put in some new dams just last year—Jacinda called them ponds—to conserve as much of the runoff as he could.

He'd talked to her about all this and she'd listened and nodded and told him, "I had no idea so much research and thought had to go into running cattle in this kind of country." And he'd thought, yes, he had skills and knowledge and strength that he took for granted, things that could impress a woman that he'd never seen in that light before.

Not even with Liz, because Liz had grown up with cattlemen and had taken it all for granted, too, just the way he did.

What did Mum see?

What did Pete see?

Pete had irritated the heck out of him, earlier in the week, with the ancient-tribal-wisdom routine that he liked to pull on unsuspecting victims from time to time.

No, it wasn't really a con, because Pete was pretty wise in a lot of ways, but Callan had felt conned, all the same. He'd felt naked and exposed.

What *did* Pete see?

What was all that biblical-style stuff about seasons turning and everything having its place and its time? He liked Pete's conversation better when it was about fence posts and calving. On Wednesday afternoon, they'd had a big, pointless argument about wildflowers.

"Desert pea? It's too soon, Pete. We had those freak thunderstorms a month or two ago, I know, but the flowers won't be out for a few weeks yet, I'd say. Maybe not until spring."

"Yeah, but happens that way, sometimes. So busy saying

it's too soon, and that's right when you see 'em, red flowers dripping on the ground like blood, right where the rainwater soaked into the ground."

"I still say it's too soon."

"You want your friend to see 'em before she goes," Pete had said. It was a statement, not a question. "You're not happy, because you think she won't."

And he was right.

Callan liked Jacinda so much, he wanted to show her dawn from Mount Hindley, and Pete's ancestors' rock carvings farther up in the gorge, and the bloodred, black-eyed Sturt's desert pea flowers blooming on his land.

"Got your camera?" he asked her, as they walked out to the four-wheel-drive parked in its usual crooked spot in front of the house.

They moved and spoke quietly because the kids were still asleep. Mum's light was on. She'd have made her early morning cup of tea and would be drinking it in bed, in her quilted dressing gown. She'd be dressed and over at the main house before Carly and the boys had finished wiping the sleep from their eyes.

"Yep," Jacinda answered, holding up her day pack. "Remembered it this time." She shivered a little.

"Cold?" he asked. It wasn't an award-winning question. Of course she was cold. So was he. They'd need to get moving before they would warm up.

"A bit, but I'm fine."

He liked that about her, too. She didn't complain. Being cold or hungry or scared or wet…or confronted by a carpet python…or teased about drooling…was never enough on its own to spoil her mood. She took things in stride, just like her daughter did.

Yeah, but there were limits.

Monday morning, five days ago, on the veranda.

Sheesh, what had he said?

You think you're the only one it's ever happened to?

Callan, idiot, you can't say things like that in a naked moment and then drop it and refuse to talk.

It was still sitting there, the conversational elephant that they both pretended they didn't see. Jac didn't know what he'd meant, and he wasn't going to tell her, so they would both just have to ride it out until the memory of Monday morning wasn't so fresh and didn't matter anymore.

Maybe papering it over with fresh memories of things like going into Leigh Creek with Carly, eating quandong pies, climbing Mount Hindley at dawn and watching yellow-footed rock wallabies come down to drink would help.

He warmed the engine and took his usual semicircular route around and out of the yard. They parked beside the dry creek bed under the same tree as last Saturday night, which was a mistake because it reminded him of…all sorts of things. But if he'd parked somewhere different, it might have looked as if he was avoiding that spot, which would just be crazy.

The sky had begun to soften in the east, but the air was still cold and the dew heavy.

"I love being awake and out of the house this early," Jac said, but she shivered again as she spoke.

Which made him want to put his arms around her to keep her warm.

He hiked faster, instead, moving his feet over the rocks the way he'd been doing all his life, forgetting that her stride wouldn't be as sure-footed or as wide. She didn't ask him to slow down until they were almost at the top of the mountain, and then her request came just a few seconds too late.

"Callan, could you—? Yikes! Ouch!"

She'd stepped onto an unsteady rock and it had tipped. She stumbled several steps and grazed her calf on another rock before almost falling to her knees.

"I'm sorry." Oh, damn! She'd already hurt herself once this week, on that strand of barbed-wire fence while he'd feared she was lost. She'd only removed the Band-Aids Thursday morning. "I was going too fast. Wanted to warm us up."

He doubled back to her, not reaching her as fast as he wanted to. He definitely shouldn't have let himself get so far ahead. She bent down and started picking dirt from the graze, wincing and frowning.

"Let me," he said.

"It's nothing. The skin is barely broken."

"What about this?" He took her arm and turned it over so she could see. She had a graze there, too, which she hadn't even noticed yet, a scrape between her elbow and wrist where blood was beginning to well up.

She made a sound of frustration and impatience. "I shouldn't have tried to go so fast."

"It was my fault. You were only trying to keep up, and I have better boots than you."

She smiled, tucking in the corner of her mouth. "That's right. Blame it on the boots, not the hopeless city-bred American."

"Don't. It really was my fault."

Together, they washed the grazes, dried them with the towel and put a couple of Band-Aids on the deepest scrapes, both of them finding too many reasons to apologize. Any awkwardness wasn't in their first-aid techniques, it was in their emotions. He felt as if he shouldn't be touching her, but that would have been impractical.

Oh, crikey!

Would he ever learn to act naturally around her?

He didn't hold out a lot of hope.

"We must be almost at the top," she said when they were ready to start moving again.

"Just about." It felt good to find something safe to talk about! "See that cairn of rocks up ahead? That marks the official summit."

"Did your family build it?"

It was a good-sized pile of stones, grading from larger at the base to smaller at the top, a couple of meters high.

"No, it's been here way longer than we have, over a hundred and fifty years. A couple of brothers, the Haymans, built it when they first ran sheep here in the 1850s."

"Do you know the whole history of your land, then, Callan?"

"Pretty much."

"And the aboriginal myths?"

"And the geology. You're standing on some pretty nice quartzite."

She laughed, intrigued and pleased for some reason. "Am I?"

"Yep, although down in the gorge itself it's granite. I can show you some maps. And I have satellite pictures, too. Those are fascinating, when you look at—" He stopped.

Or not.

Because she couldn't be that interested, could she? She was just being polite.

"Finish," she said.

"The way the land folds," he summarized quickly, "but, no, I'm done on geology. Let me know if you ever do want to see pictures. Speaking of which, get your camera out or you'll miss the sunrise."

She nodded, swung her day pack off her shoulders and found the natty little piece of digital technology. He watched her switch it on, position herself on a rock, line up her shot. There was a moment of stillness and expectation. The whole earth waited, and Jac waited with it.

Callan's body felt warm and loose from the walk, a little

dusty around his bare lower legs. He was thirsty, but didn't even want to breathe right now, let alone fiddle around in search of his water bottle. He just wanted to watch Jac watching the dawn.

She wore stretchy black shorts that finished snugly halfway down her lean, smooth thighs, and her legs were bare until they disappeared inside a pair of chunky white tennis socks just above her ankles. She had her backside parked on a rock and her knees bent up to provide a steady resting point for her elbows.

The sleeves of her navy sweatshirt were pushed up. Beyond gracefully bent wrists, her hands looked delicate yet sure as they held the camera, and she'd turned her baseball cap around the wrong way like a kid, so that the peak wouldn't get in the way of her view.

"Oh, it's fabulous…fabulous," she whispered.

The horizon began to burn and the first rays shot across the landscape, setting it alight with molten gold. She clicked her camera, got impatient with her position and stood up, circling the whole three hundred and sixty degrees twice, clicked and clicking, as the light changed and flared and shifted around her. It settled on a herd of cattle, turning them from dark blobs into distinctive red-brown silhouettes, etched with a glow. Finally, she lowered the camera and smiled.

And he came so close to grabbing that back-to-front baseball cap off her head, throwing it on the ground and kissing her, except…except…all the terrifying reasons from the other night were still there, and he didn't see how they were ever going to let him alone.

"I want to see the satellite pictures and hear about the history, Callan," she told him. "Don't think that you're ever boring about this place, because you're not."

"Yeah, it had occurred to me as a possibility," he managed to say.

"No. Not a possibility. Okay?"

He just nodded, relieved but still wondering if she was simply being polite.

"Mmm, I need some water," she said.

They both drank, then she put her camera away and asked, "Will we miss the kangaroos again?"

"We should get down into the gorge, before the sun climbs too high, yes."

He stayed behind her, this time. The sun at this height was already warm on their bare legs, but when they got lower, the gorge was still in shade. It was magical. They saw several kangaroos and a pair of yellow-footed rock wallabies, impossibly nimble and sure-footed as they bounded back up the rugged sides of the gorge after their morning drink. A family of emus showed up, too, their big curved backs heaped with the usual pile of untidy gray-brown feathers that bounced as they got startled by the human presence and ran.

Jacinda took more photos, then went to put her camera away.

"I brought breakfast, if you want it," Callan told her. "We can light the fire. Or we can head back."

She twisted to look back at him, trying to read what he really wanted, not wanting to be a time-waster or a nuisance. "Can we stay? Is there work you have to do?"

"We can stay. I'm getting pretty hungry."

And I don't want to end this, because it's too good.

She helped him with the fire. He'd brought an old pan, eggs and bacon, bread to make toast, a couple of garden tomatoes to grill, long-life milk, instant coffee and the billycan to boil the water in. They got everything ready, but the flames were still too high to start cooking. Their hungry stomachs would have to wait for glowing coals.

Jacinda looked at her day pack a couple of times in an uneasy kind of way and he almost teased her about it. Was she checking no snakes were lurking, eager to crawl inside?

Finally, she blurted out, "I brought my...Lockie's...note-book. Would you mind if I scribbled in it for a little while?"

Of course he didn't mind.

And he tried not to watch, because he knew that somehow it was private. She didn't like to feel herself under the spotlight of someone else's observation when she stared at the blank page or scratched the ballpoint pen impatiently back and forth over a wrong word—or even when she was writing smoothly and unconsciously smiling at the fact that it was going well.

Okay, so that meant he *was* watching. Sneaking glances, anyhow.

Even though the flames had still not died back quite right, he started cooking to distract himself, putting strips of bacon and halves of tomato into the pan and poking at them with a barbecue fork more than he needed to. He knew he shouldn't keep spying on Jac's tentative new relationship with written words.

He was so busy not noticing her write that he didn't notice when she stopped. Her question sneaked up and leaped at him like an enemy ambush. "Callan, tell me what you meant the other day, that I'm not the only one it's ever happened to."

He whipped around, bringing the sizzling pan with him and almost losing the freshly cooked eggs over the rim. She had the notebook open in her lap and the pen still in her hand. What was she going to do? Record his answer?

She looked startled at his sudden movement. Her gaze dropped to the pan. "Careful...."

"Sheesh, Jacinda!" he said on a hiss.

The ambush metaphor still held. He felt like a soldier, taken by surprise but on such a hair trigger that he was ready for the attack anyhow, weapon fully loaded. He bristled all over, prepared to lie under oath, stay silent under torture, neu-tralize the onslaught in any way he could.

He wasn't going to talk about this!

* * *

Wrong, wrong, wrong, Jacinda realized at once, watching Callan set the pan of eggs down on a rock without looking at it.

They'd each gotten to different places during the past ten minutes of silence, she saw. She had felt increasingly peaceful, close to Callan, at home….

And braver, because some nice snatches of language were happening on her page, and writing well always made her brave. Out of nowhere, she'd had an insight into one of the half-forgotten but very real characters in her old, unfinished novel, and suddenly that character wasn't half-forgotten anymore, but was right here, as if sitting beside Jac, her story clamoring to be told.

When she'd looked up from her writing, she'd seen Callan crouched by the fire, his muscles pulling under his shirt as he reached to poke the coals or flip the toast on the old wire rack. He wasn't saying anything, wasn't looking her way, and she thought he must be feeling peaceful, too, happy about being together like this, enjoying each other's uninterrupted company, sharing the same appreciation of nature's gifts at this fresh hour.

The question hadn't felt abrupt to her. It had felt right.

But it wasn't right.

She could see it instantly in the way he turned, the way his face changed, the sharpness in his voice, the appalled expression in his eyes.

Sheesh, Jacinda! In her head, she echoed his own exclamation.

You could have led up to it better, couldn't you, Jac? Given him some warning?

She let her notebook slide to the ground and stood up, covering the few yards of physical distance between them—

and hopefully some of the miles of emotional distance—in one breath…in four heartbeats.

"Callan." She put her hand on his arm and he flinched. "I didn't intend for it to be such a tough question."

"Okay…"

"I'm sorry, I'm too self-absorbed over this. You seemed to understand so much the other day. About the whole thing with my writing. The problem. The block. The incompleteness. And today it was flowing so well. I have to thank you, because I never imagined finding a place where I'd feel so safe, after what was happening with Kurt at home. And I just wanted to understand about you, in return, that's all. I wanted to hear from you about the incompleteness that happened to you, and what you did about it. What worked for you, when you solved it."

He froze.

Wrong again, Jac.

Hell, how could her intentions have been so good and still have led to such a mess?

He closed his eyes, gritted his teeth. When he answered, she could hardly hear. "I haven't solved it."

He broke roughly away from her, turning his back to her just the way he had on Saturday night.

Guarding himself.

Guarding against some power she had over him, or some threat she was unconsciously making. Either way, she didn't understand.

But her bravery was still in place—that sizzling sense of capability and strength that good writing could give her. And that meant she wasn't prepared to let the issue go.

"Please don't turn your back, Callan," she said and stepped toward him.

He didn't move, apart from thrusting his hands down into the pockets of his shorts. He didn't speak, either.

"You turned your back the other night, too, when we were here," she pressed on. "You know when I mean. Looking for Lockie's Game Boy, when we—"

"Yes, I know when you mean."

She reached him, but his body language practically screamed at her not to touch. It created physical pain because she wanted to touch him so much.

"I would really like to talk about this, Callan. To understand it."

He laughed, as if she was being completely naïve.

Maybe she was, because the bravery was still there inside her, only she was kidding herself that it came from her good writing.

It didn't.

It came from something else.

Desire.

She wanted Callan so much, and at some level she *trusted* the wanting—*had* to trust it because it was that powerful, and she knew, despite everything he said—and did—and didn't do—that it reflected back at her from him with equal force. He wanted her, too.

"Okay, then we won't talk," she said, standing behind him and wrapping her arms around his rigid body. "For the moment, we'll just do this…."

His torso was as hard as a board, vibrating with tension, and her touch didn't soften him at all. If she'd been feeling even a fraction less brave, less sure, she would have let him go, her face flaming with embarrassment at his rejection.

But if it was the desire, after all, that had made her brave, it was the writing that had made her see clearly and she knew…just *knew*…that he wasn't rejecting her. There was something way more complex going on here.

She slid her hands up to his shoulders and began to caress him, running from his warm, solid neck and out to his upper arms, over and over again. Soon, she let her fingers trespass farther, touching his jaw, brushing the lobes of his ears, feathering into his hair. Still, he didn't soften or move.

"Prebreakfast massage," she murmured. "The sun's on my back, so I'm getting a massage, too. Whatever's happening, Callan, don't be angry. Don't push me away."

He didn't answer, but his breath came out in a shuddering sigh.

"If you're going to tell me to stop, then you have to tell me why," she said.

Silence. She kept touching him.

"I'm not going to tell you to stop," he finally answered.

She didn't jump on his words, she just let them hang. Then she leaned her cheek against his back, slid her hands between his rigid upper arms and his sides and began to stroke them down his chest. To begin with, she stopped at his ribs, which moved up and down with his breathing. His back moved with his breathing, also, pushing against her breasts. Her nipples were hard against his body. Could he feel?

She let her caress drop lower, reaching the waistband of his shorts, and then his hips, drifting in toward the center, and she forgot about anything more she might want from these moments because they were so precious and delicious all on their own.

He moved.

At last.

His body snaked around and he held her. She wanted to kiss him, take his face in her hands and press her mouth over his, imprint her taste onto him, drink him, make him respond. More than that, however, she wanted him to talk, which meant she couldn't capture his mouth. Not yet.

"You said you were incomplete, and you didn't mean incomplete because you'd lost Liz," she whispered. "We haven't known each other very long, but you're important to me,

Callan. You're good to me. Good for me. And I trust you. I wish you'd trust me, because we can help each other better then."

"I trust you. I don't need help." She thought he was going to push her away at that point, but he didn't. After a moment, like an afterthought, he added, "But I want you. Oh, I *want* you."

"Yes…"

"But that's where I'm incomplete, Jacinda. God, can I say it? Am I saying it?" He was talking more to himself than to her. His whole body was shuddering, shaking.

"I don't understand."

"I couldn't satisfy you, that's the problem. I couldn't satisfy either of us. I haven't been able to in four years, since—" He broke off and swore beneath his breath, then looked her full in the face with his blue eyes burning. "You see, I'm impotent," he said, and she knew for him these had to be the ugliest two words in the world.

Chapter Ten

One wrong word.

All she would need to do would be to say one wrong word at this point and everything between them—the trust, the chemistry—would be shattered, Jacinda knew.

And yet silence was wrong, too, which meant she had to think fast. She held on to him, understanding the tight, rigid state of his body much better now, and she wondered how arrogant she must be to even hope that her touch could soften him, after what he'd just said.

"Thank you for telling me," she said quietly, just before the silence grew too heavy.

"Well, you pretty much gave me no choice."

"No. Okay."

"So there you have it."

She waited for him to move, to disengage physically and emotionally from their close body contact, but he stayed where he was, and so did she. "Who have you talked to about it?" she asked.

Letting her head fall lightly against his chest, she felt the strong beat of his heart. There was nothing wrong with his circulation, for sure, and absolutely nothing wrong with his ability to arouse a woman.

"You," he answered her. "Just now." His voice was barely human, more like a growl.

"Not a doctor?" She was moved—and scared—that she was the one who'd heard his confession, when no one else had.

"No, not a doctor."

"Shouldn't you?"

"Hey, do people need doctors anymore? All that trouble and expense? We can scare ourselves for free on the Internet."

"So you've looked it up there?"

"I couldn't find anything that seemed…relevant. It was all too much about side effects from illness. Prostate cancer. Diabetes. Physical things."

"So you think this is emo—?"

"I don't want to talk about it, Jacinda."

No hesitation. No doubt. The same tone he'd used when he'd said *I don't need help.*

She didn't have the right to push any further, and he'd pulled out of her arms so she couldn't even touch him anymore.

"We should eat then," she answered carefully. "You rescued the fried eggs, we shouldn't let them get cold. But first can I say again, thank you for telling me?"

"That means you're going to bring the subject up again, right?" He moved farther away, picked up the panful of eggs. Every nuance of his body language screamed at her to keep her distance.

"I'm remembering how this started, you see. Because you understood about my writer's block. We have common ground, Callan. You were the one to work that out first. If we can help each other, I don't want to let this go."

"Don't—just *don't*—talk about helping me."

"Okay." She took a breath. "Boy, that bacon smells good!"

They ate, sitting on adjacent rocks, and every bite tasted fabulous after the early morning climb and all the fresh air.

Well, she's still here, Callan thought, dragging in a long, hot mouthful of smoky coffee.

Which put her in the same category as Birgit. The blonde at the races would have been long gone by now. Jacinda would go the sex-therapist route, take his admission of sexual inadequacy as a personal challenge. He hadn't told Birgit that his failure with her wasn't his first, so she'd used phrases like *getting you back in the mood* and *scary the first time, with someone new.*

He felt defensive. Didn't want to hear any of those kinds of lines from Jacinda, the way he hadn't wanted to read the pamphlets on bereavement from the hospital. He would prefer that they spent the remaining two and a half weeks of her visit in total, monklike silence. From beneath the concealing brim of his hat, he watched her, waiting for her to pounce. It took him a while to understand that she wasn't planning to.

She ate with a mixture of fastidiousness and greed that no one could have faked. It wasn't intended to seduce, but, Lord, he found it sexy! Something deep in his body began to stir again. Putting egg, bacon and tomato inside a sandwich of two bits of toast, she opened her mouth wide and bit down on it hard and slow, closing her eyes. The liquid egg yolk burst, leaked from her lips and ran down her chin, and she opened her eyes and laughed.

Running her index finger up to push the yolk back into her mouth, she said, "I wish this could be breakfast every day.

Salt? Cholesterol? Who cares! The sun evaporates that stuff, right?" She swallowed, grinned, and then apologized for talking with her mouth full.

A small, irritating black bush fly buzzed around her face and she waved it away, her hand soft. Callan remembered how her fingers had felt on his body just now, pushing for his response. He took another gulp of coffee, to disguise the fact that his breathing wasn't quite steady.

A fantasy flashed into his mind, as complete as an edited piece of film. He would spread out a blanket on the sand—never mind that he hadn't brought one with him—and he'd fall asleep. Jacinda would seduce him without waking him. He would believe the whole thing to be a dream. She'd take off his clothes with whisper-soft movements. He would feel her breath, the brush of her hair on his skin.

The sun would climb and the air would heat up. Her naked body would almost burn him as she slid over him, wrapping him in her long limbs. He'd thrust into her, hard as a rock, engulfed by her silky heat and, because it was a dream, he wouldn't think any of those panicky, mood-destroying thoughts for a second and they'd surge over the crest of the wave together. Success before the concept of failure had even entered his head.

Failure.

The stirring, swelling, expectant feeling sank away like water down a plug hole.

Callan, just finish your breakfast.

"Do we have time to swim?" Jacinda asked, as he drained the last mouthful of coffee.

"It would be pretty cold," he said, dampening the idea down the way his body had just dampened down its own need. "The sun isn't on the water, yet."

"The water's cold even with the sun on it. I don't mind. I think a swim would be good."

For both of us, the words implied.

Therapy.

Or a cure.

Yeah, and she was probably right. The outback version of a cold shower. Not that he needed one right at this moment, but maybe she did. He knew she wanted him, and he'd left her hanging.

"We'd better put the fire out, first," he said.

She remembered the way they'd done it last week and shoveled on scoops of creek sand with the billycan, smothering the dying coals. "Is that enough?"

"It's fine. You'd have to be unlucky to start a bushfire in these conditions, even if you left it in flames."

"But you like to play it safe."

"A few minutes of work versus hundred-and-fifty-year-old creek bed trees? You bet!"

They packed up the egg carton, the jar of coffee and the rest of the breakfast things, and then she started rummaging in her day pack for her swimming costume. Callan had another fantasy. She'd forgotten it back at the house. She'd have to swim naked. They'd both—

"Why are things always in the last place you look?" she said, dragging the two pieces of animal-print fabric from the side pocket.

"Because once you've found them, you stop looking," he told her.

She stared at him, blank faced, and then she laughed. "Cattleman's logic?"

"There's an impressive intellect at work under this hat, I'm telling you."

She laughed again, and he felt better. No more fantasies invaded his brain. His muscles weren't knotted quite so tightly. The empty, angry feeling had gone. First and foremost, they were friends. He had to remind himself of that, hang on to it, trust it.

Trust her.

And not look at her while she changed.

She helped by disappearing behind the pale trunk of a huge tree overhanging the creek and he took off his shorts, boots and shirt while she was out of sight, to reveal the dark gray swim trunks he'd put on this morning just in case.

Wearing her neat, figure-hugging costume, having left her clothes in a tidy pile beside her day pack, Jacinda screamed all the way along the sand, like a jet coming down a runway. "If I take this fast, I won't notice the temperature," she yelled, then disappeared in a flurry of splashed-up water. Twisting, she launched onto her back with her arms spread out, still yelling. "Hey, are you coming, Callan? It's *freezing!*"

"After that sales pitch…" He launched toward her and ended up deeper, wetter and probably colder, competitive the way he'd been with Nicky as a child. Couldn't let any female get too far ahead of him, but appreciated the ones who gave him a good run for his money.

Like Liz.

He felt a twist of regret and loss and impatience. Why had he thought about Liz now? Why did he have to make everything so hard for himself? Liz would have been the last person to approve of the way he tied himself in knots.

Go for it, Callan.

He could almost hear Liz's voice, saying the words.

But go for what?

"Are we jumping and yelling and bunyipping today?" Jac asked.

"What, we're not cold enough already? We need to get colder?"

"We need to keep moving. The rocks up on the ledge are starting to get into the sun. They'll warm us up. I didn't yell loud enough, the first time. I want to do it again."

"Race you to the ledge," he said, and won.

Just.

"You let me get that close to a win." She was breathing hard, making her chest rise and fall in the water. He wanted to look down, ogle her breasts. He was tense and prickly and awkward and aware, and knew she felt pretty much the same. "You were going easy on me. Weren't you?"

"You'll never know, will you?"

She flicked water in his face, and then they both climbed onto the ledge.

The way they'd done last Saturday, they ran and jumped and yelled, swam and climbed and ran to jump again. "Why *is* this so good?" Jac said. The highest parts of the rock ledge were in full sun, now, and the smooth granite warmed rapidly. They sat on it, stretching their legs out and making wet imprints that shrank to a vanishing point as the moisture dried. "This should go in a self-help book."

"You ever think of writing one of those?" Callan suggested. "They sell pretty well, don't they?"

"Never, no matter how well they sell. I don't think I have enough answers for myself, let alone for anyone else!"

"I can't imagine self-help books give people real answers. I've looked at some. They always make it sound too easy. And if they do give answers… What about your novel? Doesn't a novel need answers?"

"Yes, but they're messy ones. Nice and human and flawed. Not definitive."

"But basically, with a novel, you control the universe. You can make it all work out just the way you want. That must be pretty nice."

"Not always. I mean, it is nice, but you can't always do it. You'd be surprised. Characters sometimes refuse to behave."

"Make them."

"You can't. They have minds of their own. If they don't,

then they're made of cardboard and readers can tell. I mean, I've never finished my novel so I don't know why I'm sounding like such an authority on the strength of thirty thousand words. All I know is, there have definitely been times when my characters didn't behave, and the right thing seemed to be to let them take control."

"When you talk about your writing, when you're really involved in it, your face changes." He'd noticed it before, but the change was more marked, today.

"Does it?" She pressed her hands to her cheeks, embarrassed, laughing a little. "Hope the wind doesn't shift direction, then."

"No, it's a good kind of change. Your eyes get a spark in them. You smile more. You move more. Are you working on your novel, in Lockie's notebook?"

"No." She shook her head vigorously. "No, I'm not." She paused. "At least…"

"So you are?"

"Oh…no…I had a couple of thoughts about my main character, that's all. I'm sure it doesn't mean anything. I haven't written a word."

"Are you going to try? You should. You shouldn't give up on something like that. You shouldn't let it defeat you."

She moved abruptly on the rock, shoulders squaring and bent arm snapping straight. "You are so unfair, do you know that?" she almost yelled.

Startled, he realized she was angry, not kidding around. She jumped up, headed toward the water, then circled back.

"So unfair!" she repeated even louder, and she was blinking back tears.

Before he could respond, she'd slipped into the water and started heading for the beach, her crawl messy and furious, lots of splash and not much speed. He followed and caught up easily, grabbed her wet shoulder and turned her around

just at the place where they could both stand without diffi-
culty, chest deep.

"Don't say something like that and walk away," he told
her.

"Why the hell not? You do it to me! How many times now
have you said something important about what's going on
inside you and then just walked away?"

Oh.

She meant *that*.

Of course.

"That's different," he growled.

"Why? Your manhood is of universal, earth-shattering importance, but the disappearance of my creativity...my liveli-
hood...is a minor irritation? We can chat about one in a light,
friendly way, lots of helpful hints from you about how to get
it right, while the other is this doom-laden, forbidden, terrifying, ghastly topic that has me beating myself up because I've
accidentally—despite a burning, huge need to...oh...just be
your friend about it, Callan—said and done a couple of
slightly, and totally unintended, sensitive things? Is that how
it is?"

"You're telling me the two things are related? Not being
able to write, and not being able to—?" He stopped. "You're
telling me that they're parallel? Equal?"

"Yes! Damn it! Isn't that part of what lets us understand
each other? Care about each other, even? Care, probably,
way more than is sensible, in my case." She blinked again.

Creek water or tears?

He wasn't sure.

He *was* sure that she was still angry.

And, so help him, it turned him on. He felt his heart rate
speeding up, and his breathing, and the air in his nostrils and
deep in his lungs was suddenly full of some indefinable aura
of wanting and need that he and Jacinda had manufactured

together like a powerful scent. This time, after all the false starts, he couldn't imagine it ebbing away. This time, he was sure he could get it right, because she was so different, so much more important in his life than those other women had been.

She looked like a sleek wet leopard in her animal print, with her shoulders getting tanned from the sun and her hair streaming down her back. The water came level with her breasts, floating them higher so that they swelled smooth and neat and round above the curved and normally modest neckline of her suit.

Her black lashes were spiky and thick with water, and her gray eyes seemed huge. They flashed at him. The tension in her whole body was electric.

"Jacinda…" he said.

"I'm trying *so hard* to find a way to get my writing back. I've told you how important it is. You almost… I've even thought you understood. More than I would have expected. Because of— Yes, your own problem. I've told you how it's helping me, being here. I've been…really naked to you about it, a couple of times."

"You don't think I've been naked?"

"You have. Which is why you should understand how hard it is, and not *push* me about my novel." She paused. "But I probably overreacted."

"And I didn't think," he said.

"Let's forget it."

She bobbed down into the water, letting herself float on her back with her arms spread wide, trying to relax. Her hair floated away from her like water weed and she stretched out her neck. Moisture gleamed on her fine-pored skin. The water lapped at the hip-level gap between the two halves of her swimsuit, showing her flat, olive-skinned stomach.

He didn't take his eyes off her for a second, and she must

have known he was watching her, she must have felt it like an electric current zapping between them in the water. His whole body crawled with aching desire like some dizzying illness, only the feeling was too good to be a disease.

When she stood up again, one swimsuit strap had drifted down off her shoulder, peeling the animal-print fabric halfway down her breast. Her thumb came to hook it back up, but he closed his hand over hers and said, "Don't. Please don't. Leave it down. Please."

She looked at him, and didn't need to ask why.

Which was good, because he couldn't have given her an answer. If he thought about anything…*anything*…except the immediacy of this moment, then he feared the moment would go.

In the water, they drifted against each other. The cold was unimportant. He felt her thighs, tight and cool and as slippery as satin, wrapping around him while her arms wrapped around his neck. Her eyes were wide and clear, their gaze fixed on his face. He cupped her backside in his hands and pulled her tighter against him, slid his fingers down and along to her inner thighs, where he stroked her.

She kissed him, her mouth wet and flavored with creek water, cool at her lips but warm within. He kissed her back, deeper than the other night, harder and stronger and longer. The sun dried their faces and heated their skin, contrasting with the cool water that moved around their legs.

He bent his knees and dipped her deep in the water again, kept kissing her with their faces submerged then pulled up to break the surface again and let their contact break. He still didn't speak. Couldn't. But wanted more. He found the second strap on her swimsuit, the one that was still in place, and lowered that, as well.

She didn't protest.

Not a word.

But she watched him and her eyes said, "Keep going."

He slid the tank-style swimsuit top down to her waist and her bared breasts moved lightly in the water, her nipples the color of cinnamon and strawberry mixed together. The swimsuit top bunched awkwardly so she raised her arms and he pulled it over her head, flung it toward the beach, didn't look to see if it had safely gotten that far.

She stepped back a couple of paces, to where the water only came just above her waist, and stood up, letting her body stream with dazzling wetness. She had her spine straight and her shoulders softly square. She knew he couldn't take his eyes from her jutting breasts and she didn't want him to.

The sun steamed the water from her skin and caught in her hair and she lifted her face higher into the bright light and closed her eyes. He could see just how much she loved the freedom of this place, the air and the space for miles around, no one to see them, nothing to get in the way of the sun on their skin and their primal awareness of each other.

He closed the distance, kissed her mouth, her jaw, her neck, and her tight, beautiful nipples, one and then the other. Her breathing sped up and she closed her eyes, pressed his mouth harder against her breast and arched her spine. He took her deeper into his mouth, sucking hard, lifting her higher. Each breast fitted just right, swelled just a little bit beyond the size of his cupped hands.

He was hard, throbbing, in pain.

And she knew.

Easing him into the shallows, she stroked his back, slipped her thumbs inside the waistband of his swim shorts and dragged them down. Then she lay back in the water and pulled his arms toward her so that he slid up her body, his hardness brushing the one remaining barrier of fabric between them at her groin. He heard her breath hiss in at the contact, felt her pushing her hips up so that he'd feel her again.

Oh, God.

He reached between them, cupped his hand over the warm mound between her legs. She pushed harder, and beneath the water his finger slid the fabric aside and slipped inside the two sweet folds. She gasped and writhed, her body trembling with its need for more, and he gave it to her.

But then he felt a change. She began to hold herself back, pressed her hand over his, and opened her eyes. The hesitation lasted only a few seconds, and he could see so clearly what she was thinking, the questions in her head.

Tease or keep going? What's going to make him stay aroused? What's going to keep the momentum? If I think about my own pleasure is that going to ruin everything for him?

Half a dozen other doubts and concerns, too, for all he knew.

Her hand slid awkwardly up his arm, and she whispered, "Not yet."

And despite how sure and confident he'd been just a short while earlier, that was all it took for everything to go wrong. It was like snatching at a piece of thistledown in the wind. You grabbed, and the thistledown floated farther away. You chased it and grabbed again, crushing its delicate fibers in your palm, forgetting why you'd reached for it in the first place.

"Callan?"

"I'm sor—"

"Don't apologize," she begged. "Please don't. It was my fault."

He laughed.

"It *was!* I stopped. I didn't know—"

"What to do next, because I'm such a delicate flower, one wrong move—"

"And I made it. I made the wrong move."

"It shouldn't be such a knife edge. Hell, it feels so strong between us sometimes—I like you, Jac, I want you—you'd think I could withstand twenty wrong moves and still get there."

He slid out of the water and onto the warm sand, hugging his arms around his knees, hiding the evidence of his failure. The sun beat onto his back, a slap more than a caress by this time. They should have headed back to the homestead way before this.

She followed him and knelt in front of him, her posture caving in the way he'd noticed it did when she lost confidence. Was his self-doubt contagious? She crossed her arms in front of her, covering her breasts. He didn't think it was deliberate. "What could I do to bring it back, Callan?" she asked him softly.

With no answers, thankful at least that she'd managed to avoid the phrase *help you* he just shook his head and closed his eyes.

It must only have been about thirty seconds later that Jac heard a vehicle. At first she thought it was something else. Wind in the eucalyptus trees, or one of the airplanes that occasionally flew overhead. But it got louder and she recognized the grind of an engine making its way slowly over the rough track in their direction. Kerry surely wouldn't have come looking for them yet, would she? They'd probably been gone longer than planned, but not by that much.

Oh, shoot, and where was the top of her swimsuit?

Scrambling to her feet, she went looking for it, hearing the vehicle get closer and closer. Make that vehicles, plural. There were two more driving in convoy behind the first one, she saw, as she picked up her sand-encrusted top from the hot ground. Still bare and dripping, Callan found his swim trunks and pulled them on, then crossed the creek bed to meet the vehicles, which gave her time to soak the sand off her top and pull it awkwardly down over her body.

Her throbbing body.

Her breasts still felt swollen, with hardened nipples at their crests, and she had an aching fullness where he'd touched her, and tingling skin that baked where the sun hit her shoulders and back but still felt cool along her arms and around her sides.

If they'd kept going, if Callan had been able to make love to her, they would have been discovered or at the very least interrupted. She'd never been a sexual exhibitionist, but right now in a heartbeat she'd have exchanged flagrant, shameless discovery for this feeling of failure and mess.

She felt stupid for having thought that a block as deep and real as Callan's could be overcome by a few sexy moves on her part, or even by the real and deep-rooted strength of her own desire. And she felt stupid for having believed that they'd established enough trust, enough depth, enough commitment.

Good grief, commitment?

The word fit nowhere.

She and Carly were leaving this place in two and a half weeks, in quest of a place to belong on the far side of the world. Those postcards she'd written to her brothers on Thursday at the café might have reached Adelaide by now. They were such a tiny step in creating a future for herself, but it was the only step that made any sense—the start of a plan, at least.

Move east, close enough to Andy and Dad in New Jersey or Tom in upstate New York so that they could get together every week if they wanted.

Work on her relationship with Andy, Dad, Tom and her nieces and nephews so that they *did* want to spend time with her and Carly, because Kerry had shown her it was possible and worthwhile.

Live on her savings and Kurt's ungenerous alimony for a year while she wrote…tried to write…worked out if there was a chance she'd be able to write and sell…her novel. If she couldn't, then at least Carly would be in school by that time, and Jac could get office work or possibly teach.

The plan didn't—couldn't—include Callan, his family, his land or his problems.

She found the rest of her clothing and struggled into it, her wet swimsuit dragging against the dry fabric of T-shirt and stretchy Lycra shorts. The sand didn't help, either. Her feet were covered in it, and it ended up gritty and uncomfortable inside her socks and shoes.

She could see Callan still talking to the new arrivals, nodding and gesturing, pointing to places on a map they'd unfolded and spread on the hood of one vehicle. She thought about going over there but before she could decide if it was the right thing he'd left the group and returned across the creek bed to the water hole.

"They're going to camp here," he said, and she could see how glad he was to have such an obvious and impersonal subject to talk about.

He wasn't planning to launch into a rehash of sensitive issues any time soon, and he was probably right. She wondered if they'd ever rediscover the same peace and intimacy that they'd found this morning, and that still hadn't been enough.

"They've picked a good spot!" she said, meeting him halfway.

He nodded, brushing dry sand from his forearms and calves, which gave him a good excuse not to look at her. The air almost crackled with the distance he'd put in place. How long would it last? Would she dare try to break it? Was there any point?

"They're part of a four-wheel-drive touring club," he said.

"Seem pretty responsible, and well-equipped. They're planning on staying three nights, and hiking up the gorge tomorrow. I'm glad we did our dawn climb this morning, or we'd have had company."

"Do you charge them for camping here?" She held out the towel she hadn't taken the time to use, but he shook his head and she could see he'd dried off almost completely in the sun and didn't need it. "It's your land, after all."

"We've thought about it, but it'd be more trouble than it was worth. We'd have to put up signs and garbage facilities, even a pit toilet, and that would only encourage more people to use the place."

"The water hole's a pretty sensitive ecosystem, isn't it? It wouldn't take much tourism for it to be ruined."

"We don't get too much tourist traffic out here. We're not on the main road to Leigh Creek, and our side road ends just a few clicks from the homestead, at Wiltana Bore. A generation ago, that made Arakeela a pretty lonely place, sometimes, but there're so many more tourists coming up here now, you're right, it's become a good thing."

"So you never get to know any of them? They don't invite you down to their campfire for a beer?"

"Sometimes," he said, and he sounded awkward about it, as if sharing campfire tales wasn't something he liked doing even when he did get an invitation. "We should head back."

"Yes." Pick up on his cues and leave everything unsaid? Or speak? Suddenly, that felt wrong. "Callan—"

"Can you grab the breakfast things and put them in the vehicle?" he cut in quickly. "I'd better get my shirt on or I'll start to burn."

So we're not even going to acknowledge that we're not talking about it, Callan? That's it? We're left hanging?

And yet, when she thought about it, she didn't know what else they could do.

Chapter Eleven

"Callan!" said Brant's voice on the phone a week and a half later.

"Hey…" Callan answered, glad to hear his friend and yet cautious at the same time—a stunning display of inconsistency in his attitude that was becoming far too familiar.

Beyond the closed door of his office, where he'd been working on some financial spreadsheets, he heard a background of typical evening sounds. Kerry called Lockie to help her with the dinner dishes. Water ran in a pipe. Josh accidentally turned the CD player up too loud, then turned it down again.

"We had two winners today," Brant said, and Callan could hear background noise at his end, also. It sounded like Brant's sister's voice. "I thought you'd like to know. Gypsy Caravan romped home in Albury, and Rae gave Lucite a try in a maiden event at Rose Hill." Rae Middleton was one of their trainers, based near Brant. "We weren't sure she was ready for a metropolitan race yet. Rae had talked about giving her more country starts, but she did us proud and got home by a nose. It was a small field, but it's still a good win."

"That's great." For once, Callan was able to sound as if he meant it. The racehorses took his mind off things he didn't want to dwell on, questions for which he had no answers. "I thought Lucite had some good stuff in her."

The water stopped running. He heard footsteps coming along the corridor.

Jac's.

He could recognize them easily, now.

"Mmm, you're half-asleep already, aren't you, sweetheart?" she said, just outside the office door, and he knew she must have Carly in her arms, taking her along to bed.

"Rae's got plans, now," Brant said. "She's thinking Group races in her next prep, maybe even the Melbourne Cup in a couple of years. The mare's a stayer."

"Not that Rae's aiming too high, or anything," Callan drawled, because horse racing in Australia didn't get any bigger than the Melbourne Cup. The whole state of Victoria took a public holiday on the first Tuesday in November for the big race day, and the prize purse was huge.

"Speaking of aiming high," Brant said, "I'm here to tell you that I have to be smashing you in the letters tally, at this point."

"Letters? Oh, from the Outback Wives women."

Change the subject, Branton, please.

Brant didn't. "Dusty reckons he's had about a hundred and fifty, and he's written back a nice fat *no* to all of them, because of Mandy. Me, I'm up over two hundred, and they're still coming."

"Yeah, and I'd be somewhere in between," Callan admitted. He had given a bundle of replies to Rob this morning, and had mailed several more two weeks ago in Leigh Creek, along with Jacinda's postcards to her brothers.

He heard her come back along the corridor, and then her

voice again in the kitchen, muffled by distance and the closed office door. "She couldn't even stay awake for a story. Anything I can help with, Kerry?"

"No, love, Lockie and I are doing fine, here."

"I'll be on the veranda, then."

Writing, Callan guessed.

"And Dusty and I are going to have to crawl over broken glass as punishment, at some point, for putting you through this whole *Today's Woman* deal?" Brant said into his ear. "Is that the message I'm getting?"

"Something like that."

There was a silence at the far end of the phone, then Brant asked cautiously, "So you're not going to meet any of them?"

Brant didn't know that Jacinda—who had to count as one of "them"—was staying here, and had been for three weeks. Now would be the obvious moment to tell him.

The words stuck in his chest and wouldn't come.

Brant didn't have to know, Callan decided. Because right at this moment, he just wasn't up to putting the necessary positive-yet-casual spin on the whole thing. He would end up saying too much, giving away more than he wanted to. Letting Brant and Dusty see how much of a mess he still was after four years without Liz was what had gotten him into this situation in the first place. He should learn to hide his damned feelings better.

But if it hadn't been for the magazine and its Wanted: Outback Wives, he never would have met Jac….

He tried that idea on for size and it felt so weird that he couldn't contemplate it.

He didn't want Jac and Carly to go…but he was counting the seven remaining days. He'd dragged those swim shorts of his onto his body seconds after he'd first heard the campers down at the water hole ten days ago, but he still felt naked whenever Jac was around.

Her presence in his house was so warm, it enriched all of

them…but when he found himself pricking up his ears for the sound of her voice, he felt ill and attempted to avoid her for hours afterward. He wished they'd never met…but he couldn't picture the universe without her, now.

He didn't know how to handle any of this.

Friendship was such an unsatisfying word, sometimes, but anything else held more pitfalls than the worst track on his property held ruts. He'd been sending out some pretty strong signals, since his failure with Jac down at the water hole, that she should keep her distance, that if she was ever tempted to try some more of Birgit's helpful sexual therapy then for heck's sake just damn well *don't,* and over the past week and a half she'd been scrupulous about it.

They hadn't so much as touched.

"What about you? Who have you met?" he asked Brant, since he considered attack to be the best form of defense, and a crucial strategy in male friendship. "I bet they've all looked like the back end of a bus, because who else would look at a sheep farmer like you?" Gratuitous, jokey insults usually worked pretty well, too. Anything to get this onto a safer level.

"I have met many female bus ends in my time, Callan, mate, for sure, and recent samplings have lowered bus-end technology to new depths," Brant said. "Now Nuala's got some wretched European friend arriving tomorrow in a state of crisis, and the words *on your best behavior* have been heard beneath our roof. I wish she'd hurry up and get married!"

"The European friend?"

"No, Nuala! Because then she'll be Chris's problem and I'll get some peace. Bloody wedding's not until September."

"You'll live," Callan drawled.

"Not if the European friend decides to stay until then."

They talked a bit more about their horses, and he ended up being glad that Brant had called, which he hadn't been at all sure about at some points during their conversation.

After he'd put down the phone, he went into the living room and stepped over to the window that looked out on the section of veranda where Jac had taken to sitting, in that rickety cane couch that needed either repairing or throwing out.

Yes, she had one of Lockie's notebooks in her lap and a pen in her hand.

He wouldn't disturb her.

But he envied her.

She'd been writing like crazy two hours every night for days, and a couple of times during the day he'd caught her snatching a moment to jot down some phrases in a folded up bit of paper she apparently kept in her front jeans pocket. She kept a pencil in there, too, a tiny stub of a thing that fit snugly there and didn't poke into her when she sat down.

He could see the fresh creativity flowering inside her, could see the miraculous, glowing effect it had on her, and she kept bloody well *thanking* him for it. *Thank you for making this possible, Callan. Thank you for showing me your beautiful land. Thank you for giving me peace and safety when I needed it most. Just for everything.*

And her gray eyes shone when she said it, and her cheeks went pink, and energy and satisfaction sang in her whole body, and dear God how he envied her!

The only consolation was that he didn't think the envy showed.

He managed to keep himself tightly enough bound inside that nothing showed, and he worked as hard as he'd ever worked in his life, overhauling the engine in the truck, doing the final work on the mustering yard with Pete, riding out to tag cattle, checking lines of fence and fixing broken strands of wire or putting new posts in places where the fence itself probably didn't need to exist at all.

"Take Jacinda for some company," his mother had suggested a couple of times.

"No, she might want to write."

"She's only writing in the evenings."

"She probably feels she can't write in the day, because there's too much to do. You know she likes to help out wherever she can."

"She doesn't need to do that every day. Take her with you, and she can sit under a tree and write while you work," Mum had persisted.

She knew nothing about what had happened two Saturdays ago down at the water hole, but she'd probably started guessing all the wrong things.

"But if she needs the computer—" he'd said.

And he hadn't been surprised when Mum still wouldn't let the subject go. "She seems to like writing by hand."

Still watching Jacinda through the window, Callan saw her pick up her pen and scribble several lines, before looking into the distance with a searching expression, then writing another few words. It was dark out, but the evening was still mild. She'd kicked off her shoes and curled her bare feet up onto the couch, and she was in short sleeves. A pool of light fell over her page, and half of her body, from a clip-on lamp he'd set up there for her last week.

On an impulse, he went out to her. "I'm driving out to Wiltana Bore tomorrow," he said, "to do some maintenance on the windmill. Do you want to come? See a different part of the property? You can sit in the shade and sip cool drinks and write, while you watch me work. See how the other half lives."

She nodded slowly. "I'd like that." Then she gave a sudden grin. "I mean, you head out of here every morning in a truck or on a horse and you claim it's working. It'd be good to get some proof."

"I'll put on a star performance." Humor was one of the things working best between them right now.

"Ooh, in that case, I'll take photos!"

"We'll leave right after breakfast," he told her, and felt a little less tense.

When Callan had gone back inside a moment later, Jacinda wondered about the invitation. Kerry had probably suggested it. The two women had good-humored tussles with each other about how much Jac should help around the place, and how much her writing time should be protected.

Jac wasn't yet convinced that she had anything worth protecting, while Kerry had begun to treat the subject with reverence, pronouncing the words *your writing* as if they were spelled with capitals. Jac appreciated the fact that her creative endeavors weren't considered a frivolous hobby, but she still felt like a fraud.

And she felt like a fraud climbing into the four-wheel-drive beside Callan the next morning, with her notebook and pen in the small backpack that had become known as hers. They were bringing morning tea but not lunch because he'd said the job should only take a couple of hours.

How much writing would she really get done?

Why had he asked her, when for the past week and a half he'd avoided any time alone in her company?

He was back to playing the Flinders Ranges tour guide, it turned out, with the unstated subtext that these were things she should see before she left.

Which was getting to be soon.

Six days from now, they'd probably be out at the airstrip, waiting for Rob and the mail plane to arrive.

"It's harsher country out this way," Callan told her as they drove. "You might not like it."

It's the tour-guide routine I don't like, she wanted to tell him, *even though you're getting pretty good at it.*

The country *was* harsh, and somewhat farther from the homestead than the "few clicks" he'd claimed one day recently. Fifteen kilometers slid by on the four-wheel-drive's odometer before Jac saw the tank and windmill, with a large group of glossy, red-brown Santa Gertrudis cattle gathered around it, drinking from the metal trough that the tank fed into. The rocky ranges looked distant from this point, as the parched land flattened in the east toward Lake Frome.

Callan got out his tools and his oil for greasing the windmill's moving parts, while Jac unpacked the flask of iced coffee they'd brought, found some shade beneath a scrubby tree, set up her camp stool, her drinking mug and her shady hat…and couldn't write a word.

She wasn't blocked; she was just restless—distracted by Callan's familiar body at work, full of questions, almost ready to take flight in the light breeze along with a hawk she could see soaring overhead in the usual yawning blue. After five minutes in her folding canvas chair, she got up again, put down her notebook and pen, poured mugs of cold, ice-cream-thickened coffee for herself and Callan and wandered over to him. He stood at the base of the windmill, whose daisy-petal iron blades creaked as they turned in the breeze.

"Anything I can do?" she asked.

"Nothing's coming with the writing?"

"Not right now. I might, oh, describe the cattle, or something, in a minute."

"Go and say hi to 'em, they won't bite. Actually, they'll probably run."

"I wish they were on the other side of that fence, to be honest."

"I don't, since that's not my land!"

She laughed. "No? You mean your land does end? There is life beyond Arakeela Creek?"

He clicked his tongue. "So I'm told."

Skirting the cattle, who were far more interested in water than in her, Jac went closer to the fence. It was impressive, over six feet high, a fitting border to Callan's kingdom, she thought. Coming back to him, sipping the icy coffee as she walked, she said, "No wonder you're always fixing fences." She gestured back at the line of netting and posts. "I didn't know Santa Gertrudis could jump that high." She smiled.

Straight-faced, he answered, "They've been taking lessons from the 'roos. You don't often see it, but you'll be impressed if you do, a whole flock of Big Red Santas going boiing-boiing-boiing." He bounced his hand up and down, giving her a strong and cartoonlike mental image of the "flock" of leaping cows.

She laughed again. "You are such a nut!"

He grinned back at her and their eyes met, but that didn't feel comfortable—friendly kidding around felt fine, but not eye contact—so they both looked at the fence once more.

"Seriously, though, this fence isn't my job," Callan told her. "It's the Dog Fence."

"The what?"

"Over five and a half thousand kilometers. Longest fence in the world, dividing the north from the south and keeping the dogs on the other side."

"Because people in the south of this country don't like poodles and cocker spaniels?"

"Well, poodles, they're pretty deadly, yeah, but worse are the dingoes—the wild dogs the aborigines brought with them twenty thousand or so years ago. Dingoes and sheep don't mix. Settlers built the fence originally to keep the rabbits out of the north, but the rabbits just laughed because they were already there. So then the fence switched to keeping the dingoes out of the south, out of sheep-grazing country, and that works pretty well. It's patrolled for breaks, or drifted sand."

"Patrolled. Half of your boundary fence is actually patrolled." The fact made this place seem even more like his own personal kingdom. "But you don't graze sheep here at Arakeela," she remembered.

"Some properties in the Flinders still do, and of course farther south."

"I can't believe it, a three-thousand-mile fence."

"Write about it," he suggested.

So she did.

And she wrote about the sound the windmill made, and the sulfurous, salty tang of the water, and the rich, almost cherry red color of Santa Gertrudis cowhide in the sun. Then she looked at Callan perched on the top of the windmill with a big metal tool in his hand and wrote about him, and realized that one of the male characters in her novel had changed, over the past week or so.

Her broad-shouldered Chicago lawyer, Russ, moved and looked and laughed like Callan now, and...oh drat, she had to face this because Russ himself had been trying to tell her so for days, only she hadn't wanted to listen...Russ didn't want to be a lawyer anymore. He'd thrown down his briefcase in an act of rebellion and picked up a wide-brimmed cattleman's hat instead.

What the heck was she going to do with him?

When they got back to the house, she asked Kerry, "How are you managing? Is Carly being a nuisance while the boys are doing school?"

"No, she's fine. She's always fine!"

"W-would it be all right if I kept writing this afternoon?"

"Isn't that what I've been telling you to do?"

"And do you think Callan would be okay with me creating some new files on his computer? I know the boys will want to use the school one."

"He's offered you his computer whenever you want, Jac." Kerry patted her shoulder.

"Well, I might start right now, then."

Callan had already gone off on his next task, after making some sandwiches the size of doorstops to take with him for his lunch. His office was quiet. Jacinda closed the door to encourage Carly not to disturb her, and was immediately surrounded by the vivid and complex aura of Callan's personality.

The space was simple, practical, unpretentious. The computer was almost new, but the battered desk it sat upon could have counted as a colonial-era antique. Beside the mouse pad sat a brightly painted plaster drink coaster that one of the kids had made for Callan's coffee mug, and on the wall in a long line above the window, he'd tacked up paintings, also done by Lockie and Josh.

Most of the bookshelves were filled with cattle-breeding journals, horse-racing manuals, tomes on *Tax for Primary Producers* and the like, but there were three or four shelves that looked more like exhibits in a natural-history museum, set out with neat displays of aboriginal stone axes and spearheads, or interesting rock samples, or snake skins and bird nests and feathers.

There was also a picture of a medium-blond young woman cradling a newborn baby in her arms, and Jac knew, because she'd seen other pictures of the same woman in several places around the house, that this was Lockie with Liz.

Russ.

I'm supposed to be making decisions about Russ.

Who really, absolutely, seriously refused to be a lawyer anymore.

She found Callan's word-processing program, set up a folder called Jacinda—Novel, and created a new file. The words flowed fast, and soon she didn't even hear the sound of the kids or Kerry.

First, she typed in some of the handwritten scenes she'd worked on over the past few days, and when she came to the end of those, she just kept going, starting a new file for plot and character notes and one for the lines of dialogue that kept coming out of Russ's mouth even though she didn't yet know where they'd fit in the book.

She ended up switching back and forth between all three files as new ideas came to her, sending each file to the bottom of the screen when it wasn't immediately required, and putting things in the wrong file occasionally when she got really absorbed. A couple of times she searched the Internet for research, and left some of the most useful sites at the bottom of the screen, also, so she could access them quickly if she needed them again a page or two further on.

At one point, her concentration broke for a moment and she thought about Callan and Wiltana Bore and that nutty image of the Santa Gertrudis herd leaping like cartoon kangaroos. She grinned to herself. A warm, giddy, happy feeling flooded into her.

Callan, you are such a nut....

Russ needed a sense of humor, too.

Yes! Something else she should have seen in him before. Her fingers moved again on the computer keys.

At one point, Kerry tiptoed in and whispered, "Tea," then tiptoed out again, leaving a steaming mug and a piece of lemon cake on a plate near her elbow. At another point, Callan must have arrived back, because she was dimly aware of his heavy footfalls coming along the corridor and passing by. She forgot about him and kept writing, and suddenly it was six o'clock and Kerry was calling her for the evening meal, which they usually ate at this hour.

Remorseful that she'd left Kerry with the household chores and all three kids for so long, she quickly closed her files and the Internet sites and went to make sure that Carly washed her hands.

Despite the remorse, she knew it was the best day of writing she'd done in years.

* * *

Jac hadn't closed her files properly, Callan discovered when he went into his office after dinner and his shower, to check some Web site information on cattle vaccination.

Mum had told him Jac had been writing on the computer all afternoon, and then he'd seen for himself how she had hurried to the dinner table with a guilty look on her face, saying, "I'm sorry, I should have stopped an hour ago."

He wondered if she'd remembered to back up. Probably not. This computer had one of those key-fob-sized removable drives and he kept it in a bird's nest on the bookshelf, which wasn't the most obvious location. He took it out of the bird's nest, leaned past the swivel chair and plugged it in, then copied in the files. At the bottom of the screen, she'd left one named Bits, which made him smile because that had been the name of one of their dogs here at Arakeela, long ago.

He opened it, and that was indeed what it contained. Bits. Snatches of notes and writing that she hadn't found a place for yet, some of it in paragraphs, some of it just single lines. Not thinking that it could be private—after all, she'd said this was a novel, intended for a whole audience of readers—he took a closer look.

And found himself.

C's silhouette against this improbable sky belongs like a puzzle piece snapped in place, Callan read, leaning his hand on the desk as he scrolled the mouse down. *His muscles work, his body moves, his eyes fix on what he's doing and I watch all of it, thinking about all the ways this body is different from the pumped-up ones I've seen in L.A. gyms.*

The breeze shifts and the windmill turns its metal daisy face. Southern Cross *reads the windmill company's name on the rudder blade, as it swings more clearly into view.* Don't fall, C, *I silently beg. And I know he won't. There's a trust I*

*have in his body—its skills, its strength, its utter compe-
tence—that I've never felt before. I would let this man's body
take me anywhere. I would lean on it as far as the ends of the
earth. I would cradle it and protect it, believing it would
break in a thousand pieces while protecting me, if breaking
was required.*

*This is what a woman wants. Or (let's not generalize!) it's
what Megan wants from Russ, anyway. Not just the physical
hunger, but the physical trust. It was never enough for her
that Russ knew contracts and civil statutes and partnership
deals. She needed a body as well as a mind. Maybe she's
more like an animal (I'm more like an animal) than I thought.
That's why Russ being a lawyer just didn't work!*

Behind him, the door opened, and he turned to see Jacinda
herself, her hair pulled back in a ponytail, the sleeves of her
cotton top pushed to the elbows and splashes of dish-washing
water on her front. Her cheeks were pink from standing over
the steaming sink, and she had the aura of energy he was
starting to realize meant she was still riding high on the good
writing she'd done today.

"Callan, I'm sorry to bother you," she began, "but I
couldn't find the removable drive before dinner, so I
didn't—" She stopped, and her voice changed. "Is that one
of my files?"

He ignored the question. "You wrote about me."

This crystallized her attention even more than the open
file. "You've *read* it?"

Still he ignored her. "C. That's me. That's today. Up on
the windmill at Wiltana Bore. You put me in your book."

"You read my work without asking."

They weren't listening to each other—or only enough to
make both of them angrier. Callan stood with his hand resting
on the mouse, and Jac might have thought he was threatening to delete the whole file, the way her gaze zeroed in on

his finger then flicked angrily back to the screen. Right now he didn't care if the file did disappear. "I'm your research material, and you never said."

"This is draft stuff." She was indignant, impatient. She pushed her sleeves up higher and propped her hands on her hips. "Not even that. Character notes. You're not in the book, Callan. And you *read* it!"

"You'd left the file onscreen and I was backing up for you, that's all. I read it because…" Hell, this sounded stupid! "We had a dog called Bits, once. You've said it's a novel. How can that be private, when you hope someday people will pay to read it?" Any hint of defensiveness disappeared as he realized again what this would mean. "Pay to read about me, Callan Woods. Me, stripped raw."

"It's not you," she repeated through gritted teeth, her patience exaggerated. "It's notes. And *it is private*. This is how writers work, Callan. We take all these little strands and mix them up and mull over them and in the process they change and lose that personal quality, but to start with, in this form… Do you know how naked it feels to have *anyone* read that raw stuff?"

"Do you know how naked it feels to read about 'C' up on the windmill, with his trustworthy body!"

They glared at each other again. Jac's eyes flashed darker than usual, her cheeks got even pinker, and the little gold dangly earrings she wore flashed, too, as she jutted out an angry jaw, and he thought, *This is sexual frustration. This is irrational. We are both irrational, and over the top, and crazy. We are making a big sexually frustrated mountain out of a tiny privacy-issue molehill and I don't know how to stop, because I want her so much it feels like an illness.*

And I don't want her to leave in six days and take a part of me with her in her damned book, because what's she going to leave behind for me, in return? What am I ever going to get out of this, since the one thing we both want, I can't deliver?

He closed his eyes and hunched his shoulders, still gripping the mouse and feeling overwhelmed.

"So it's bad that I trust your body that much?" Jacinda said. She didn't sound quite so angry now.

"I don't know why you would." He let go of the mouse, leaned on the desk, whooshed out a breath. "How many times has it let you down, now?"

"Not many," she said softly, stepping closer. "I'd be up for more. It's you who's running for the hills, Callan. That's what this is really about, isn't it?"

"Yeah, for you, too, and I wonder why." He added harshly, "Maybe I just don't want the ego-orientated sexual-therapy approach you're prepared to offer. The Jacinda Beale patented cure."

"That is a really awful thing to say!"

"And I don't want my body in your book, Jacinda. I don't want any part of me in your book."

"Well, that's your problem, not mine!" she snapped back at him, and in an instant they were bristling and snarling at each other again, like two angry dogs. "Because I've told you, Russ is *not you!*"

He turned away from her, tired of the stalemate they'd reached.

"I'm checking the e-mail," he muttered. "Your files are backed up. I keep the removable drive in the bird's nest, next time you need it."

Chapter Twelve

Jacinda didn't stay to watch Callan's list of new e-mail messages cascade onto the screen. She was too angry, too hurt and too confused.

Deep down, she knew that they were both right to be angry…privacy had been invaded on both sides…but not this angry. She would have said that they trusted each other—that him reading her work shouldn't have felt like such an invasion, and that her using him as a key into Russ's character shouldn't have felt like such a piece of theft.

Carly was already asleep. Restless, hugely keyed up and on edge, Jac went into their room and checked on her anyhow, in an attempt to get her emotional compass pointing back in the right direction, but it didn't help.

Even bending down and inhaling the sweet, familiar scent of her daughter's hair and whispering, "You and me together, sweetheart," didn't help, because she knew she needed Callan in her life, as well, the way Megan was starting to need Russ.

She prowled out of the bedroom again and went onto the veranda—the place where she'd first put real words down on paper again, the place where she and Callan had shared that first really strong connection, beneath the moonlight on her first night here.

All those "firsts." Any day now, she and Carly would be starting the "lasts." Their last visit to the water hole, their last egg-collecting expedition in the chook pen, Carly's last morning as an honorary student at the School of the Air. The more personal "lasts," Jac's last things with Callan—last cup of coffee, last hug. Those, she didn't even want to think about.

But she couldn't help it.

Last joke, last shared grin.

She remembered those kangaroo-jumping cattle again, and got that same silly grin on her face.

Oh, hell, she couldn't stay angry with him!

She was in love with him.

He found her still standing there several minutes later, and he didn't seem angry anymore, either. The guts had gone out of the emotion, the same as they had for her, but whether he'd come to the same realization as she had about what this meant, she didn't know.

"There's an e-mail for you," he said. "A-dot-Dugan, at one of those big American addresses. I didn't open it. Is it just junk?"

"No," she said blankly. "A. Dugan? That's Andy. Andy Dugan. My brother."

Omigosh, Andy had replied! He'd actually replied, within a couple of days of receiving her postcard!

She felt a ridiculous surge of feeling and the prick of tears. "Can I take a look right now? Are you busy on there?"

"No, I'm done. Of course you can look."

She stepped toward the doorway into the house where he stood holding it open, and it was probably the closest they'd gotten to each other in days. She saw him draw in a breath and lift his hand as if to touch her, but then he thought better of it and turned away.

"Just switch off the monitor when you're finished, can you?" was all he said.

"Sure."

He half turned back again. "And can we forget about yelling at each other just now?"

"Oh, please, yes! Both apologize, maybe?" she suggested.

"I overreacted. I'm sorry."

"So did I, and I'm sorry, too."

Apologies, however, were sometimes the easy way out. Sitting down at Callan's desk, Jac opened the e-mail.

Hey, Jacinda, it was nice to hear from you! she read.

Andy told her some items of news—his wife, Debbie, had bought an art-framing business, their second boy would be starting college in the fall—and asked her some questions about her life. What was she doing so far away? Debbie had noticed recently that her name wasn't listed on the credits of *Heartbreak Hotel* anymore. How come?

It touched Jac that he and Debbie even remembered which soap she'd written for, and she e-mailed right back, answering his questions as best she could without dumping too much on him. She also told him, *I'm thinking Carly and I may relocate to the tristate area soon, and it would be great to see you when we do.*

"So your brother got your postcard," Callan said to her when she emerged from his office a little later and met up with him in the kitchen.

"Yes, and it was a nice e-mail in reply. I wonder if I'll hear from Tom. Upstate where he is, he may still not have gotten the card."

Andy's e-mail gave a healthy lift to her spirits, which was a pity, in hindsight, because this only meant they had further to fall the next day, and by ten in the morning they'd come crashing down like an airplane in a tailspin, hard on the heels of Lucy's phone call from Sydney.

"I haven't wanted to worry you," she said, "but Kurt's been calling."

"The hang-ups?"

"He's not hanging up anymore, he's staying on the line. I—I had to let you know. I know it's not what you want to hear. He's got to the point where he's threatening and abusive, now, and he's convinced that I know where you are."

"Did you tell him? Oh, Lord, did you?"

"Jacinda, mate, I don't know! You're on some farm in outback south Australia that's civilized enough to have e-mail and a phone."

"Have you told him that? Have you told him anything? What kind of threats?"

"That he'll track you down. That Carly will disappear and you'll never find her, because you're no good for her and he's the best father who ever lived." Lucy's voice came through jittery and thready with fear. "Jac, he's sounding weird and scary—drugs, maybe?—and just now he told me he had plane tickets to Sydney and he touches down in two days."

"Tickets, plural?"

"For him and…I can't remember the term he used. Body-guards. Entourage. His paid muscle, anyhow."

"That'd fit," Jac had to admit. Kurt loved having black-shirted, eye-shaded security people walking three paces behind him most of the time. In the past, she used to joke about it, but he'd never been able to laugh about things like that.

"He knows where I live, doesn't he?" Lucy said. "You gave him my street address when you stayed here before."

"Yes, I did. Oh my God, Lucy, I did." He was Carly's father, after all, and at that point he hadn't seemed anywhere near this out of control. "I'm so sorry!"

"And he says he's coming," Lucy said. "Can you find out if it's true? He probably thinks you're still here, and when he finds out you're not… I want to call the police, but I won't yet. Not until you've talked to someone in California, because maybe none of what he's saying is true."

Kurt had never been prone to empty threats. Feeling sick to her stomach, Jac didn't tell Lucy this yet. "I'll call you back," she told her friend, "after I've talked to Elaine."

It was five in the evening in L.A. and calling from the phone in Callan's office, she got her former boss on her cell phone, in the middle of bumper-to-bumper traffic on the freeway. The connection kept threatening to cut out, which made the conversation even tougher than it needed to be.

"I can't talk detail on that, right now," Elaine said in a guarded tone.

"Because you have someone there?"

"That's right."

"Not Kurt?"

"No, honey, but you know that particular bank has a lot of branches in this area."

"Right. But you can listen."

"And I am."

She summarized Lucy's phone call. "Does it fit with what's happening at your end, Elaine?"

"This traffic. It's a mess."

"Elaine, I'm losing you."

"Connection's fine here, at the moment."

"Not the connection. What you meant. A mess? Kurt's a mess? I just want to know if Lucy should contact the Sydney police. And I want to know if Carly is in danger." Her voice cracked, she sucked up a sob, and at that moment Callan's office door opened and there was her daughter, blond and big-eyed and the most precious, important thing in the world. "Everything's fine, honey," she said brightly.

"Does that mean we should finish now and I should call you back?" Elaine asked.

"No, I meant— You should definitely call me back, but I was talking to Carly. Carly knows everything is fine," she added for her daughter's benefit.

"But you don't?"

"No, not at all."

"I am going to call you back, okay? I promise."

"When?"

Elaine said guardedly, "When I have more information."

But she didn't call back all day, and when Jacinda tried her cell phone, her landline and her work phone, she got machines and messages every time.

Just before dinner, figuring that it was around one in the morning in L.A. and Elaine wasn't going to call back tonight, she called Lucy again and said, "If you want to talk to the police in Sydney, go ahead, but we don't know what flight he's on, or even what airline, and there's no guarantee he'll travel under his own name. I'm sorry. I'm so sorry to have involved you in all this, Lucy. And I wish there was more I could tell you."

"This is her ex-husband?" Kerry asked Callan, while Jacinda was putting Carly to bed.

"Yes."

"What's going on?"

"Apparently he's making threats. He told her friend he's coming out here."

"Here to Arakeela Creek?"

"He doesn't know that this is where she and Carly are, but Jac's afraid he'll do something to Lucy to get her to tell him." Callan shook his head, knowing it sounded bizarre. "Jac is very jittery about it. I don't know if she's right to be."

"She wouldn't say anything to me. Not really. A problem at home, that was all, and she was waiting for an important call. I want to hug her and tell her everything's going to be all right, but you're right, we just don't know. Carly has picked up on Jac being so tense. She's a perceptive little thing. They're leaving in less than five days, Callan."

His mother spoke the words tentatively, then left them hanging in the air. He wanted to yell at her, "You think I don't know that?" but he didn't. She meant well. She was asking something from him—an idea of where Jacinda and Carly might fit in his future, if anywhere—but he couldn't give her that because he didn't know.

Mum left the house to cross to her little cottage a few minutes later, after saying good-night to the boys. She liked a quiet hour or two on her own before she went to bed, but Callan couldn't help wondering if there was more to her prompt departure this evening. Was she tactfully leaving the other two adults alone? What did she expect to happen?

Nothing did. Only this ache of tension and uncertainty and failure deep in his bones.

What could he do for Jacinda?

Nothing.

Hadn't he already proved that more than once to them both?

By eight, Lockie and Josh had conked out for the night. They had the sound, steady sleep habits of active kids, and weren't as aware of Jacinda's tension as her daughter was. Jac had spent longer in the bedroom putting Carly to bed tonight.

When she came into the kitchen at last, as Callan was making tea, he asked her, "Asleep?"

"Finally. I read two stories and sang three songs, and she was still restless, but finally when I patted her back she drifted off."

"What are you going to do?"

"Read, maybe. I'll have some tea, if there's enough in the pot."

"I meant about your ex-husband's threats."

"I need to hear from Elaine."

"He can't kidnap Carly off my land, Jac. He can't hurt you here." It was true. He believed that. But it sounded lame.

"You wouldn't think so, would you?" she said. "But something's not right. Why is he making these impossible threats? I'm upset for Lucy. I need to be able to tell her if she could conceivably be in danger. It's like an episode from a bad spy show on TV. I don't understand what he's trying to do, or why. I'm going to keep trying Elaine in the morning. She promised she'd call back!"

"Are you going to be able to sleep?"

She shrugged. "Eventually."

Eventually, Jac did sleep.

She must have fallen off at about midnight, and by then she was so tired that she slept deeply for a solid two hours. Then something woke her when the electric clock radio beside the bed read 2:09. She didn't know what had roused her, at first, and lay there with her heart pounding in blank fear, her emotions immediately locking back into the state of nervous tension they'd been in all day.

Creak…thump.

That noise.

I know that noise.

It was the flap of the screen door leading to the veranda, she realized, and there it was again. Creak…thump. Creak…thump. It was swinging wide open on its hinges and hitting the wall. Carly tended to forget to close it sometimes, so Jacinda knew the sound well.

Carly.

Twisting, Jac looked over to Carly's bed, but there was no moon tonight and the room was pitch-black. She had to feel her way across the space, her tired eyes questing for the dim shape of a humped quilt and a head on the pillow.

The bed was empty.

And it was stupid to panic about it because Carly hadn't been…couldn't have been…kidnapped by Kurt in the middle of the night…although Kurt was still to blame. After sensing her mother's stress all day, Carly was sleepwalking.

Creak…thump. The screen door flapped again. She had probably gone out to pat the dogs on the veranda.

Jac switched on the light in their room so that she could see her way down the corridor without waking Callan or the boys in their nearby rooms with too much sudden brightness. She passed through the living room and, yes, the front door was open and the screen door was flapping, just as she'd thought.

But Carly wasn't with the dogs. They snoozed on their old blankets, opening their eyes long enough to say a doggy version of "Hi, Jac, what are you doing here in the middle of the night?" before losing interest and snoozing again. The blankets were crooked along one edge, as if they might have been scuffed out of place by a little girl's knees, so maybe she had been here at some point.

Jac checked the cane couch, but Carly wasn't there, either. She walked all the way around the veranda, hampered by the lack of moonlight, then she found the flashlight that Callan kept on the windowsill beside the front door and went out to the chicken coop, in case Carly had gone on a midnight egg hunt. But the chooks were fast asleep, lined up on their perches, and the gates to their run and coop and the vegetable garden were all shut.

Back in the house, with her heart and breathing beginning to get faster, she checked Carly's bed again in case she'd just…what…*imagined* its emptiness and that flapping screen door?

She hadn't.

The bed was still empty.

She woke up Callan, shaking his shoulder and speaking before he'd even moved.

"Carly went sleepwalking, Callan, and I didn't hear her until the screen door woke me up, and now I can't find her. Anywhere."

He sat up, dragged his fingers across his creased eyes. "Sorry, say that again." His voice was deep and creaky with sleep, and he smelled warm, and like almond-scented soap. The white T-shirt he usually wore to bed stretched across his chest, twisted from the way he'd rolled in the bed.

"Carly went sleepwalking outside. The screen door woke me up, flapping."

Creak…thump. It did it again as she spoke, moved by the night breeze, and only then did she realize what this implied.

"Carly must have left it open," she said. "But that doesn't mean she only went through it fifteen minutes ago, does it? I—I got to sleep around midnight and now it's two thirty. She could have been wandering out there for two hours."

Callan threw back the bedcovers and stood, his bare feet slapping onto the wooden floor. "She's not with the dogs?"

"That was the first place I looked. I went all around the house, and out to the garden and the chicken run."

He nodded, but didn't speak, then crossed the room and flicked on the switch beside the door. They both blinked in the sudden light. He grabbed a windproof jacket and shrugged into it over the T-shirt, dropped his pajama pants, hauled jeans over his long legs and naked hips, and slid his sockless feet into his old elastic-sided riding boots. He was ready in less than a minute.

"She can't have gone far," he said. "And it's not a cold night, thank goodness."

"But it's supposed to be hot again tomorrow, isn't it?"

"Low thirties," he confirmed, using the centigrade scale that temperature was measured in here. She knew that meant at least ninety degrees, and Carly would have no water with her. "But Jac, those temperatures are hours away. Don't think that far ahead."

"How can I help it?"

"Get dressed. I'll grab another flashlight. We won't wake Mum and the boys yet."

But Kerry heard them calling Carly's name around the outbuildings within a few minutes, and appeared at the front door of her cottage in her dressing gown. "She's sleepwalking?"

"She must be," Jac said. She hugged her arms across her body. As Callan had said, it wasn't a very cold night but, in her haste, she'd only slipped into a thin angora sweater, a colorless dark gray in the dimness, as well as panties, jeans, socks and running shoes. "But I didn't hear her go."

"She can't have gone far," Kerry promised, just as Callan had.

Jacinda didn't believe them. Carly could be tenacious when she walked in her sleep. What kind of an idea did she have in her head? There could easily be no logic to what she had done. Could she have gone to the water hole? She'd never been down there on foot, only on horseback and by vehicle. She probably had no idea of the distance at night, on her small legs, even if she did know the right direction to set off in.

Or would she have gone to visit the horses? She'd been getting more interested in them over the past week or so, and less scared of their size and unpredictable behavior. A few days ago, Jac had let Lockie lead Carly around on the quietest of them, a ten-year-old gelding, which was the one

Josh usually rode, and all three children had been so cute about it.

"That's great, Carlz!" Lockie had kept saying to her, while Carly had worn a huge grin on her face.

Josh had half walked, half skipped—backward—about ten yards in front of them, watching their every move and giving frequent cautions.

"Isn't he a great little horse? If you fall off, don't scream and scare him, Carlz."

Jacinda smiled at the memory, but then the smile turned into a half sob, because if Carly's tame little ride the other day had encouraged her to go looking for the horses in the middle of the night…

The animals weren't stabled but left free in their paddock, which had to be at least ten acres in size. Callan nodded at her suggestion that Carly might have gone in that direction and together they walked past the outbuildings toward the fence and gate. Jac's left foot hurt with every step. She'd pulled on her sock so carelessly that it had bunched into a crease that would give her a blister if they did much more walking tonight.

A blister wasn't important, but if they did walk as far as the water hole and it slowed her down… The issue crystal-lized into a small, self-contained agony that was a subset of the vast agony of Carly's disappearance, which itself came on top of Kurt's bizarre, threatening phone calls to Sydney that she still didn't understand.

Should she stop and fix the sock?

Which would waste more time? Fix it? Leave it?

The bite of pain and the torment of indecision remained with her.

When they reached the paddock fence, Callan played his powerful flashlight over the dry ground until he found the horses in one corner, asleep.

"I can't see her," he said needlessly, because Jac had been watching the moving pool of light along the ground as intently as he had. "But I didn't sweep the whole paddock. Could she have fallen asleep on the ground somewhere?"

"I— She could have. She's so unpredictable."

Jac couldn't go on speaking, but her thoughts just wouldn't stop.

As Callan painstakingly swept the flashlight beam back and forth through the huge field, Jac remembered everything he had said to her the night she hadn't returned from her walk before dark, all that stuff about survival in this country without food or water and how a human being didn't last long.

She remembered his warnings about snakes, thought about the cold depth of the water hole beyond the first shallow slope of sand if Carly did somehow get that far. She couldn't swim.

She pictured the cattle grids where fences and tracks met, and imagined Carly trying to cross one in the dark and slipping between the thick metal bars. Would her leg get jammed or broken?

She remembered the pitiless terrain stretching beyond Wiltana Bore, the stories of doomed explorers in the nineteenth century, and the name of a mountain she'd seen on the map not far north of here—Mount Hopeless.

"I can't see her," Callan said at last. "But there was something over in the northwest corner—a shadow—a shape. About her size. It's worth taking a look."

He unhooked the chain that kept the gate shut and let Jacinda through, then followed her, and they tramped through the paddock. Callan kept his flashlight beam trained on the place where he thought he'd seen a shadow, while Jacinda pointed hers toward the ground ahead of them.

The circle of light should have been comforting, but somehow it wasn't. It created a barrier between them and the darkness, turning the vast nightscape into an alien universe.

Trying to go faster, Jac tripped more than once. "Is it too soon to call?" she said. "If it is her, shouldn't we call her?"

"Yes, go ahead. If it is her, she hasn't moved, though, so she might be asleep."

"She'll wake up if she hears my voice." She called her daughter's name over and over, but there was no sound or movement in reply.

After a couple of hundred yards, Callan slowed and stopped. "It's nothing," he said heavily. "Just a dip in the terrain. It flattened out as we got closer, and now it's disappeared. It's not her."

Jac's legs felt as if they wouldn't carry her any farther, and the blister on her foot must have burst. It stung insistently, a final piece of meaningless cruelty that somehow reminded her of Kurt and his meaningless cruelty, reminded her of Elaine failing to call her back yesterday, of Lucy feeling threatened in Sydney, and the possibility of Kurt himself finding his way out here by chartered helicopter, so that even if they found Carly tonight and she was safe...

Her knees shook so hard that she began to lower herself to the ground in the middle of the paddock, gasping for air, no strength left. Callan caught her and gathered her up into his arms. He didn't speak, but his body was warm and hard and strong and she needed it more than she'd ever needed a man's touch in her life.

"Help me, Callan," she gasped. "Help me."

"Anything, Jac." He pressed hard, urgent kisses into her hair. "God, you must know that by now. *Anything.*"

"You told me how easy it is for someone to die out here, if they get lost."

"I should never have said that." His voice dipped and rasped. "I should never have scared you like that."

"No. I needed to hear it. Because it's true. I can work that out for myself. The way the day heats up, even in the middle of what's supposed to be fall. The way the laundry dries so fast." Her voice cracked. Such a stupid thing, laundry drying in half an hour, but it reminded her of how soon a human being would dry out and crave for water. "But now Carly's lost. If we don't find her…"

"We will. Don't even say it."

"How do you know we will?"

"Because I'll die trying."

For several heartbeats, they just held each other, but Jacinda felt precious time trickling away and soon pulled back. "We have to keep looking, but I don't know where. Where do we try next? How do we do this?"

"Listen, it must be three, by now, or later." He ran his hands down her arms over and over as he spoke, in firm strokes that he might have used on a frightened horse. That was how she felt—like an animal in terror, beyond rationality. "If there's no sign of her by first light—that's only a couple of hours away—we'll call the emergency services and they'll start a full-scale search. She can't have got far."

"Stop saying that. When we don't know what direction she went in, even a couple of miles is too far. She'll be terrified if she wakes up in the dark with no idea of where she is and how she got there. Oh, Callan!"

He kept stroking her arms, wouldn't allow her panic to overwhelm him, or respond to her impatience. It helped just a little. "First, let's go back to the house," he said. "We should check through it again, and then we'll have to wake the boys."

And finally something clicked in Jacinda's mind that she'd been too panicky to realize before.

"Check through it again?" she echoed blankly. "Oh dear Lord, I didn't look in the house!"

"You what?"

"I didn't check to see if she'd come back in the house."

His hands stilled on her shoulders. "You said you did. You said you went all around the house."

"I meant the outside of the house, on the veranda."

He squeezed her waist, the movement shaky along with his voice. "You didn't say that, Jac, sweetheart."

She pressed her fingers to her head, heart pounding even harder. "You're right. Oh dear God, you're right. I heard the screen door and I was sure she'd gone outside. Both times before when she's walked in her sleep, here, she's gone out to the veranda. And even when I realized it was the wind making the door flap, I didn't make the connection. I didn't think it might mean she'd come back into the house."

"Let's check."

"Yes. Oh, yes!"

They both broke into a run, stumbling back through the horse paddock to the gate. As they reached the track that led between the outbuildings, Kerry came around the corner of the feed shed. "She's nowhere here. I've checked behind every hay bale and every bag of grain. Oh, Jacinda…"

Not stopping, Callan called back to her, "We're checking the house more thoroughly. She definitely came out through the front door, but she might have gone back in. She may still be there, asleep somewhere that Jac didn't see her before."

Kerry muttered a fervent prayer that Callan was right and followed them slowly, still wearing her dressing gown and slippers, while Jacinda felt ill with this new hope mingling with the cold pit of fear still inside her.

Carly might be in the house.

But she might not.

It had been so quiet before. If she was anywhere inside, then she must be sleeping peacefully again or Jac would have heard her movements. Passing through the living room earlier, she hadn't noticed Carly then.

Please let her be there, please let her be there, please let her be there…

Ahead of Callan, she sprinted up the veranda steps, clattered across the old floorboards and swung open the door, not caring how much noise she made. The living room was empty, the dining room, the kitchen. Along the corridor, she passed Callan's office on one side and his bedroom on the other. She switched on the lights.

No Carly.

"She's not in the bathroom or the laundry," Callan said behind her.

And then Jac got to Lockie's room and there she was.

Carly.

Her precious, innocent daughter.

Fast asleep, like an angel.

Snuggled next to Lockie in his single bed.

Safe.

Jacinda moaned with relief. The strength simply drained away from her legs the way it had done out in the paddock, and just as before, if Callan hadn't been standing behind her to take her weight, she would have fallen.

"She's here," she whispered. "There with Lockie. Look! Oh, thank God, thank God!"

In comparison with Jac's immediate, concrete fears about heat and thirst and lack of shelter, she couldn't consider that Kurt's bizarre threats still presented a danger. Carly was here. She was safe.

And Callan would keep them all that way, or die trying.

He'd said so, and she believed him.

She began to cry, with sobs that shook her whole body but managed to stay silent because she didn't want to wake the sleeping children and let them see how scared she'd been. Callan held her from behind, his arms wrapped hard and tight around her waist, beneath the soft weight of her breasts, his chin resting on her shoulder and his head tilted toward hers.

"It's okay," he soothed her. "Everything's all right now." He brushed his cheek against her hair, but didn't touch her with his mouth. Even in her sweeping flood of relief, she noticed it.

"I know," she answered him jerkily between her sobs. "That's why I'm crying. Because everything is all right, and I've just spent half an hour imagining all the worst ways it might not have been. Oh, and Callan, there were so *many* disasters I could think of!"

He laughed softly, squeezed her tighter. "Makes life interesting, out here."

"I'm not looking for that kind of interesting!" She leaned back against him, wanting so badly to turn into his arms but not sensing the right signals from him. Even now, with feelings running so high, he had that wall in place.

"And nothing happened," he said, "so you can go back to being bored tomorrow."

"Don't tease me."

"I'm not," he whispered. "Not really. I just want you to stop shaking."

"Then keep holding me, please." His arms and his body heat felt very, very good.

They watched the two sleeping children in silence for a few moments. Lockie was curled on his side, facing away from the window and into the room. Carly had wedged herself between him and the wall, and was lying on her back with her hair tangled around her on the pillow and one leg kicked free of the sheet and light cotton blanket. Her face was as soft and relaxed as a sleeping kitten's, and if Jac listened very carefully, she could hear both children breathing.

Carly feels so safe here, she realized. She feels as if she belongs. Otherwise, she never would have come to Lockie in the night. *I feel as if I belong, too, but in just over four days, we're going away.*

She almost said it.

Callan, I want to stay.

But then they heard Kerry's footsteps, and the creak of the screen door once again. "Is it safe to let you go now?" Callan asked.

"Only if you get me an enormous mug of medicinal brandy. once you've told your mom everything's all right."

"I'll check the pantry and see if there's enough for both of us." He opened his arms and let her go, and she leaned against the doorjamb instead and watched him as he walked away.

"Hot chocolate will do," she said to his retreating back.

"Mum?" Jac heard Callan say a moment later, in the living room. "Carly's fine. She was in the house all along, cuddled up with Lockie."

Kerry came out with all the heartfelt thanks and relief that Jacinda hadn't been able to express out loud. She made her way slowly down the corridor, still leaning her hand against the wall as she went because she felt so shaky.

"We're having some hot chocolate, Mum, do you want any?" Callan asked as Jac reached the living room.

"No, thanks. I'm going to head straight back to bed." She hugged Jacinda. "Callan can lock the doors at night from now on. We don't worry too much about people breaking in. around here. I never thought we'd have to take precautions against someone breaking out! She's such a sweetheart, Jac. I was so worried!"

Jac hugged her back. "You're a sweetheart, too, Kerry. Oh. I'm still weak at the knees!"

"Are you going to put her back in her own bed?"

"I'd better. Lockie would probably thank me for it because sometimes she kicks!"

Chapter Thirteen

"Want to sit on the veranda?" Callan asked, appearing from the kitchen with two mugs of hot chocolate in his hands.

"That would be great." Jac had become very fond of that old cane couch.

She'd transferred Carly back into her own bed with no trouble, just now. Lockie had woken briefly as she leaned across him to attempt the awkward maneuver of gathering a sleeping four-year-old into her arms.

"Are you taking her back to her bed?" he'd asked sleepily.

"Yes, did she wake you when she climbed in?"

"It's okay. I think she had a bad dream. I made up a story for her and she went back to sleep, and then I did, too."

"Thanks for taking care of her so well." She'd hugged Lockie, once again close to tears.

For all sorts of reasons.

Out on the veranda, with only a little light spilling through the living-room window from the lamp Callan had left on, the hot chocolate smelled…different.

"What did you put in this?" Jac asked him, catching the aroma as they both sat down on the couch. Callan had taken off his jacket and kicked off his boots.

"Baileys Irish Cream."

"Ah."

"I was serious about the medicinal brandy, even if you weren't."

"I can easily be persuaded to be serious about it." She took a cautious sip. It tasted fabulous, made her forget about the broken blister still smarting on her foot and soothed the adrenaline still pumping in her system. "How much did you put in?"

"Just a thimbleful."

"Good…I think."

"You've seen the kind I mean, a thimble for a seamstress with this huge, enormous thumb." He outlined its shape in the air, the size of an eggplant.

She laughed, and he grinned back at her. He knew she liked it when he made her laugh. "You know what I keep thinking about?" she said.

"What?"

"Those cows you were teasing me about at Wiltana Bore, jumping like kangaroos, boiing-boiing-boiing."

"They'll recognize it as a separate breed, soon. The Jumping Santa Gertrudis."

"It's such a silly picture in my head. I can see it like a movie scene. They've got these serious expressions on their long faces, you know, with those flared, supercilious nostrils, and their tails—like fancy curtain cords with a big tassel on the end, nothing like kangaroo tails!—their tails are swinging up and down, and their knees are bending like folding chair legs, and for some reason it's just…funny. Every time it comes into my head."

He was still grinning, pleased. "Yeah?" Complacent, also.

He definitely knew that she liked it when he made her laugh.

So how come he didn't know everything else she liked about him? How come he wouldn't let her get closer, or even consider letting her work with him through his terrible emotional and physical block? She'd fallen in love with him, she didn't want to leave this place, and there was this impossible thing standing in the way.

Callan, I want you, but I know if I told you that, you'd feel the pressure and shut down again. Do you realize how little time we have left? Four days! Is there no way we can get past this?

She didn't even know how to ask.

They sat in silence for several minutes, letting the hot chocolate make them sleepy and the Bailey's Irish Cream infuse their limbs with its relaxing slow burn.

Carly was safe.

In her relief, Jacinda wasn't frightened of Kurt's threats right now. For Lucy's sake, and possibly Elaine's, she had to deal with them as soon as she could, but they seemed like shadowboxing, completely impotent compared to the genuine danger she'd glimpsed tonight when she'd thought that her daughter might be seriously lost.

Impotent.

Hmm, there was a word, and it didn't—shouldn't—couldn't—apply to a man like Callan.

He had said tonight that he would find her daughter or die trying, and she had believed him utterly. She knew his strength and capability would never let her down, and would never turn into the kind of meaningless show of force that Kurt resorted to so much.

This had to count for something. It had to give her some hope.

She finished her hot chocolate and put the empty mug

down on the veranda floor beside the couch, then slipped off her shoes and those troublesome, blister-making socks. Callan was still drinking, his mug only half-drained. She stopped fighting the sag of the couch and let it ease her closer to him, then leaned her head against his shoulder.

"Thank you for staying calm enough to realize my mistake about checking in the house," she said.

"No worries."

Which meant "you're welcome" and was just as much of a formula as the American phrase, she now knew.

After a moment, she tried again. "Lockie woke up when I reached for Carly. He told me she'd had a bad dream and he'd made up a story to get her back to sleep. He's so good with her, Callan, and she obviously feels so safe with him. I love watching them together."

"He's a good kid. All three of them are. I know Josh can be a bit prickly and territorial, sometimes."

"He's fine. It's natural. We're new in his world, and he's not convinced that we belong."

Do we belong, Callan?

If he'd understood her unstated question, he didn't answer it.

Silence fell once more, and she didn't know if the electricity in the air was the good kind, or not.

"Cold?" Callan asked, when the pause in the conversation had stretched halfway to the starlit horizon. He sounded awkward.

"Yes, getting to be." She was still only wearing that single layer of fine angora and her jeans.

The hand-knit mohair blanket was folded and draped over the back of the couch as usual. Callan hadn't waited for her response, but had put down his now-empty mug, reached around and was sliding the blanket across their legs before Jac understood his intent. At which point she practically stopped breathing, because a man only did something like that if he was looking for an excuse.

Didn't he?

She waited, not daring to speak or move.

She waited for a long time.

Nothing.

Nothing but a tension that you could have cut into slices, it was so thick. She could feel the warm pressure of Callan's thigh against hers. She could feel his breathing, the only movement he made. When she dared to look at him, she saw so many details that she loved—the fine lines around his eyes because he'd spent so much time squinting in the sun, the determined angle of his jaw, the smooth curve of his lower lip.

Would they sit here physically warm but emotionally frozen until morning? It could only be an hour or so away by this time.

"Help me."

For a moment she thought she'd heard him wrong, the words were muttered so low and with such intensity. "Callan?" she whispered.

He said it again, pressing a hot hand over hers, resting on her thigh, and squeezing it until it almost hurt. "Help me, Jacinda," in just the same, desperate, last-ditch, heartrending way that she'd said these exact words to him out in the horse paddock more than an hour ago.

Help me, or I'm lost to hope forever.

Help me, or I don't know how I can survive.

Help me, because you're the only person in the world who can, and I've never asked anyone for something this important before.

Understanding all these things that he didn't say, she turned to him, freed herself from his grip and took his face between her hands, hope and responsibility choking her throat. "Will you really let me?" she whispered.

He closed his eyes and nodded, and Jac knew there was no room for any more doubt or any more questions, let alone any mistakes. This was it. The last chance he'd ever allow either of them.

The pressure felt intense, and for at least a minute she didn't have the slightest idea how to begin. She simply sat there holding his face softly between her palms, listening to the breaths he couldn't manage to keep steady, and watching his motionless, expectant mouth and flickering lids.

"Oh, Callan…" she breathed.

It felt like the first time she'd held his hand and jumped into the water hole. It felt like the first time she'd ever been kissed, years ago. She knew she was running out of time. Another moment and he'd lose faith that she wanted this at all.

Frightened about the impending significance of every touch, she brushed her mouth lightly across his. At first, his lips stayed motionless, and she wondered automatically, after just a few seconds, is this not working?

Well, it won't work, you foolish woman, if you're going to think like this every step of the way.

Get it right, Jac.

The first step is your own attitude.

His mouth was so beautiful, perfect to tease. There was no hurry, she reminded herself, and no hardship in taking this slowly, letting the tension build. With one hand still cupping his face and one resting lightly against his shoulder and bare neck, she took her time with every soft, slow kiss and let go of the pressure, the urgency, and even the possibility of failure. When she felt this way about him, when she loved him this much, surely there was no such word.

His eyes stayed closed, which allowed her to get greedy.

She could watch his face between every kiss, study the shape of his cheekbones and his chin, see the moment when her mouth trailed away from his once more and made his lower lip drop open on a sudden in-breath of hungry need.

He wanted her back.

The press of her mouth. The taste of her.

Yes. Good.

She pulled her head back a few inches more, anticipating that he'd try to push forward to her in his impatience.

Oh, no, Callan, not yet. Feel what you're missing, first. When he leaned toward her, she touched her fingertips to his mouth, warding him back. "No, not yet," she whispered and brushed her fingers slowly across to his jaw and away.

This time, she made him wait longer for her kiss, letting her lips hover just a fraction of an inch from his so that he could feel her warmth but couldn't find the contact.

Not yet, not yet.

Feel me, and wait.

Ah, he'd opened his eyes. "What are you doing to me, woman?" he muttered.

"Nothing," she whispered back. "Just loving you. In my own sweet time. In my own lazy, lazy way."

He groaned.

Then he took control. His mouth closed over hers, the kiss deep and full, his tongue sweeping against hers, with the taste of chocolate and sweet, alcohol-laced cream still strong. Jac was already aching and swollen, her nipples tingling against the soft, clingy caress of her sweater, but she could wait. Oh, when kisses were this good, she could wait for a very long time.

He began to touch her, brushing his knuckles across the swell of her breasts, through the knit fabric's inadequate barrier. "You cut a few corners getting dressed just now," he said softly.

"Is that against the dress code around here?"

"Not at this hour. It…uh…might be a requirement, from now on. It's great." He cupped her through the fuzzy angora, and it tickled. Well, there should be a sexier word than *tickled* for this. It felt so soft and she was so achingly sensitive. "Are my hands cold?" he asked.

"I can't tell."

He slipped them inside the lower band of the sweater. "Can you tell now?"

"They're…mmm…they're fine."

"Good. So far, so good."

"Good all the way, Callan, no matter what bumps we hit and how long it takes."

"I like the bumps I'm hitting now."

"Mmm, yeah, I'm pretty fond of those ones, too."

They laughed and he kissed her again, his cattleman's hands deliciously rough on her skin despite the tender way he touched her. She touched him in return, running her hands over the muscles that spoke of meaningful strength and vast physical experience, and dwelling in places where her touch made him shudder with need.

"You know what?" she whispered eventually.

"What?"

"I'm still having a problem with the dress code. It's too formal."

"You could be right."

"Can I make some suggestions?"

"I'm in your hands."

"If I can follow through on my suggestions, there'll be quite a bit more of you in my hands." She plucked at the waistband of his jeans, showing her impatience at the barrier.

"In that case, suggest away," he whispered.

"The T-shirt could go."

"That only leaves me with the jeans."

"Those must go, too. I'll keep you warm, I promise."

"If I comply with this new dress code, do I get a wish list of my own?"

"A dress-code wish list?"

"I think the dress code is already established. To achieve compliance with current standards, you'll need to lose the sweater and the jeans and what's beneath them." He slipped a hand across her breast again. "If anything," he added with scrupulous attention to probability.

"So what's your wish list?" She sat up, crossed her arms obediently and pulled the sweater over her head, knowing he was watching every move. When she'd tossed the sweater aside, he wrapped his arms around her and buried his face in the valley between her breasts, a low sound coming from deep in his throat.

"That we stay out here," he said. He began a trail of slow kisses up toward her throat. "That we...maybe...make each other laugh a little bit instead of staying all earnest about this."

It was a plea for emotional protection, Jac understood. "We seem to be pretty good at making each other laugh," she agreed.

"It's nice, Jac. I love it."

And I love you, she thought.

She didn't dare to say it yet.

"It's very nice," she agreed instead.

"Mmm." He kissed her neck. "What were we talking about?"

"Nothing. We'd finished. Dress code, wish list. We're done with the planning stage...." Jac replayed those last words in her head and decided they sounded a little scary, a little too heavy on the expectations. She didn't give herself or Callan time to freeze up over it. "Now we're into im-ple-men-tation," she whispered, her breath caressing his ear.

"Good grief, I had no idea that was such a sexy word," he mumbled. "Can you say it for me again?"

She drew out the word even longer this time, her tongue caressing the *l* and her lips pouting on the *tion*. Then she added, "Hold still, Callan, I'm taking off your T-shirt...."

Oh, and when she did, he was so beautiful. He pulled her against him and his chest was a wall of warmth and hard strength. Her breasts squashed between them, the contact intimate and tender, male against female, so right and perfect, meant to be.

She reached down for the fastening of his jeans, but the fabric had pulled tight there because of the male awakening beneath, and she fumbled and couldn't slip the hard piece of metal through. "Need an expert?" he said, shifting back.

"Yes."

She watched. He pushed his hips forward and twisted his hand on the fastening. She'd never before experienced this shameless need to see a man, to see him hard and straining against the faded blue denim, then freeing himself and springing outward as he unzipped the jeans and worked them down.

She touched him and he shuddered at the light sensation on the taut satin skin. She lay back along the couch and pulled him on top of her, and he slid his hands inside the back of her jeans and cupped her, pressing her closer even though she arched her hips upward, as desperate as he was for full contact.

"Jac... We have to lose the jeans."

They fought over the task, fingers getting in each other's way. He rolled to kneel on the floorboards, and dragged the denim and the slip of underlying lace down her legs in a single movement, while she lifted and shimmied her hips. Then he trailed his mouth the whole way up her body, lingering in all the places she wanted him to.

By the time he reached her mouth and they were lying length to length along the couch, she was in a white heat of wanting.

And he was ready for her.

The old cane creaked beneath them, its sagging center holding their entwined bodies like a giant cupped hand. She wrapped her legs around his body and arched back, aching for his first thrust. It was clumsy. The couch sagged too much. They couldn't find each other.

It doesn't matter, she coached herself inwardly. *It doesn't matter. We'll get there.*

Then, out in the chicken run, Darth Vader crowed.

Hell, it was almost morning. Opening her eyes, Jac could see that the sky at the horizon had just begun to grow pale. She feverishly attempted to calculate how much time they had left. Forty minutes? Half an hour? Then she felt Callan's slackening impatience and heard his shuddering sigh. "Oh hell, Jacinda, I'm sor—"

"Don't say it! Don't you dare say it!" she told him fiercely. She gripped him so hard with her legs that the muscles of her inner thighs hurt. "Don't you dare pull away!"

"The kids'll be awake soon."

"Not this early! It's still almost pitch dark. Shut up, you bloody rooster!" she hissed at the creature, over her shoulder, in the direction of the chicken run. "Callan, I have to tell you, your alarm-clock system here needs some adjustment."

"Jacinda—"

"*No!* You wanted to laugh, we're going to laugh. You didn't want to get too earnest about this. Well, we're not! This is funny. Ridiculous, and typical, and funny. We have a conspiracy going on between a puritanical couch with a hole in the bottom of it and a spoilsport of a rooster, and we're not giving in to it! I don't know what kind of agenda those two have got going, whether it's a work-ethic thing, or the idea that bed is the only acceptable place for this kind of behavior, but Callan, damn it…damn it…"

She stopped gabbling, stopped the doomed attempt to

make him laugh, and just started kissing him because that had been so good, that had gotten them both so, so close.

Close to the edge.

Close to each other.

He lay on top of her, and even though he kissed her back, with a warm, soft mouth, she could tell he wasn't feeling the magic, the way they both had been before. So she stopped kissing him, threaded her fingers through his scented, slippery hair and pulled his head down to her chest. "Talk to me," she said. "Tell him about those other women, the ones who were so wrong for you that this could happen."

He swore.

"Tell me, so I can hunt them down and kill them with my bare hands."

At last he laughed. "Oh Lord, Jac…!"

"I want names, ages, occupations, distinguishing marks."

He laughed again, then he rasped out a sigh. Then with his head still pillowed on her chest, he told her about the blonde at the races and the Danish girl camped down at the creek, and when he had finished, he almost broke her heart when he said, "And I don't know why I expected this time to be any different."

She had a choice.

Nurse the broken heart, or fight to fix it.

She chose to fight, because she knew his heart had to be broken, too, for him to say something like that. She echoed his statement. "Why did you expect it to be different, Callan? Don't you know the answer to that by now? Because—"

She wanted so badly to say, "Because I love you," but that was still just a little bit too hard, when it brought with it so many decisions about a radically different future, so she bit it back and said something almost as important. "Because this is me!"

"Hmm?" He lifted his head for a moment.

"This is me. Just me. No one else. Not a blonde. Not a backpacker. Definitely not a sexual therapist. Me." She gripped his shoulders and spoke so fiercely that she was almost yelling. "I went bunyip-jumping with you when I was terrified about it. I laughed at your kangaroo cows. I drink my coffee the same way you do. Don't—*don't* put me in a basket with anyone else, when I'm nothing like those other women and by now you have to know it. That hurts. It really hurts, Callan," she finished on a whisper, and buried her face in his hair.

Jacinda was right.

Callan lay on her, protecting her from his weight by resting one side of his body against the back of the couch. Beneath the softness of her breasts, he could feel the rhythm of her breathing against his cheek, and she was right. She was nothing like those other women.

And yet he'd still failed with her.

That was the point where logic had stopped and emotion—blind fear—had kicked in. But she was right. Something was different, because he was still here, feeling the way she held him and kissed him, any bit of him she could reach. Hair and ear and temple and eyelid. He hadn't shut down and turned away, and neither had she.

She still had more to give. She wanted to keep trying.

She was right. It was different. They knew each other, and she cared about him, and they were both still here.

Something hard and painful in his heart began to let go and break away. He felt renewed and ready to go forward, no longer stuck in the same sad, pessimistic place he'd locked himself into.

Jacinda.

Because of Jac, he could do this.

Without speaking, he shifted and slid along the couch until

he could share the pillow where her head rested, then he held her breast, feeling its warm, rounded weight and the nipple that was still peaked with desire. He began to caress her, forgetting about dawn, the past, the kids, the sag in the couch. Her skin was so fine and soft. She smelled so familiar and sweet.

"Jacinda…" he said, and she understood what he wanted and what he was telling her, just with the whispered sound of her name.

She turned toward him and they half rolled until he lay beneath her. She bent to kiss him, her mouth hot and moist. Her nipples brushed against his chest while her thighs parted and pinned him down. He couldn't believe how fast his need accelerated. Zero to sixty in five seconds. Sixty to a hundred in ten more. His body remembered exactly where it had been twenty minutes ago and exactly what it wanted.

She was ready, and this time there was no clumsiness. He lifted his hips and slid into her, his breath catching halfway to his lungs. Ahh. He held her soft, satiny cheeks and pulled her even closer, so that the sweet sensation of the way she enclosed him grew even more intense.

Unbearably intense.

And when she moved against him like this, opening wider, pressing harder, matching his rhythm, sliding her body on his, raggedly breathing out his name, the whole universe seemed to zero in to this single place, this one segment of time and they surged over the crest of their wave together and clung to each other for sheer survival.

He was still lying with his eyes closed, motionless and breathless and lost, when he felt her fingertips press gently against his mouth. What was this about?

"In case you're planning to say something I don't want to hear," she whispered in explanation, when he opened his eyes and frowned at her.

He laid his hand over hers and slid it away. "Like what?"

"Etiquette-book stuff." She kissed the corner of his mouth.

"You mean th—"

"Yes. I don't want to hear it. You can tell me that the earth moved, if you want, but nothing beginning with *th*. That's banned."

"Did the earth move for you?"

"Like the San Andreas fault." She grinned. "Oh, damn, now I want to say it to you. Thank you, Callan."

"You said it was banned."

"I'm inconsistent."

"Jac—"

"I'm still inconsistent. You are not saying it. You are beautiful, and wonderful, and complete, and you are not saying it."

She sat up and stretched, giving him a slow, creamy smile like a satisfied cat. Then she reached for her sweater, untangled the sleeves and dropped it over her head.

Darth Vader crowed again. Callan had the vague idea he'd been hearing that sound at intervals for quite a while, now, and when he looked at the sky it was on fire at the horizon and pale blue everywhere else. Over at the cottage, his mother's kitchen light was on, and inside the house he heard a couple of thumps. The kids were up.

He found his jeans and dragged them on. Jacinda was watching him, the lower half of her body wrapped in the mohair blanket. They smiled at each other, tired and replete and very content.

"It's going to be a beautiful day," he said.

"I dreamed I was in Lockie's bed," Carly said to Jac, finding her on the way to the bathroom and reaching up for a morning hug.

Wearing the jeans she'd only just managed to climb into in time out on the veranda a minute ago, Jac crouched down to small-daughter level. "You *were* in his bed, honey, for a couple of hours. You must have been sleepwalking, because you went outside to the veranda."

"Did I?"

"I think you might have gone to pat the dogs. But then you came back in and went to see Lockie, and you had a bad dream. He told you a story and you went back to sleep, right beside him, but later on I came and carried you back to your own bed. Do you remember any of that?"

Carly shook her head and laughed. "No! I did all those things?"

She'd been told about her nighttime wanderings before, and always found it very silly and funny that she could do all those things in her sleep and not remember the next morning.

Jac thought about telling her that they'd thought she was lost out in the open, but that would involve admitting how terrified she'd been, and Carly was already too closely attuned to Mommy's emotional barometer. It was almost certainly why she'd begun to sleepwalk in the first place.

Because Jac had been so overwrought about Kurt.

Still holding Carly lightly around her little waist, she felt her stomach lurch. She'd shower and change, and then she'd try calling Elaine once more, because whether she panicked about it or not, whether Kurt's threats were real or simply games, she had to find out what was going on.

When she came into the kitchen after her shower, she found Callan there with Carly and the boys, making breakfast. It was only a few minutes after seven, but this still made it a slightly later morning than usual. Pouring two mugs of coffee, Callan smiled at her across the room and she smiled back, and got a warm, goofy sort of happy feeling inside, that she could see in him, also, glowing like ripe fruit in the sun.

Yeah, aren't we great?

Wasn't it good?

Isn't this a beautiful morning?

Mmm.

"Want—?" he began, but the rest of his sentence was cut across by the sound of the wall phone ringing.

Elaine.

Jac knew it would be Elaine.

She was the first one to reach the telephone, and when she snatched it up, she heard her former boss's voice. Callan poured milk into the coffee mugs and put them in the microwave, then dropped bread into the toaster.

"Honey, I'm so sorry I didn't get back to you yesterday!" Elaine said. "Things were so crazy, and then I worked out the time and it was going to be the middle of the night down there so I had to wait. It's around eight-thirty by you now, right?"

"Seven."

"So I still got it wrong. That's weird."

"Never mind about working out the time difference, Elaine." She was already sweating and newly on edge, her hands clammy and cold. "Just tell me what's been going on."

"Well, it's all over now."

"All over?" Dear Lord, what did she mean?

"I couldn't talk yesterday because I was with Lauren," Elaine said.

Lauren was Kurt's new wife, a blond twentysomething, with ambitions even larger than her surgically—

Yeah, well.

That was water under the bridge, now.

A year ago, Jac had wasted quite a lot of precious emotional energy on hating the woman, but the bad feelings had gone when she'd realized that Lauren could have been any one of a hundred near-identical variations on the same theme…and when Jac had discovered that she actually felt sorry for her.

Kurt was the problem, not the trophy babe he happened to choose.

"But you can talk now?" Jac prompted Elaine. "So please don't make it cryptic!"

"Honey, Kurt's ill."

"Ill?"

"Mentally ill. He's been diagnosed with bipolar disorder."

Jac came out with an incoherent sound of shock and saw Callan's concerned look, across the room.

Elaine went on quickly, "Manic depression, they used to call it, and it's very treatable. It's been building over several months, but he's in the hospital now, medicated and resting."

"That sounds—" Her mouth would barely move.

"Yes, it's the best thing for him," Elaine agreed, brisk and sympathetic, as if Jacinda had come out with a coherent line. "He was completely exhausted. He was barely sleeping, supposedly putting all these fabulous projects together, but most of them don't exist. And Lauren found out he was having her followed."

"Poor girl! They've been married less than a year!"

"She called me, we were in the car, yesterday, going to their house. He wouldn't listen to us, we had to get professional help. It was a crazy day, in more ways than one. He's been getting increasingly delusional over the past month or two, talking about the president directing a movie he'd written that would bring about world peace, and calling people on the Fortune 500 list to ask them to invest in it. *And* sending Jacinda Beale look-alikes to your daughter's preschool, and threatening to fly to Sydney and take her."

"Those bits I knew," Jac said weakly. "I'll call Lucy right away and tell her she doesn't have to worry now."

"Those are the bits that scared you, but trust me, things were scarier at this end, for a while yesterday, when he wouldn't accept that he had a problem."

"So—So— None of what happened…all his power games…even the divorce…?"

"Honey, listen to me, you and I both know that Kurt is and always has been a power-hungry control freak, so don't go thinking that you divorced your husband when he was ill and needed you. This has developed since then. And when his medication has been balanced right—which may take time— he'll still be a power-hungry control freak, except not a de-lusional one who's going to threaten your friends and try and kidnap your daughter. Okay?"

"That's—that's—"

"It's good news," Elaine announced, since Jac couldn't work out what it was, right now. "It means you can come home and get on with your life and be safe with Carly." After a tiny pause, she added, "And we can even talk about you coming back to the show."

"I don't want to come back to the show." The words fell out of her mouth before she even knew she was going to say them, but then she heard them echoing in the air and knew that she wouldn't take them back.

Kurt or no Kurt, writing block or no writing block, she didn't want to go back to writing dialogue for *Heartbreak Hotel*.

"You see, I've started working on a—"

"Don't say a screenplay," Elaine cut in. "Please, please, if you care about me at all, do not say a screenplay. I had the drinks waiter from the studio catering team give me his screenplay yesterday, while I was on the phone listening to Lauren sobbing in terror about Kurt at the other end, and it was the twentieth unsolicited and previously undiscovered gem of movie-making brilliance I've been privileged to receive this week."

"It's not a screenplay, Elaine, it's a novel."

"Thank God! Someone else's problem!"

"And—and I think Carly and I might be moving back east, to be nearer to my brothers and my dad. You know, and for a change."

There was a silence at the far end of the line. Then Elaine said blankly, "Leave L.A.?"

"I think so."

"Wow."

"I think it's the right thing." Jac caught Callan's expression as he pulled the mugs of coffee from the microwave. She couldn't read it, but she knew he was following everything she said.

"Wow!" Elaine said again.

"Yeah, it's been an interesting few weeks."

"And on that note, I should go. Back to my interesting life, interesting work and tedious, tedious amateur screenplays. I'll see you when you get back, though? You'll have to pack up your life here, first?"

"And I'd like to visit Kurt. Of course you'll see me, Elaine."

"We can talk detail, then, okay?"

"Sounds great." A few moments later, she put down the phone.

The kitchen was suddenly much quieter. Carly, Lockie and Josh shoveled in their eggs and bacon and gulped their hot chocolate. Pippa had somehow wangled her way inside and was thumping her tail against the table leg, her eyes trained hopefully on the food. Kerry would probably be over any minute now.

And Callan was watching Jac, his face as intent as Pippa's but his agenda much less clear. "Here's your coffee, Jac," he said quietly. "I was going to ask if you wanted toast."

"Everything's fine now," she told him. "Well…it's more complicated than just *fine,* I guess, but I'll explain later on, once the kids are doing their school."

"It's safe for you to go back."

"Yes."

She waited for him to say, "Don't! Stay!" but he didn't, he just repeated his question about toast and she accepted some, knowing she would barely manage three bites.

Chapter Fourteen

"That's everything?" Kerry asked.

She stood back and looked at the suitcases lined up on the dusty ground beside the four-wheel-drive. Her shoulders slumped a little and a helpless expression flitted across her face.

"I've checked pretty thoroughly through the house," Jacinda said.

"Yes, so did I," Kerry agreed. "Is Callan...?" She turned toward the veranda steps.

"Looking for his hat, I think."

Kerry nodded. "Well..." She looked around again. Sighed. Straightened her shoulders. "Where's Josh?"

Callan had appeared, hat on his head. It was tipped too low over his eyes, Jac thought. "Josh is in the feed shed and won't come out," he said. "Jac and Carly, he says to tell you goodbye."

"Should you make him—?" Kerry began.

He shook his head. "I'm not going to force the issue."

He began to load Carly and Jacinda's suitcases into the back of the vehicle.

They were leaving today.

Since Friday, time seemed to have sped up, and never before had Jacinda been so aware of a human being's powerlessness in its grip. She'd hung onto every moment, savored it, made memories like photographs, telling herself, *I have to remember this. I have to lock this in, so when I think back on it, I'll be able to feel it again and know how strong and how important it was. Even if I never have a reason to come back.*

She'd told herself this while feeding the hens, picking lemons in the garden and helping the kids with their School of the Air. She'd said it to herself on Saturday when they'd all gone on horseback down to the water hole once more, this time with Kerry and the dogs as well. She'd said it as she'd kneaded bread dough, and when she'd watched Callan ride on horseback into the yard with Pete after an overnight boundary ride yesterday afternoon.

Most of all, she'd thought it…felt it…when she and Callan had made love together, on the old cane couch at night and on a blanket spread over a shady curve of the creek bed on Sunday just before noon.

Never in his bed.

She'd noticed that.

It had frozen inside her like a splinter of ice in her heart, and it meant that, deep down, she wasn't so surprised that he was letting her go today. Why would he try to keep her here when, after all the emotional distance they'd traveled together over the past four weeks, all the ways they'd healed and changed and been good for each other, he still wouldn't let her fully into his life?

"Lockie, say goodbye to Carly," Callan growled at his elder son now.

"G'bye, Carly." Lockie lifted his little friend off her feet and gave her a hard squeeze. She could barely breathe, but she was laughing when he put her down again.

"Bye, Lockie," she said.

He turned to his dad. "But when are they coming back?"

"Now's not the time to talk about that, okay?"

Lockie knew that tone in his father's voice. He didn't argue, just gave Jac a quick goodbye hug as well.

"Aren't you guys coming out to the airstrip, Kerry?" Jacinda said. The suitcases were in. The rear door was shut.

"Best not," the older woman answered. Her smile was wide and stiff. "I'm rotten with goodbyes. I hate them. If I was eight years old, I'd be with Joshie, hiding in the feed shed. Let me give you a hug, love."

I'm going to cry, Jacinda knew. *I don't want this. And I don't think Kerry wants it, either. She doesn't understand why Callan is letting us go. Why is it happening?*

She had waited since Friday for Callan to talk about the future, about how he felt. It was *obvious* how he felt, she often thought, but then he said nothing, he kept her out of his bed, and she began to doubt, and the words she wanted to blurt to him stayed shut away inside her.

I love you.

I want to stay.

Sometimes, like Kerry, she felt as if she were eight years old. She was a kid who desperately wanted to be asked for a sleepover at her best friend's house and couldn't believe the best friend hadn't suggested it. Just how sinfully rude would it have been to bring up the idea herself?

Callan, I love you and I'm sleeping over. For the rest of my life.

She couldn't do it.

Not when he hadn't made love to her in his own bed.

Not when he and Pete had disappeared off to the far horizon for twenty of the last precious hours of her stay.

"Bye, Kerry," she said against a shoulder covered in sun-heated cotton, fighting the tightness in her throat and the sting of tears. "I can't tell you how much this has meant to me, these past four weeks."

"It's flown by. We've loved having you. Carly is precious."

"I don't want to go." But the words came out muffled against Kerry's shirt, and no one heard.

"Jump in, Carly," Callan said.

He opened the rear door and, as always, it creaked because of the red desert dust that had worked its way into the hinges. Jac wondered if she'd ever again hear a creaking car door or the flap of a screen door against a porch wall without thinking of this place, and of him.

Lockie threw a stick to Flick and Pippa, then ran after them as they chased it, calling, "Come on, Pippa, come on, Flick, race you to the shed." Jac thought he was probably scared he might cry. She climbed into the front passenger seat, didn't even make her usual frequent mistake of going around to the wrong side. She'd gotten used to the fact that the driver sat on the right in this country.

By late this afternoon, she and Carly would be in Sydney. On Thursday, they'd fly home, and it would still be Thursday when they got there, with a list no doubt several pages long to prepare—all the things they'd need to do before they moved east.

Jac had had an e-mail from Tom last night, and a second one from Andy this morning, saying that he and Debbie would love to see her if she came east. Dad was getting pretty vague, but he talked about her from time to time. He'd asked Andy recently if Andy thought it was the right thing to have sent Jacinda to live with her aunt, all those years ago.

I told him it was the best thing he could do at the time, Andy had written. I'm not going to hurt him by encouraging regrets at this point in his life, Jacinda, but it would be great if we could make more of an effort to stay in touch, wouldn't it, even if it's just through e-mail?

Callan started the engine. Kerry waved and smiled madly for a moment, then turned abruptly and hurried up the steps, across the veranda and into the house. Carly kept waving, even though—if you left out Lockie, Pippa and Flick, just about to disappear around a corner of the feed shed—there wasn't anyone to wave to, anymore.

Carly was sad about leaving, but too little to really understand just how hard it would be for them ever to come here again, let alone how much Jac felt she and Carly were losing as they made these awkward goodbyes.

They drove out to the airstrip, and Jac could already see Rob's mail plane approaching over the dry, rugged mountains to the south. The plane's wheels hit the earth just as Callan brought the four-wheel-drive to a halt. He switched off the engine, but then he didn't move.

Waiting for Rob.

Waiting for Rob with his whole body in a knot of tension and not saying a word.

Jac couldn't take it anymore.

"I'm going to stretch my legs," she said, opening the door and sliding out. "Carly, wait here, honey, till we're ready to walk to the plane."

Carly nodded, her gaze dropped down at something in her lap, and Jac leaned back into the vehicle and looked more closely to see what she was doing. She had a tissue spread like a napkin across her thighs, and she was painstakingly pulling apart some lavender flowers she must have picked from the garden shortly before they'd left, and dropping the bits of lavender onto the tissue.

Jac could smell them now. "So you're busy and happy with the flowers?" she said.

"Uh-huh. I'm making aloe-vera tissues."

"Are you, sweetheart? Good girl. They'll be lovely." She shut the door carefully and circled away from the vehicle.

But Callan followed her, which meant they had to stand together, watching the mail plane coming toward them with its wake of rust-red dust like the train of a regal robe. Callan watched with particular intensity, it seemed to Jacinda, as if his focus on the plane and Rob gave him an excuse not to focus on her.

It really was unbearable.

"Don't wait," she told him. "Rob's here. He's waving at us, giving us the thumbs-up. There's obviously no problem with the aircraft, which means we'll be taking off again in a couple of minutes. There's no need for you to wait. I'm the same as your mom. I hate goodbyes."

I hate this *goodbye.*

But then she saw that Rob had one of those damned mailbags he brought every week, so of course Callan needed to wait. He saw the mailbag, nodded at Rob and gave a thumbs-up back to him, and then he kept looking at the bag, tense and intent, as Rob began walking toward them.

Jac gathered her courage and turned to him for that last hug she'd been dreading for half her stay. "Callan—" she began, not having the slightest idea of what she could say as an exit line without crying.

"Do you think you could come back?" he said.

"I'm sorry?" she answered weakly, while thinking, *No, this is wrong. This isn't what I wanted.*

If she'd hoped for anything, it would have been *Don't go.* Not this. *Come back* wasn't necessarily even something people meant when they said it. It was the kind of thing flight attendants said on airplanes.

We look forward to seeing you again next time you choose to fly with us.

Next time you're passing by Arakeela Creek, do stop in for tea.

She looked up at Callan and found a tight face with eyes still half-hidden beneath the brim of his hat. They had their arms around each other, but it felt clumsy and uncomfortable and not right. "I know you have to leave," he said. "But I want you to come back."

"Callan—"

"Come back and—"

"G'day, Callan, hello Jacinda." Rob had almost reached them, his strides confident and long, his expression cheerful. "I've got it, mate. It's right here in the bag. Are you ready for it?"

"Ready for it?" Callan echoed in a strange tone, letting go of Jacinda and almost pushing her away. "I am stuffing this up so totally, Rob, it's not funny. She thinks I have a good sense of humor, she didn't know I could be the butt of my own joke, but yes, I am ready for it. Can you give it to me, then give us a minute or so?"

"No worries." Rob tossed him the mailbag. "I'll give you as long as you want."

Jacinda had no idea what was happening, but she didn't like it. Callan was eager about some package delivery, while her heart slowly burned to ash inside her?

With the mailbag in his hands, Callan didn't seem to know what to do with it. He held it, pleating it up in his hands the way women pleated the open top of a stocking, then he rummaged inside.

Rob had gone off to pull bits of bark off one of the few pieces of decent vegetation beside the airstrip. His body language said that he was being as tactful as a simple man knew how, but Jac couldn't see the need. Meanwhile, was Carly still making her "aloe-vera tissues" in the backseat of the vehicle?

She craned to look. Yes. Good.

"Jacinda, will you marry me?" Callan said in a desperate tone, and her head whirled around.

He had a blue velvet box in his hands. It was open, and inside was a ring. She saw the bright wink and dazzle of diamond and gold in the sunlight, and couldn't speak. He pinched it awkwardly between his fingers and pulled it out.

"I know you have to leave now," he went on. "I know you have to wind up your life in L.A., but after that, don't move east to your brothers. I've seen you building on that plan the whole time you've been here and now I'm telling you to just give it up. Maybe that's too selfish. I don't care. Come back here with Carly, and be my wife."

He flipped the ring over and over in his fingers. Jacinda couldn't speak, could barely breathe.

"I had to get this over the Internet," Callan said, stumbling over his words. "I don't know if it'll fit, if you'll like it."

She did. It was simple and finely made, and right now a ring made from braided horse hair would have been more than good enough.

"I didn't even know if Rob would have it with him this trip, but if you say yes…if you think you might manage to say yes…I didn't want you to leave without something like this, you see. I want you to carry it with you, because… This has probably been the worst proposal in the world…."

"It's getting better by the second," she said shakily.

"But…you're carrying my heart, too, and if there's any danger of you forgetting that, when you'll be so far away…" He stopped, then tried again, slipped the ring onto her finger—it was a couple of sizes too big—and laced their hands together. His voice was so husky it was barely there. "I just wanted you to have this so you'd know, every moment of every day, that I love you, and you're carrying my heart."

It had definitely not been the worst proposal in the world.

"Yes, oh, yes!" Jacinda gasped out.

"Yes? You'll come back? You'll marry me?"

"Yes, because I love you and you're carrying my heart, too, but, Callan…" Jac started to cry, because it was the best proposal in the world but the timing was still terrible. "*Now* you say this? When Rob's waiting to take us away? The propellers are still spinning." She stroked his face. "Couldn't you have picked a time a tiny, tiny bit less like the absolute last minute?"

Was she laughing or crying? She didn't know anymore.

"But I didn't know what you'd say." Callan held her close, his head bent and his forehead pressed against hers. "I thought maybe for you this was just…an interval. You gave me everything on Friday morning, more than I'd imagined or dared to hope for, but then you seemed to hold back, little by little. You had your plans for moving east. You were so happy this morning when that second e-mail from Andy came."

"You never had me in your bed. We never slept together, Callan. We only made love. In other places. *You* held back, and then you disappeared with Pete. I didn't know what to think."

"I'm a one-woman man, Jacinda, that's all."

Something cold stabbed in her stomach. "But you want to marry me…" Her mouth felt numb. "Even though I'm not the woman?"

"Oh, hell! No! No! One woman at a time! That's what I mean. And this time it's you. The woman is one hundred percent you." He kissed her, fast and sure. "But I had to say my last goodbye to Liz before I could ask you to marry me and share my bed and my life and my future. That's where I went with Pete, to a couple of the places I used to ride to with Liz that I haven't shown you yet. Pete knew. To say goodbye. Now the only woman in my life is you. If you want to be."

"Oh, I want to be! And I don't want to go. I'd lost any hope that you'd wanted something like this, and now I have to go. Rob's waiting. The airstrip, Callan? Not the water hole on Saturday. Not even the chicken run this morning. The airstrip? Now? With the propellers going?" She was still laughing and crying at the same time, with the ring slipping too loose on her finger.

"If it had all gone pear-shaped, you see, if you'd said no, you couldn't exactly have called a cab to pick you up and take you and Carly to a nearby motel. I didn't want to make everything awkward if I had it all wrong." He kissed her lightly once more. "Gotta think of things like that, out here."

"Oh, trust me, I'm going to be thinking of things like that all eight thousand miles of the journey home!"

Rob detached himself from the scraggly tree he'd just stripped half-bare and wandered across to them. "I have a bit of a schedule today, Callan," he said apologetically. "My boss might think I should be getting on with it."

Callan got a hunted look on his face and Jacinda held him harder. "Another five minutes?" he said.

Rob grinned. "From the look of the two of you, I don't think five minutes is going to be anywhere near enough. Jacinda, how about you change your flights out of Broken Hill and Sydney over the phone, and I come back for you next week?"

Jacinda and Callan looked at each other. "Yes!" they both said, and laughed because they'd been too desperate and emotional to think of it themselves.

Five minutes later, when they pulled up in front of the house, Pippa and Flick came racing around the corner of the feed shed and greeted the vehicle as if they hadn't seen Callan, Jac and Carly in a week. The screen door squeaked on its hinges and flapped back against the veranda wall, and three people appeared, each of them with eyes exactly like

Callan's—a glorious overload of piercing blue. They must have heard the four-wheel-drive, and two of them—the smaller ones—were grinning.

"Jac, you came back," Kerry said in a shaky voice, too emotional to smile.

Lockie and Josh had questions. Carly couldn't get herself unstrapped from the backseat. When she showed Lockie her "aloe-vera tissues" a cascade of tiny bits of lavender rained all the way down the front of her little dress. Jacinda told Kerry about the ring and the proposal and the short trip she and Carly would be making back to the U.S.—the west coast to deal with arrangements, and then the east coast to visit family.

Kerry wondered why they were talking about it out here when they could be inside discussing the details over a cup of tea. The boys asked if they could maybe have the rest of the morning off school. Callan said yes, knowing he'd just been conned, and Pippa and Flick barked as joyously as if they'd been given the same reprieve.

Chaos, all of it, like the day four weeks ago when Jacinda and Carly had arrived.

Fabulous, safe, friendly, normal, reassuring family chaos.

My chaos, Jac thought. She sighed and smiled and leaned back against Callan's sun-warmed shoulder as he wrapped his arms around her from behind and nuzzled her neck.

"Welcome home," he said.

* * * * *

HOTEL MARCHAND

This riveting new saga begins with

In the Dark

by national bestselling author

JUDITH ARNOLD

The party at Hotel Marchand is in full swing when the lights suddenly go out. What does head of security Mac Jensen do first? He's torn between two jobs—protecting the guests at the hotel and keeping the woman he loves safe.

A woman to protect. A hotel to secure. And no idea who's determined to harm them.

On Sale June 2006

HMITD

The Marian priestesses were destroyed long ago,
but their daughters live on. The time has come
for the heiresses to learn of their legacy, to unite
the pieces of a powerful mosaic and bring light to
a secret their ancestors died to protect.

The Madonna Key

Follow their quests each month.

SPECIAL EDITION™

Welcome to Danbury Way—
where nothing is as it seems...

Megan Schumacher has managed to
maintain a low profile on Danbury Way
by keeping the huge success of her
graphics business a secret. But when a
new client turns out to be a neighbor's
sexy ex-husband, rumors of their
developing romance quickly start to swirl.

THE RELUCTANT
CINDERELLA

by CHRISTINE RIMMER

Available July 2006

*Don't miss the first book from the
Talk of the Neighborhood miniseries.*

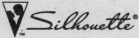

COMING NEXT MONTH

SSECNM0606